Suite Enemy

A Sapphic Romance
Lavender Quinn

Contents

Blurb

An old enemy. A second chance. A hotel filled with memories and haunting fantasies. Welcome to BED.

Taylor, a former teen star on the verge of a comeback, walked away from her acting career years ago after suffering a devastating heartbreak. When she accepts a birthday party invitation at Hotel BED, Las Vegas' newest playground for debauchery with an exclusive high class twist, she once again comes face to face with her oldest enemy, and her only love.

Gabriella has spent years building the career she has always wanted. Now, a respected showrunner at her best friend's sinful hotel, Gabriella has a choice to make; redemption or revenge.

Determined to free herself from Gabriella's past influence, Taylor sets out on a mission of self-discovery and exploration in the place that could hold the key to it all, but Hotel BED is Gabriella's kingdom and in the five days that Taylor has to regain her freedom, she will once again learn that there's more than one Queen she'll have to outmaneuver in order to find peace.

By Lavender Quinn

Hotel BED Series Duology #1
The Intimate Beginnings of Taylor
Suite Enemy

Author's Note

Suite Enemy is the first book that I wrote about Taylor and Gabriella, although it serves as their conclusion. Their relationship was so big in my mind, I thought it deserved a prequel. If you have been reading this far, I thank you. You may never understand the impact your support has had on me, but I want you to hear it from me, anyway.

Thank you.
Thank you.
Thank you.

Content Warnings

Healing is not a linear process. Please be kind to yourself. This book features toys made for sexual pleasure, and contains graphic sexual scenes, exhibitionism, kitten play, knife play, biting and role play.

This one's for me.

Chapter One
Taylor

THERE ARE ONLY TWO reasons I, an L.A. native, would entertain the idea of traveling through the one-way, congested streets of Downtown Los Angeles on a weeknight. It has nothing to do with the nightlife, the shopping, the museums or the picturesque view of the skyline.

Nope. I only travel to Downtown L.A. for my best friend and the black-owned coffee shop across the street from her condo. I haven't got a clue of what their coffee tastes like, but their blueberry scones and hot chocolate are amazing.

Nicole answers her door after the toe of my shoe bangs on it a few times. She waves me inside of her apartment with her phone firmly planted to her ear. The coveted L.A. skyline greets me through the large windows. The first half of the apartment is all city views and lights with her bedroom door facing out toward the scene.

I set the tray holding unclaimed coffees on the kitchen counter, unlace my boots, place them on the shoe rack and sit cross-legged on the couch. Nicole hadn't bothered explaining why I needed to leave my home in Santa Monica to speak with her in person, instead of over the phone, through text messaging or video chat. Nothing looks out of place. If we're embarking on a covert mission to separate her from her fiancé, more preparation is necessary.

We've done it in the past with mixed results. On the one hand, the plan was a success. On the other hand, my heart has never recovered.

Her brown long-haired chihuahua, Kendrick, struts down the hallway and bounces into my lap without an attempt at consent. I stroke him behind the ears and watch his tail sway back and forth in enjoyment. Lucky for him I'm partial to chihuahuas, no matter the hair length, for reasons I'm prohibited from talking about under Nicole's roof.

Kendrick barks and growls, his eyes focused on the front door. A knock sounds seconds later.

"What a smart boy you are," I say to him while setting him on the floor and rising to my feet. Kendrick runs ahead, his barks growing louder and his growl more aggressive. Chihuahuas are notorious for their terrifying front with very little results in the long run. As soon as I open the door, he'll most likely go running and leave me behind to deal with the intruder myself.

I can't make out the voices on the other side, but they sound friendly. I hike myself up on the tips of my toes to see a group of women chatting in the hallway. Their faces are recognizable. Judy Park is currently playing the role of a young woman trapped on a remote island with a nefarious group of characters on Monday nights. Maye Johnson is doing rebellious teenager shit on cable TV and Christina Lopez is the eldest daughter on a sitcom. They are all former child actors, though Christina is still on the show she started on as a kid.

I unlock the door and allow the group of women space to enter. They all greet me in a chorus of *heys* and *how are yous*. True to form, Kendrick barks at them while simultaneously backing up to the other side of the room.

I eye Nicole suspiciously as she rounds the corner to greet the group. As two people who grew up in the entertainment industry, our friend group consists mainly of people who also work in the same space. You see the same faces often and everyone knows everything about everyone. I consider most of these women to be my friends — individually, but together the four of them form a collective I have opted not to be a part of.

"How have you been, Taylor? It's been a while." Christina licks the spilled coffee off the lid of her cup. When Nicole asked me to pick up three extra cups of coffee, I assumed others would be in attendance. I just didn't expect *them*. For one, Nicole has forbidden me from hanging around Christina in any capacity. I don't know the entire story, but it has something to do with Christina expressing a tiny bit of interest in me. Christina doesn't have a sketchy past as far as I know, but since my breakup with my ex-girlfriend, Nicole has been overly protective.

Other than Christina also being from a Mexican family, I don't notice any similarities between her and Gabriella. Christina is funny with great comedic timing. Gabriella is very serious. Christina's laugh can fill an entire room. Gabriella doesn't laugh. She smiles. It's a beautiful smile that she always tries to suppress. Probably even now. They both have tanned skin and dark hair. Gabriella's hair is shiny and curly. The type that looks wet even if it isn't. Christina's hair is straight and I've never seen it look any different.

"Everything's good. Are you all recording an episode tonight?" Maye, Judy, Nicole, and Christina started a rewatch podcast of their old shows about a year ago. When Nicole asked me to join, I declined. I support the show as a listener, but revisiting my life on *Sunny and the Dreamers*, the show Nicole and I starred in together, would remind me of the very things I have tried so hard to forget.

Three pairs of eyes shoot at Nicole, who suddenly looks very uncomfortable being the center of attention. "Well, with the new show starting, the viewers have been requesting more information about it, and since you are the star—"

"Nicole," I warn.

"Taylor, come on! You're going to have to do press for this. There's no way around it," Kendrick barks again at the sound of Nicole stomping her feet on the hardwood floor. I take a deep breath to calm myself for the sake of the riled-up puppy.

"Press is different."

The internet is a cesspool of nosey people with long memories and nothing but time on their hands. The press I can deal with. My longtime manager, Zara, will make sure I'm only interviewed by people who love and respect me and who wouldn't ask questions I'd be uncomfortable with or that could paint me poorly. Years ago, I made a mistake. I paid a high price for it and I won't have people continually throwing it in my face.

"People love you." Nicole walks over and places her hands on my shoulders. "And they want to hear more about your past life as Dream Daniels and your future as Hope Harlee."

I landed the lead role in the newest network TV medical drama, *Saving Hope*, as a resident of Serenity Hope Hospital, whose sole mission is to convince the top cardiologist in the nation to treat her rare heart condition. That is if she can stop herself from falling in love with her first.

It's a big deal. A network TV show with a majority BIPOC ensemble cast and two queer leads. Nicole has a supporting role as a resident. It's the first time since we were pre-teens that we'll be on screen together.

"Ok, fine." I point my finger at her and stare menacing at the rest of the group. "I have to be out of here by nine. If we're not done by then, that's too bad."

They all assure me I have nothing to worry about. "We already went through and selected the questions. There will be no surprises and no drama," Nicole says. I take one glance at my cell phone and note the time before following the group down the hall to the spare bedroom where they record.

There are only two reasons I would drive from Santa Monica to Downtown L.A. on a weeknight, but there is one specific reason I shouldn't do so on a Thursday. I have an appointment. And I don't like to be late.

I arrive home in time to shower. I don't bother dressing afterward. There's no point. Excitement courses through me as my hands trail over my smooth skin. I bite down on my bottom lip when my fingertips brush over the sensitive area below me. My arousal is barely present. I shake it off. It's too early for me to start anything now.

The warmth from the HVAC unit greets me upon arriving in the kitchen. I bounce the camomile tea bag up and down inside the white ceramic mug before blowing across the top. Despite the heat, the cold quartz countertop prevents me from leaning up against the island. Normally, I would wear socks to keep my feet warm, but I can't tonight. Not yet.

I already prepared the kitchen nook. I cleared the wooden bench of all pillows. The table is free of all settings. Even placemats. The tall bay windows create a perfect space for me here.

I sit at the table, sliding over to the spot closest to the outside view, blowing over my mug, and sipping my tea. It doesn't take long before I hear the sounds of something scraping across the concrete outside.

A glance tells me Kyle and Monica have emerged from their house to the backyard that separates us. I have barely spoken to them since I moved in. I watch Monica sit first, removing the dry bikini top from her skin and dropping it to the ground.

From my position, Monica is facing away from me. The top of her dark hair blocks my view of Kyle's lower half. Kyle straddles Monica, tossing her hair to the side when she kisses her.

I close my eyes, welcoming the rising heat from my seat. The grip on my mug tightens. I won't let it go until I can barely maintain control. Kyle moans. I know it's hers because Kyle expresses her pleasure through labored breaths, while Monica moans out single phrases.

Following Kyle's rhythm, my hips roll backward and forward. By the sound of it, Monica isn't only enjoying the fullness of Kyle's breasts. She's exploring somewhere deeper.

My hips rise to disconnect from the friction I'm creating with my body, only to return to the movement seconds later. Sex is a drug first fed to me by my captor. The highs are amazing, filled with adrenaline and lust. The lows keep me coming back for more.

I stand to stretch by placing my hands over my head and arching my back. The floor-to-ceiling windows do nothing to hide my naked body. Out of the corner of my eye, I see Monica and Kyle change positions. They are both watching me now with Kyle's breasts pressed up against the back of the lounge chair and Monica kneeling behind her. I can imagine what they're doing. It's a position I've been placed in many times before, but that's not what matters now.

Now, it's my turn.

My knees spread as I lower myself down onto the table. The chill from the wood cools down the heat.

I cup my breasts. The feel of them, round and slick, causes the inside of me to clench. My senses tell me they're watching me. All my body knows how to do is respond. I trail my fingers past my belly until my arousal covers the tips of them. They bend in memory of her and every night she ordered them into action. I moan, arching my back. I go further, trapping them in between my folds, sliding up, down, and around in a circular motion.

My feet lift, giving me more room to explore myself. The cries of Kyle and Monica blend with the sound of my increasing pleasure. Her voice is also present, though they'd never know it. She barks orders at me to influence my body's behaviors, all for her entertainment.

The table bangs against the wall in rhythm with my hips. My breasts bounce at the action, jiggling in the moonlight. I imagine what she would say to the sight of me. Her words would be dirty and encouraging. My knees bend back and I feel the pressure of her hands on my skin. My fingers dip inside, but only as far as she'll let me. She always makes sure she's in control. Even when others are watching. My thumb brushes over the hood of my clit. I do it again, increasing and slowing the speed as much as I need—as she demands.

My breaths shorten. A few choice words escape from my lips. "Fuck." The tension knotting in my stomach is almost too much. Years ago, I would have stopped, too afraid to achieve my own pleasure. Things are different now. She taught me how to be a good girl. And a good girl never stops coming.

I free my fingers from inside of me, gliding them up and down once again. I add a third, rubbing it against my sleek skin. It's not long until they're ready. The three of them cake in me, sticking together in my excitement, and my desire to please those who are watching me, especially her.

I enter again, slowly adjusting to the fresh addition. The feel of my body stretching to adjust forces my neck to stretch out. My eyes slam into Kyle's. Her hands are now pressed up against the window while Monica moves in and out of her from behind. Their lounge chair is long forgotten.

She wouldn't want them to be this close. They'd have permission to look from afar, but with only a few feet separating us, there would be trouble.

Kyle's lips, trapped between her teeth, encourage me. My wrist moves into action, thrusting all three fingers. Thrust. Thrust. Swipe. I maintain my rhythm, grazing my thumb across my clit every third time.

The heart rises again. I move faster, refusing to dislodge my hand from the only place on my body pleasing me. Waves crash through me, sending my hips shooting up. I rub my clit until my knees lock and my breath catches in my throat.

My aching thigh muscles relax as my legs slowly drop back down onto the surface. I wait a few minutes to catch my breath before turning around to face them.

Kyle remains on her knees, but this time her lips wrap around the strap Monica used to enter her. I use my pleasure-free hand to wiggle my fingers in goodbye before sliding off the table and making my way back to the shower.

I should've stopped before now when I realized they had moved too close and gotten too comfortable. She'd be mad that I hadn't.

My one-bedroom back-house apartment was a steal. I have no interest and roommates, and living in someone's backyard is the perfect excuse to have no one come over. Especially when you may not get rid of them in time for the show.

When I moved into the back of Kyle and Monica's house two

years ago, I did not know this would become our weekly situation. Being watched while naked is an old pleasure, but I didn't do it on purpose the first time.

It had been a late night. Later than now. I'd been dancing to the music in my earbuds when I looked up and saw them propped up on the edge of the pool watching me. I didn't stop dancing. I let my hands roam across my breasts and down my thighs in rhythm to the beat. Kyle moved behind Monica, one hand lifting the thin fabric of the bikini top, the other disappearing in the water underneath. That night, I didn't touch myself until I got back into my bedroom.

I thought it was over after that. An embarrassing moment that we would all pretend didn't happen. Except one day I came home to two notes:

"Don't hide from us."

K.

"Sharing is caring :)"

M.

And my nook became my new stage.

They have extended the offer for me to join multiple times in the past two years. And not by note form. Whenever there's a chance for either Monica or Kyle to catch me leaving the driveway, they ask me over for dinner. I always decline. I know where dinner is supposed to lead.

I want to join, but I can't. It's an urge and a resistance that's been difficult for me to understand over the years. I can imagine the sex in my mind. It's amazing. I've never had sex without her. She's the answer to everything. And the cause.

She was the producer of my bedroom. The keeper of my love. My heart's assassin. I hate her and love her all at once. I haven't seen her in years and only hear echoes of her existence when I travel down to San Diego, where she's from. And yet, traces of her remain imprinted on my skin.

I keep my vagina free of hair, nice and slick and ready. The purpose of pubic hair is to absorb moisture. If it's not there, it can't snatch away from my arousal. I get wetter faster and stay wet much easier. That's how she liked it. And I always did what she wanted.

She was once a dream I never wanted to wake up from. If there was one thing she taught me, it's that everything imagined isn't always meant to be. That's why all interactions with my neighbors stay on the other side of the glass, where I'm safest.

I place my clean and naked buttered body between the sheets. My phone chimes. I swipe it off the end table, squinting my eyes at the bright and blinding light. The email I read is the third of its kind. I ignore it. The last time I responded to Chasity Coleman, I found myself in an Orange County mansion, too depressed to escape.

Chapter Two
Gabriella

THE PALM OF MY hand covers half my face as I contemplate the death of my career. "Why the fuck does she sound like a murder victim?" This is not a horror show. It's a sensual production scheduled to premiere to hundreds of hotel members in a matter of hours, and my female star moans like she's being stabbed in the back with a hatchet.

"Get rid of her fucking now and find me someone else. Someone who doesn't sound like they're being hacked away by a chainsaw." I lock the hands I have been refraining from pulling out my hair in front of me, upset that there's nothing to strangle except air.

My assistant scrambles away, her long braids flapping behind her. I watch her pull the performer off stage, hand her a robe and escort her from the theater. Casting the performers for the show can be tricky. Balancing production quality and member happiness has become an issue. Members sometimes think that because they throw a lot of money at the hotel, they should be able to get anything they want, including jeopardizing my show for their ego.

That's not to say I don't run a tight ship. I do. But you can't be mean to everyone. I know how to smile and nod along with the best of them. And then tell them no, when it conveniences me. I hate politics. Everyone should just do what I want.

My knuckles rap against the room door three times before I knock again. She answers, dressed in a red robe with mesh sleeves covered at the end in feathers. I stop my eyes from rolling back into my head and lean against the doorjamb instead, crossing the arms of my leather jacket.

"Get on stage."

Nancy is one of my stars. The women love her high femme energy with her toned thighs, flat stomach, flawless makeup and expressive performance. And the men—they just want to fuck her. Either way is a win for me. The only thing she needs to do is lie pretty and receive pleasure. She's good at it and she moans like a baby angel flying through heaven. I need her on stage.

Nancy pouts. Her blonde highlighted hair is in a sleek, perfectly straightened ponytail. Her light pink-and-rose-gold manicure matches the key dangling from her neck perfectly.

I follow her inside the room, ignoring the piles of clothing she has stuffed in a few of the corners. Her partner isn't here at the moment, but it's Friday, and partners that don't live at the hotel during the week usually appear on the weekends. I may have met her, but I don't care enough to remember.

Weeks ago, Nancy attempted to give me an ultimatum about how many shows she was willing to perform. I ignored her and then the team couldn't find her before rehearsal today, replacing her instead with the murder victim. I won't ignore her again.

"Will you get me into Gloss?"

Gloss is a private party for selected Significant members. Nancy isn't a Significant. Her Partner status prevents her from joining exclusive gold events.

I watch her eyes widen as my fingers trail across her neck. Her feet step backward until her back connects to the end of her vanity. I keep pushing. Nancy obliges by lifting her hips to sit where I direct her to. My thumb runs down her throat.

"Are you threatening me?"

"No!" She blurts it quickly and loud enough for any witnesses to hear.

"Good."

Her hand clamps down on my wrist, failing to stop my fingers from closing around her neck. My lips glide across her jaw, leaving traces of my red lipstick. Nancy's eyes flutter closed. She reaches for me, releasing my wrists and tugging at the ends of my ponytail, far more curly than hers.

"Never tell me what to do."

Her hips shift forward. Her knees open to make space for me. My tongue darting out to taste her skin is a surprise. Nancy moans, extending her neck, giving me more room to grip. Her fingers tug on the edge of my jacket.

My teeth pull at her diamond-pierced earlobe.

"You'll get into Gloss when *I* let you in." Her eyes inch open. She stares at me before nodding in understanding. I move away before she has the chance to pull her body closer to mine.

"You're on in thirty."

I don't make my way back to the theater after the door shuts behind me. I need a break. The job is getting to me. I'm usually more professional with the talent than I was with Nancy. I'm supposed to be unattainable. Something they wish they had, but are afraid to access. The fairy in their dreams, but the ghost in their nightmares.

The identity of the Keeper of Gloss is unknown to members. I know who they are. And it's not me. However, Nancy doesn't need to know that. Rumors are good for business.

I breeze by the managers standing in the waiting room of Chasity's office and enter unannounced. She continues talking on the phone, waving me over to the chair in front of her desk. Confused, I pull out my phone. Other than the message from my mom that I've left on read for the last few days, I have received nothing new.

My fingers scroll down far enough to Eryn's last message to me. I don't need to click on it to know what it says. She sends the same thing every year. *This is your annual reminder that you're an asshole.* Taylor's sister never really liked me much, and the breakup sent our relationship over a cliff. In the beginning, I replied with grace. I even said sorry once. I'm strangely grateful for her annual reminders. Her messages were proof that Taylor hadn't moved on. They meant I had time. Not that Eryn's messages were the only evidence. Taylor is never photographed with anyone besides her best friend and other actresses she claims as friends. If she had been with someone, I'd know it.

"We have a problem," Chasity speaks before her headset untangles from her hair and clashes on the desk.

"Oh?"

"She's not responding." My eyes narrow. Chasity has been my best friend since middle school. Other than a brief few years after college when we didn't speak, I've always had her back, but not with this.

I take a deep breath and try to keep the anger I feel from rising to the top. "That doesn't sound like an 'us' problem."

Because it isn't. Chasity is on a mission to get Taylor to the hotel for her birthday party in two weeks. She emailed and didn't receive a response. She called and was sent to voicemail. She texted and was left on read.

"She doesn't want to talk to you." I don't know what happened during the summer Taylor spent with Chasity. I know the result of that was Chasity's dream — this hotel.

"You should try calling her."

The answer is an instant no. I can't. Our relationship ended with her abandoning me without a second thought. We're complicated. With the way our relationship began, we were doomed from the start. The sacrifices I made for us meant nothing to her in the end. If I am ever in a room alone with her again, I don't know what I would do to her.

I leave Chasity's office before she annoys me more than she already has. Going to my boss to talk shit about my job wasn't the best choice. Taylor is a tricky subject for me. One I go back and forth on every day, sometimes multiple times a day. I'm not ready to have Taylor back into my life in any capacity. I don't hate her, but I'm still very pissed.

What happened to us changed my life in a big way. It wasn't her fault. It was mine. I accept responsibility for all of it. That takes a lot for someone to do. It's easier for people to pretend they are not the problem. I was the problem. Then. That time. Not always, but during particular moments. And that moment sucked.

We were a team. Sometimes your teammates fuck up. Sometimes your partner isn't perfect. Instead of her talking to me and forgiving me for it, she ran.

I don't hate her. But I don't know if I can forgive her for not choosing me.

Delicacy is busy with people lining up to enjoy their sweets after traveling. I dodge the wheeled carry-on pieces of luggage and duffle bags. Technically, it's against the rules to have luggage in any of the restaurants. Bellhops are supposed to take personal items directly to guest rooms to prevent people from cluttering up the hallways. But people don't always listen and some staff are too afraid to enforce the rules.

No one questions me when I sit on a stool in the kitchen. Danni glances up, the squeak of the chair bringing attention to my arrival. "You're early." They walk to the pantry, remove the plastic wrap from the tray and place it in front of me. "I was going to take it to your office, but since you're here..." The three cake slices all look delicious. Chasity doesn't like cake, so she leaves the job to me. It's one of the best perks of my job.

I dig my fork into the confetti slice and laugh. Danni smiles. Their high cheekbones force their eyes to appear smaller. Chasity would lose her shit if I ever approve a vanilla confetti cake for her birthday.

They point one finger down at the vanilla cake.

"That one's for you."

I've been trying to keep Danni out of my bed since they started six months ago. At first, I dismissed them, but their inherent goodness is too contagious.

It started with them asking me to test small pastries not yet offered at Delicacy. The small pastries became personal-sized cakes and then cakes became pies. Cake tasting for hotel events was obligatory, but everything else was optional. I keep accepting the many options they give me. And that's not okay. Sometimes I think I have to stay away from Danni. They're too good and I've been burned by a good one before.

I lick my fork clean before diving into what I think is chocolate ganache. Its sweet creaminess melts against my tongue. My chair squeaks some more as I swing my ponytail from side to side in glee.

"That looks good. Let me try." Danni opens their mouth and waits. I know they don't need to try the very cake they baked, no doubt tasting it themselves during each step. I scoop up another chunk of ganache before hovering the fork between us. Our noses are inches from each other. Danni's eyes flutter down to my lips. My hips twitch.

Damn. I take too long. Danni shifts in uncertainty before backing away.

"Hey." My voice is barely a low whisper. Everyone around us keeps moving around the kitchen, but Danni stops. They don't need me to tell them to turn. They do it automatically.

"Come here." The crook of my index finger beckons them forward until they place their elbows on the steel table between us. Their eyes only focus on me. I like it this way. There's a thrill I get from being in control of my partner, even when we're in a crowded room. Taylor had the appetite to perform almost non-stop. I didn't mind it. As long as I was the one producing the show.

I don't know to what extent Danni likes to relinquish control of their actions, to have someone be in command of their desires. All I know is when I speak, they listen.

"Open." Their lips part slowly. Small pieces of chocolate ganache dangle from the fork. I lick my tongue out slowly and use the tip to swipe at the lowest piece.

The chocolate sweetness settles on my tongue and I moan. Danni's eyes brighten a little, growing wide in anticipation of something more. When their gaze shifts downward to watch the fork capture another slice, I bring my hand down with a bang. "Look at me."

Their guilty eyes snap up in compliance. I feel no remorse.

"Stay," I command and wait an entire breath before raising the fork again. This time, their gaze remains steady.

The fork enters and hovers over Danni's tongue. Saliva pools. They don't move to swallow. "Very good."

The corners of their mouth twitch into a smile, but they think better of it at the last second. I keep them there, contemplating what my next move should be. This game could be dangerous.

I pull the fork out of Danni's mouth and clasp it between my lips. It's just as delicious as the first scoop. "Mine." I'm saved from Danni's disappointed glare when another chef calls out to them for help. I say nothing as they leave me sitting alone at the table.

I gobble up the last slice of cake quickly. It's the one I know the best: Tres Leches. My Mexican heritage sometimes makes people do that. They think my favorite food is tacos and my favorite drink is tequila. While I love tacos and can enjoy a shot of tequila when necessary, my favorite food and drink are not offered at any restaurant. It lives over 270 miles away. Still, Danni does a good job with the Tres Leches cake. My mother would complain, but she complains about everything.

Since Danni hasn't returned, I call out my preference, knowing they're nearby, listening. "The chocolate one's the best." I imagine them smiling in a pantry somewhere or decorating a cake in the next room. The image conjures up a light feeling in the middle of my chest. Maybe I'll see Danni soon after all.

Chapter Three
Taylor

"TAYLOR, YOU HAVE TO come." Chastity's tone on the other end is about as nice as she can muster. She's never been good at pretending to be kind or sweet. This covert command is the best she can do.

I answered the phone without thinking. When the familiar number on the caller ID flashed across my screen, I slid the green telephone symbol across. It would be helpful if technology advanced enough to warn me with big bold letters: "DON'T ANSWER IT! SHE'S CRAZY!"

Alas, it isn't and now I'm stuck on the phone with my ex-girlfriend's ex-best friend, smiling at passing crew members as she tries to convince me to fly to Las Vegas for her birthday party.

I certainly do not plan to book any flights to Vegas in the upcoming week. I'm of the minority opinion that Vegas isn't all it's cracked up to be. For one, I don't gamble and for two, Vegas is hot. To escape the heat, you have to travel from hotel to hotel and battle through the heavily nicotine-filled casinos to stay cool.

After voicing this concern, Chasity rebuts by reminding me we are in January when Vegas is typically colder and rainy and not sweltering. I try to argue that having to travel from hotel to hotel to stay out of the rain isn't any better, but Chasity has an instant retort.

"You won't be traveling to any other hotels, Taylor. The party is only happening at my hotel, and my hotel has everything that you could ever need."

I pause, trying to come up with a new excuse. "How many days is this party for, anyway?" I can practically feel Chasity's eyes roll as she sighs.

"Did you even bother reading any of my messages?"

Not really. I respond to myself and not aloud to her. I had read the beginning of the first message, but stopped after, "*Hey, Taylor! I wanted to invite you to my birthday party...*"

"The party is for five days," Chasity continues in my silence. "You'll get here on Monday and then leave on Saturday. Treat it like a vacation."

"Chasity, how am I supposed to ask for five days off of work in such a short amount of time?"

"It wouldn't be short notice if you had asked for the time off a month ago when I sent the text." She's right, and it isn't exactly like I have to ask for time off. The episodes ordered by the network are already in the can. They plan to air the pilot episode in two weeks. It's nice to know that they believe in the show enough to have us film more than one. By episode three, we'll know if we have a full season order.

I don't tell any of this to Chasity. It was her ex-best friend who almost ruined my career.

I feel my phone vibrate, informing me of a notification; a text message from Eilene. "*See me in my office,*" is all it says. I interrupt Chasity's tirade about my inadequate text message etiquette.

"Look, Chasity. I'm happy for you, but I don't think I'll be able to make it to your party. I'm sorry."

This time, it's Chasity who pauses. "Ok, Taylor. Maybe some other time." And then she hangs up.

I sit on the corner of Eilene's desk, right where I know I shouldn't. I started visiting Eilene in her office after my summer with Chasity. I caught her by surprise. It was almost cute how concerned she pretended to be. That look on her face didn't last long. Soon after, she regularly summoned me to her office and slid her hand up my skirt, though today–because of the chilly L.A. weather, I'm not wearing one. However, there are always workarounds.

She initially contacted me for a role about a year after my breakup. I turned it down on account that I wasn't ready to do anything more than I had already committed to. I had a steady job on a reality competition show for kids. That was enough. A few weeks after I turned it down, I received a text message.

"Don't take this the wrong way, but I'm secretly happy you didn't take the role."

I did not know who sent it. Zara was also happy I hadn't taken the role, but that was because she was certain I hadn't gotten over my breakup. She didn't need to leave me an anonymous message. She told me in person.

There were other possibilities. None I wanted to engage. Minutes later, another message came. *"If you had, then I'd have to stop fantasizing about you in my office."* Followed by more. *"On my drive home."* And more in rapid succession. Each more confusing than the last. *"In my shower and my bed."*

It was definitely not Zara. Zara's always been more of a family member to me than a manager. She'd more likely chain a chastity belt around me than chain me to a bed.

Even without a response, the messages kept coming. They followed me through the summer, and that's when I reconsidered. Gabriella wasn't coming back. She hurt me. I left her. That was the end of that story. If I wanted something more, something different,

I was going to have to go after it.

For the first time, I performed for someone who wasn't my girlfriend. My hands snaked down my panties and pushed up the cups of my bra almost every night, after every chime. Not because they told me to. Gabriella always had, and they never did. I did it because I wanted to. I allowed myself to have a fantasy that didn't include her.

Eilene and her sister, who is also her business partner, were the only two that made sense. I imagined them both at different times and sometimes at the same time. I know it's wild, and probably something I'll never admit to their faces. Performing solo was the first step. Performing in person was the next. I've been mostly successful at it.

Eileen checks the office door. I forgot to lock it. Gabriella would say I kept it unlocked on purpose. Eileen doesn't scorn me for it. She's an older woman with light streaks of gray in her hair. If I had to guess, I'd place her in her early 40s. But I don't care, so I never guess.

My sexuality isn't a secret. Fortunately or unfortunately, at some point, it was Primetime news. There was a time when I thought I had to make myself more visible for women to acknowledge me. Eilene somehow knew I was going to be a willing participant and I'm not talking about sex with a woman. I mean everything else. She was almost right.

Similar to my problem with Kyle and Monica, I'm all show and no action. It's a surprise she keeps calling me back. There hasn't been a time when I've left her office with dry panties. Too bad she's never been able to get them off me.

I always have a half dozen scenarios playing in my mind while I'm here. My head between her thighs while she sits in her executive chair is my favorite. There's also the one where she pushes me down on her desk and gets on her knees behind me. Her fingers melting into me while my neck hangs off the side of the desk is also a good one. And I can't forget the one where she forgets about the window. I look at that window now. The blinds are pulled down. In my fantasy, the whole damn thing is cranked up. The others involve crying employees who've just received poor performance evaluations or someone walking in on us because I forgot to lock the door.

Oops.

No matter the weather, Eilene always wears a skirt. One of those long pencil skirts with the slit in the back. I think it's so we always have easy access to her. I say *we* because I can't be the only one she's holding appointments for.

My hair is in a very professional low bun today with a part in the middle. I stopped gelling down my baby hairs a long time ago, but I did leave out a few curly stands from my corner edges.

Eilene has grabbed my hair in the past, which I don't dislike per se, I just only seem to love it when someone specific is doing it. And that person hasn't been around for a long time.

Eilene runs her fingers up my stretchy black jeans and buries them in my white collared shirt. She kisses my chin, then my jaw. I lean back on my elbows when her hands reach to unfasten my pants. She snakes her hand inside as soon as the zipper slides down. It's a tight fit, but she has no problem finding her favorite spot over my underwear.

Picking underwear for this occasion is a tricky decision. If I go full commando, I risk dampening my jeans. Cotton soaks up the moisture, but doesn't feel so good gliding against the skin. For a session with Eileen, nothing less than satin panties will do.

Her wrists wind in a circular motion as soon as she finds it. I bite down on her thumb when she places it in my mouth. Even if

I didn't like it, I'd do it, anyway. I'm a good girl. I know how to follow instructions. I am well trained.

Eileen's fingers never stop rubbing against me. I pant soft enough for only the two of us to hear. The thought crosses my mind to cry out louder, but I quickly push it away. Now is not the time.

"You like the way I touch you." Her lips kiss my ear when she whispers into it. I shudder out a "yes." Eilene likes dirty talk. I don't hate dirty talk, but I can do without it.

We jump when there's a knock on the door. Eileen's fingers snatch away. I quickly hop off the desk and fix my clothing. I look at Eileen, who gives an approving nod and then opens the door. An employee, I'm not sure if I've ever seen before, stands on the other side. Eileen smiles, invites them inside, and then makes room for me to leave.

"Let me know what you think about the script once you have time to read it over," she says to me. I give an enthusiastic nod, walking past the employee—currently not crying—on the way out.

After making sure I'm not being summoned anywhere else, I slide into the back of my car, shimmying out of my jeans and freshening up with my Eileen Pack; wipes and a fresh new pair of underwear. Cotton this time.

There are several things I know to be true about my sexual needs. One, I love being watched. Two, I love the taste of my partner. So far, that's only been women—a woman. But I imagine if I gave a man the opportunity, or if Gabriella hadn't intervened like she had, then I'd also like the taste of men.

My phone chimes with a notification. A new email.

To: Ttownes@mail.com
From: ChasityCEO@hotelbedlasvegas.com
Subject: Invite & Itinerary

Taylor,

I wanted to send you the invite to the party (again) and the itinerary just in case you change your mind. Your plane tickets are also attached. The flight leaves on Monday at 8:15 am. That should give you enough time to relax in your hotel room before we begin all the fun.

Hope you make it, Chasity.

Her persistence is undeniable.

The lineup for the competition show I've been a judge on for the past few years is flexible. They have pleasantly surprised me with how undemanding they've been. The show has remained a steady success, so I guess there's not too much for them to complain about. I alternate judging and hosting duties depending on the topic. My favorites are the holiday specials. The promotional-themed ones can also be fun.

My phone chimes again with next week's shooting schedule. There are two tapings scheduled for next week. When I started to not appear in every episode, my fans were quick to inform the network of their outrage. I had to release a statement–something I hate to do–to douse the flames.

Hi everyone. I can't believe the amount of love and support you've shown me over these last few days. You're all so amazing! Please don't worry about my time on Next Big Creator, I remain a judge and co-host of the series. The producers have been excellent in allowing me to accept and experience other opportunities outside of the show, which is why you do not see me in every episode. Trust that when it is time for me to move on, you'll be the first to hear the news–from me. Rest assured, my little daydreamers.

Releasing statements is how I've had to tell my fandom and others to mind their business when no one is asking their opinion. Fans mean well, but sometimes they can be too much.

I think about Chasity's invitation for hours before deciding. There's no logical reason I haven't been able to initiate sex with anyone since Gabriella. Or at least follow through. Kyle and Monica are waiting and willing, and only a few feet away. Eileen would call me to her office every day if she could. And before them, there have been others. Others who have enticed me and intrigued me only for me to walk away completely confused about who I am and what I want. Sex isn't supposed to be this hard.

My thoughts wander back to Chasity's hotel, and an idea forms. Chasity's original idea for BED was to offer a place for people to discover their sexual needs and desires. It could be the perfect place for me to figure myself out separate from Gabriella and her demands. My ex-girlfriend's ex-best friend might be worth my time, after all.

By the end of the night, I send two emails.

To: CharmedProductions@mail.com
From: Ttownes@mail.com
Subject: RE: Next Week's Availability

Hi Steve,

Is that mermaid week I see? I call dibs! I'll let Whitney wrangle the kids during circus week. She's always been so much better at it than me ;). See you all in two weeks!

Taylor Townes.

To: <u>ChasityCEO@hotelbedlasvegas.com</u>
From: <u>Ttownes@mail.com</u>
Subject: RE: Invite & Itinerary

See you on Monday. And oh, happy birthday.

Chapter Four
Gabriella

"What the fuck did you do?" The email stares back at me, mockingly. She's coming. Chasity looks back at me with a grin stretched across her face. We are in my office, the last show of the night is being performed on the theater's stage. The guests are dead silent, their mouths too busy either on each other or wide from the shock of their experience. We appreciate the feedback of both reactions.

"I did it." She throws her hands up at the feat that just might unravel me.

Chasity and Taylor are similar in the ways that they are different. They are both so damned hard headed. Taylor expresses her stubbornness through her actions. Vocalizing intentions is rare for her. I had to be hypervigilant with Taylor; watching what she was doing rather than what she was saying. Chasity completely disregards people's emotions. For weeks, I told her I didn't want Taylor coming to BED, and she never listened. And now she expects me to be happy about her dishonoring my wishes.

"I need new friends." I toss the phone back to Chasity. It lands in her lap.

"Well, your other best friend will be back tomorrow. You can talk shit about me then." She reaches for the bowl of chocolates on the desk, not bothering to excuse herself.

"I'm not ready." I've been preparing for this moment for years, but it's come faster than I expected. Ideally, it would be another year or two before I approached Taylor with the prospect of us repairing a relationship.

I have spent my time at BED creating an environment where she'll be the most comfortable without the threat of prying eyes or clout chasers wanting to link their name to the next scandal. Everything's not yet in place. I need more time.

Chasity reaches across my desk and gives my hand a slight pat. "You are ready for this, Gabriella. I believe in you. You've moved on from what happened. If she hasn't, then fuck her. That'll tell you who she really is."

"What if I see her and I don't love her anymore?" Sometimes I think the Taylor I remember, the one I loved and sacrificed for, wasn't who she was in real life.

Chasity lifts her shoulders in uncertainty. "Won't that be a good thing?" She takes a seat in the chair next to her.

I could never quite grasp how much Chasity liked or disliked Taylor. They got along fine when we were younger and she clearly tolerated her enough to ask for her help that summer, but then something seemed to change.

"It would certainly be better for your new working relationship." Chasity lifts my hands to hold them in her own. She's smiling and hopeful I'll change my mind about taking charge of her latest media proposal. I don't return her enthusiasm.

"Chasity..."

"There's no better way to show her how much you've evolved since college. She knew you when you were drawing in your notebook. You were a writer on a critically acclaimed show, expanded your talents, made your connections, and—"

"Now I work with my best friend at her slutty hotel in Las

Vegas."

Chasity's eyebrows raise at me in response. "Director isn't a bad title."

"Of course not." I've earned it. The road to get here wasn't easy. I worked many jobs and countless hours to achieve my dream and realize my independence.

"So show her how much she's missed out on. Then convince her to stay."

I push my seat away from the desk with my feet resting on the edge. "For you or for me?" I don't even know the answer to that anymore. Four years ago I was determined to make anything work. I had a ring hiding in a drawer in my dresser and no hand to put it on. It was so difficult to look at that I eventually had to get rid of it. That's not to say I couldn't get it back. I could. Only I'm not sure I want it.

"For us," Chasity says while patting my knee and plucking another piece of candy from the dish. "We're a team, remember? Gotta help each other's dreams come true."

"If not us, then who?" The words float from my breath instinctively. I've always had to take care of myself and Chasity has always been very good at making sure her needs are met—sometimes with consequences.

"Exactly."

I take a deep breath, my thoughts and plans building around an image of Taylor. My favorite. I try not to think about what she looked like when she left. While she is beautiful when she cries, I've never enjoyed causing her tears.

"I can give you an episode. We'll stream it for the guests the same day and see what the reaction is. Taylor's good. She won't need a lot of prep. It'll be a quick edit."

The only response from Chasity is the gathering of more candy.

She changes her mind and drops two out of the six pieces she held in her hand on her way out the door.

For the next few days, I gear up for Taylor's arrival. A big part of me screams to leave. There are a dozen hotels I can stay at on the strip where I won't have to be subjected to my ex-girlfriend. Chasity argues against it whenever I bring it up. She says I'm being dramatic, but for the first time in my life, I think I'm being protective.

The gold key that hangs around my neck feels heavy. Not even Danni's flirtatious baked goods can convince me everything will be fine. And they try.

"You're thinking about this all wrong," says Shay, my other best friend. We met through Chasity. She was there with Taylor the summer they achieved the concept of BED. By the sound of things, they didn't get along. "This is your moment to either prove her wrong or get revenge. Take your pick."

Proving her wrong will be easy. Despite the limitations placed on me, I graduated from college on time and did not encounter any blacklists. Hollywood is good at excusing destructive behavior. I was working my way up the Hollywood ladder when Chasity called and asked me to join her in Vegas. I couldn't say no to the opportunity of writing, producing, and directing shows with a nearly unlimited budget. There were no regrets until now.

"And if she refuses to see it?"

I might be cruel, but Shay is cold. She's an unapologetic bitch with more self-crafted enemies than friends. People want to like

Shay. She just won't let them.

"Well, that's easy. Do what you've always done."

I don't need to think long about what she means to respond, "Punish her." Punishments are tricky for Taylor. She is as good at pretending she doesn't understand the concept of them as she is pretending to not be a celebrity. Taylor has had plenty of time to practice being normal as a child growing up in show business and with me, she's had plenty of practice shockingly breaking rules she put in place. She forces punishments and then feigns innocence. There's nothing innocent about her. She always knows exactly what she's doing.

"Do you have the itinerary?" My phone responds in confirmation of Shay's forwarded email. "This is just backup," I say, more to myself than to Shay, who's following close behind me on my walk to the spa, Embrace. "I'll see what it's like to speak with her and then, if she's stubborn, then so be it."

"You gotta do what you gotta do."

"She might leave me no choice," I shrug. It's almost the same as when she used to box me into a corner in the past, whether she knew it or not.

We walk through the spa door. "I need to see every masseuse who's scheduled for the party," I bark.

The girl behind the desk of Embrace stares back at me. I snap my fingers in quick succession. I don't have time for this shit. "Now, Tinkerbell. Let's go!" She lurches forward and disappears through a door to the back.

"Can you believe the service here?" Shay says, snickering to herself. Neither one of us is usually at Embrace. Our business is elsewhere. The staff here probably function fine otherwise, but I need them to be better with Taylor coming.

The girl comes back with another, shorter one. They're wearing the same black lace uniform, but the new one looks at me with recognizable fear in her eyes. Good. We're getting somewhere. She'd probably look taller if Embrace staff wore heels. Instead, they wear comfy lace slippers with memory foam inside. I remember Chasity's assistant wearing them around and testing them out before the last purchase order.

"Hi. I apologize for the wait. I'm Paloma. Neena said you wanted to meet with some of the massage therapists. Is that correct?" Paloma presents exactly as she should. Her uniform is neatly ironed with sharp creases visible where appropriate.

I cut my eyes at Neena for not delivering my entire message. I refuse to repeat myself. "Get me the best masseuse this hotel offers."

Paloma nods at my words. "For you? Or..." she looks at Shay, who grins to herself.

"Why are you asking so many questions?" I point to the door she emerged from. "Go back there and bring back the person who's assigned to massage Taylor Townes during the party. That's it."

She opens her mouth to speak. I interrupt. "You ask me another fucking question, that's your job." Her lips pull close and purse together. She turns on her heels and disappears behind the door I directed her through. Neena's eyes shift around and then she, too, decides it's best to follow Paloma to the back.

"Who the fuck manages this place?"

Although I'm not looking for a response, Shay offers one anyway. "What do you expect from Tasha?"

I groan. Tasha. Ms. Good vibes and good energy. She does everything at a snail's pace and then blames it on the stars' alignment. Embrace must run pretty efficiently for her to stay employed.

"Why are we here, exactly?" Shay takes a seat on the white sofa in the waiting area. I remain standing. We shouldn't be here long enough for me to tire. "Are you going to tell them to refuse service to Taylor?"

"Of course not." That would be silly. Massages aren't harmful. I don't care about the person. I care about the provider. Taylor is good at looking innocent, but she can be tricky if you don't know what to watch out for.

Paloma emerges from the back with a woman I've never met. She's tall and thick. To someone else, she could appear physically intimidating. Her hair is a coiled halo around her head. Her deep dark skin is shiny, absent of hair and blemishes. She's gorgeous. Taylor will like her.

"Hi. I'm Leo. I'll be servicing Ms. Townes during the party." Despite her powerful energy, her white smile is warm and inviting.

"Hi, Leo." I hold out my hand for her to shake. She takes it. From the corner of my eye, Shay leans forward with her elbows on her knees. "Ms. Townes–" I am unprepared for the powerful emotion that causes my throat to contract and my chest to tighten. "–is a close friend of mine and I want to make sure everything goes well."

Leo looks relieved at my explanation. There's a mix of something that settles near my heart that I wouldn't dare vocalize aloud. Especially not with Shay sitting so close by. I shift through the emotions while nodding along to Leo's words. I untangle the sadness from the disappointment and tuck away the small circle of anger that sits on top of the regret. If I had to sum them all up in one word: grief.

Chapter Five
Taylor

MY SHORT FORTY-FIVE-MINUTE FLIGHT from L.A. to Las Vegas is wildly uneventful. Chasity was nice enough to fly me out of Burbank, instead of the chaotic mess that is LAX. After my confirmation of attendance, she responded to my email with the number of her chauffeur, just in case I can't find him when I arrive. I have no trouble locating the large man who stands at baggage claim with a black suit and purple and gold tie. Call it a hunch, but something tells me that the man wearing the purple and gold tie, the same colors on Chasity's invitation, is the one for me. The nice big man introduces himself as Greg. He rolls my small carry-on to the trunk of the car and we are on our way to the hotel. He doesn't ask me questions about myself or make small talk, which I prefer. I can tell he's well-trained in being discreet with Chasity's clientele.

The drive from the airport to the hotel takes less than fifteen minutes. The strip is less packed than in the summer, but there are still plenty of people, both tourists and entertainers, out and about. Greg steers the car down Tropicana Ave to Las Vegas Blvd, and at the end of the strip sits Hotel BED. The front of the hotel doesn't look like much. From the view of the strip, it blends in with all the other tall glass buildings, but once Greg turns and continues down the long, winding driveway, the view changes, and I'm amazed.

"It's best for privacy that no one knows what they're looking at from the outside," Greg sounds, apparently sensing my shock. I nod in understanding. Of course it makes sense to not have a flashing neon sign that says *you may find your husband here*!

Greg pulls the car up to the double doors, where another man is waiting. As is customary in Las Vegas, I attempt to tip for the service but am surprised when I'm denied. The courier smiles at me. "All complimentary of Ms. Coleman, ma'am."

After Greg grabs my bag, I follow him to a different entrance. The sign overhead reads Member Services. Inside, I am asked to produce my driver's license and my invite to the party. My driver's license is scanned into a machine before I am given a gold necklace with a key pendant attached to it. The woman behind the counter, who wears a white lace top and fitted black trousers, explains my necklace will allow me entrance into the hotel and access to all available amenities. The key unlocks nothing. It's a status symbol amongst members and guests. Another attached pendant, a gold tag with an etched barcode, is my actual key to my room.

I glance at her silver necklace and pendant before entering the black iron double doors leading into the lobby.

Hotel BED has more of the look of a luxury high-rise apartment than your standard brothel, or at least what some people think a brothel looks like, but sex is definitely on the menu. The way Chasity used to speak about it, the entire premise of Hotel BED is to provide a place for people who want consistent sexual intimacy in a safe and comfortable environment. Because of this, one's sexual partner is placed on reserve to please them and only them when it's time. A BED partner may live in the hotel for months in their reserved suite, waiting for the hotel guest to return from their business trip.

At its inception, we decided on four membership levels. I

wonder how many there are now. That summer was a whirlwind for me. I probably shouldn't have been there. It wasn't the first questionable decision I had made since losing my life's love. It was only the start.

Although I guess some may argue that being in a relationship with Gabriella was the beginning of ill-advised decisions and truthfully, I would tell those people to fuck off. I loved that girl. I've tried hard to hate her, but it's not Gabriella I regret. It's her choices. Things could've been different if she had behaved differently. Instead, she wrecked me, and I found myself volunteering for Chasity's cause the next summer.

Helping Chasity fulfill her dreams became a better distraction than being on set. I'm sure I was difficult for Chasity to work with. She wasn't used to having to handle me. That was Gabriella's job, and she enjoyed every second. I did too, at first. I took those memories with me and used them in my new pursuit.

My goal at Chasity's Orange County mansion was unknown, even to me. Chasity and I argued about my role there. She didn't think I was taking on enough clients. I didn't think she had any idea what she was doing. We were both right. Well, I was right and Chasity was attempting to be controlling, but I'm an accomplished actor. Not even my manager dictates which roles I take and which I leave on the table. She can make suggestions, sure, but I'm the talent, and being the talent makes me the boss.

She didn't understand. None of them did. My clients were shy. They needed to go at a slower pace with individualized attention. They watched from afar and then followed my lead the next time. Not everyone is a natural at role play.

And besides, I don't take orders from sugar babies. Her mommies provide her with a substantial amount of money. I only caught small glimpses of them throughout the weeks. They looked how you would expect—gorgeous and powerful. They've poured even more into this hotel and agreed to sit Chasity at the helm. It's what she wanted. That summer was about convincing them she could do it. Obviously, it's been a success.

My favorite part of the summer wasn't trying to forget Gabriella. It was the few times we all got together to discuss business. I had no experience in hotel management, but I've had sex in enough of them to have an opinion. The perks we discussed, and the ideas we all had, came with a hefty price tag. The numbers we were throwing around back then were outrageous. Now, I can't imagine how real they've become.

Chasity assigns me to a suite for the week. The suite is, unsurprisingly, decorated in different shades of purple, black and gold. A large living room separates a modest dining room and kitchenette. I attempt to open the door closest to the kitchenette. The knob rattles in my hand, but doesn't turn completely. It must be the connecting door to another suite.

The door on the other side of the living room opens to reveal a bedroom with an enormous bathroom attached. I unpack before I realize there is already clothing hung up on my behalf, with each outfit tagged for the day and type of event. I continue putting my things away in the space available. Once done, I pull out my phone to review the itinerary. Lunch is first. Followed by a trip to the spa and then dinner.

Attached to the itinerary is a task list for us to complete on the first day of our arrival.

1. Go to Lavish to finalize nightwear and costumes.

2. Go to Indulgence to select your personalized gift bag.

3. Have fun, Bitches!

I search through the email attachments, but do not see a map of the hotel to locate Lavish and Indulgence. I contemplate taking a nap before heading to lunch, but with so much time between lunch and dinner, it's best to eat breakfast first.

The rules attached to the email specify cell phone use is restricted throughout the hotel and no photographs and video recordings are allowed. There's a manual in the top drawer of the nightstand where a Bible might be if this was a different hotel.

The purple faux leather cover has gold foiled lettering centered on a floral pattern. Chastity's face is on the first page, along with the hotel's logo. The pages that follow all add to the legitimacy of her dreams; the mission statement touting inclusivity and diversity, the charitable efforts made possible by the contributing members, and of course, her building plans for the future. I skip through most of it, feathering the pages past my eyes with a flick of my thumb.

It's nothing I haven't heard before and there was no way for me to verify if any of it was true. Gabriella and I talked little about Chasity when they were friends, and once their friendship ended, she stopped mentioning her altogether.

I leave the room and head down for breakfast. There are plenty of signs pinned to the walls that point me in the right direction, despite not having a map.

I'm both impressed and surprised that in a hotel that caters to sex and desire, there aren't any sex-themed breakfast selections. There are no vagina-shaped papayas or peeled bananas lying around. *Chasity keeping it classy.*

As I devour my avocado toast I hear, "Taylor? Taylor, is that you?" The muscles in my back and shoulders tense immediately.

The use of my birth name is a clue that this person is probably not a crazed fan spotting me at a place where I wouldn't want to be recognized.

I slowly turn around to see a white woman with strawberry blonde hair peeking toward me. "Oh my God, Britney!" Our unified squeals earn each of us odd looks from other buffet attendees.

In true Britney fashion, she skips the rest of the way to my table to take the seat next to me. "I can't believe it's you. Can you believe this place? I can't believe that she did it!"

I nod as Britney marvels at our surroundings. Buffets are a big thing in Las Vegas. Everyone has their favorite, and Chasity doesn't seem to have spared any expense on the lavishness of her restaurant.

I take a large bite of my meal. Avocado toast is already a bougie California option. Chasity's avocado toast is extra bougie. First, there are four variations to choose from; one sprinkled with everything bagel seasoning, another topped with green onions, radish and jalapenos, a tomato and balsamic glaze version, and finally the best version, avocado toast with lemon juice and red pepper flakes. I can hear the jokes about a California girl turning her fancy restaurant into a California eatery. But as we say, they hate us 'cause they ain't us.

Britney takes time to arrange her breakfast, a smoked salmon eggs benedict and a glass of orange juice, onto the table in front of her. "How do you think she did it?"

I shrug before replying, "Maybe the loophole is that you're paying for the all-inclusive membership with all the amenities, and not the sex?" Contrary to popular belief and despite its sexy reputation, sex work is not legal in Clark County, where Las Vegas is located, though it is legal in other counties within the state of Nevada.

Britney shakes her head at my legal loophole theory. "If that's the case," she pauses to place a slice of salmon onto a piece of English muffin, "then those strip mall massage places wouldn't get busted all the time."

I tilt my head from side to side, signaling that I could see her point.

After finishing a bite of her eggs benedict, Britney leans in and whispers, "Or...she's banging the chief of police. I saw a billboard with her face on it on the way here. The first woman elected sheriff in Las Vegas history." Britney covers her mouth and laughs, trying not to draw attention to our table with her joke. I laugh along as well, but we both know it's more plausible than we want to admit four years after the fact. If not Chasity, then surely someone she knows.

For the rest of breakfast, Britney and I fill each other in on what life has been like since leaving college, putting our Chasity gossip on hold. Britney graduated from school and then became a high school teacher. Knowing her past, my eyes narrow a bit at that information, but I don't let on that I am questioning her career choice.

I started college fully intending to continue my career as an actor. My breakup with Gabriella almost ruined everything. It was my sister Eryn, who pulled me out of bed to go to work every day. Once I was on set and in my trailer, I could snap out of it, but getting there took work.

After breakfast, Britney and I wander around the hotel, traveling up and down floors and trying to get a peek behind closed—and sometimes locked—doors.

We are both eager to figure out all of what BED offers. What parts has Chasity kept? What has she changed?

The second floor of the hotel seems more populated than the first. We pass other guests as they walk in and out of the shops, each more elegantly named than the last. Britney and I take notice of the colors of the guests' necklaces, trying to distinguish who's on which tier. Britney snickers at a few of the couples that she thinks look sexually incompatible and swoons at her ideal type: older distinguished members with younger partners. I warn her about gawking at people, but she welcomes the idea of there being some sort of consequence for her actions. She bats her eyelashes at me. "You know I like to get into trouble." My body tingles at her words. *I know. Me too.*

Seeing Britney and realizing that BED hasn't been all jokes and giggles makes me excited, but also a little uneasy. What do you say to someone who you shared such intimate moments with, but haven't seen in four years?

"Oh, wow, Brit, you're a teacher? Remember when you wore nothing under your skirt to our Greek Mythology lecture?"

Does she even remember that? I hadn't. But the moment she mentioned becoming a teacher, it suddenly all came flooding back to me. That memory—and others.

At the sight of an employee standing to the side of the walkway, greeting and smiling at members, Britney's eyes glow. Bouncing on the balls of her feet, she walks over to him. "Excuse me, sir!" Now that Britney has found her target, I have to quicken my pace to keep up.

He instantly gives her his full attention, smiling as she approaches. "Yes? My name is Paul. How may I help?"

"Well!" She places her hand over her heart and giggles. He maintains his smile. He's much younger than Greg had been, but older than Britney and me. While observing him, I notice he, too, wears a chain; silver with a silver rectangle pendant, no key.

"My friend and I," Britney explains as she gestures towards me, "are in town for Chasity's birthday party. We were told there were things to be picked up at Lavish, but we don't know how to get there. Can you help us?"

"Of course. If you follow me, I will show you the way." Britney and Paul walk side by side as he leads us down the hallway. I stay a few steps behind, silently laughing at Britney's antics. Secretly, I think she thought Paul was an expensive-looking security guard. He turned out not to be, though I'm sure there are some around here somewhere. Eventually, Britney will find them.

We pass more shops along the way to Lavish. Some storefronts have glass windows making it possible to see inside, while the windows of others are impossible to see through. A woman dressed in a pink long-sleeved lace romper with a short black apron stands between a set of opened black double doors. The tailored apron looks like a short flowy flirty skirt rather than the traditional homemaker. She is beautiful, with deep brown skin and a black braided ponytail traveling down her back. She gives a slight smile and nods to Paul as he passes with Britney. As I approach, she smiles. I smile back, maintaining direct eye contact as we pass one another.

Paul and Britney stop at a different set of double doors, identical to the ones we have just passed. He pauses before providing us with an explanation, "This is Lavish" and then he opens the doors, leading us inside.

The inside of Lavish is quiet, but busy. There are multiple staffers assisting groups of members with their shopping. I can better identify the staff from the members. Regardless of their presenting gender, staff roam around the store and other parts of BED in two distinct outfits: lacy tops and short flirty black aprons, or suits with purple and gold ties. From what I can see, every staff member in Lavish wears a chain around their neck. I notice their necklace combinations vary. Paul's chain is silver and has no key attached. Some staff have rose gold chains, with and without keys and with silver tags.

Before departing, Paul introduces us to Michael, another employee. *Silver key and tag. What does that mean*? Michael gives us a tour of the shop, showing us the different lingerie options. He explains they can tailor any item to fit us exactly. If we want to mix and match, that's available as well. Staff will deliver purchases to our rooms within twenty-four hours. Options have been pre-selected for us to approve, based on the themes.

Michael leads us over to two built-in wall tablets, where he scans the tags on our chains. Our pre-selected lingerie options reveal themselves.

"Oh, wow! She really knows us." Britney studies the outfits on her display.

I can see what she means. My casual nighttime selection is a comfy short set. Britney's? A lacy black bra set. My outfit for fantasy night is a one-piece red shimmery Mrs. Claus ensemble. Britney's outfit is a preppy schoolgirl. For mystery night, we both have different variations of an old detective uniform and for BDSM night, straps. More straps for me than for Britney, whose design leaves no straps to support her breasts.

Britney squeals in excitement. "I love it all! We don't need to change a thing."

Michael looks at me as I stand motionless. I nod at him in agreement. My picks are perfect, almost as if I had chosen them myself, but that's also what makes me nervous. What exactly does Chasity have planned for us?

After confirming our orders, Michael assures us they'll be delivered to our rooms before tomorrow night, when the first event is supposed to take place. We thank him, but as I depart the store, I realize Britney is not leaving with me. "Are you coming?"

She waves me away. "You go ahead." Her eyes roam the many racks of fabric. "I think I'm going to stay awhile."

I wave goodbye to her, making my way out of the dark double doors. The walkway is still as busy as it was when we entered and the woman across the hall, the one in the pink lacy top with the long black braid, is still standing in the doorway of the other shop. Her eyes find mine after smiling at a couple walking by. As I walk to her, her stance shifts with her head cocked a little to the side, curious.

She responds to my greeting with her name. "I'm Kacey. How may I help you?"

"I'm not sure. I'm here for the party and I don't know a lot about the hotel." That isn't what I mean to say. I want to ask her about her necklace. *Gold chain with a gold key and a silver tag*. But at the moment, it sounds rude to ask.

"Oh, right. Well, this is..." she gestures to the room behind her, "...is Indulgence, the toy store. Are you here to select your items?"

I nearly forgot all about getting a gift bag from Indulgence before setting off with Britney. I have to admit that I didn't think Indulgence would be a sex toy shop. A personalized gift bag sounds more like a fancy gift shop than a fancy sex store. I nod to Kacey, confirming my fake intentions before following her inside.

Indulgence is just as quiet and busy as Lavish was. Also similar to Lavish, there are multiple staff walking around, assisting members with their purchases. Curiously, though, there is nothing to buy. I look around the shop to find any inkling of any sex toy and see nothing, only black boxes on the walls. Kacey leads me toward a kiosk and explains I can view and then select whichever item I want.

The kiosk looks exactly like the one at Lavish; a sleek black tablet stand securely stabilized to the floor. The large screen displays a welcome message in gold lettering.

"After you're done, I'll take you to the back to get your items." Kacey's smile is warm and reassuring. I'm sure I'm not the first person who has come into Indulgence with no clue what I am doing. And it's not that I'm a stranger to sex toys. I've been trained to enjoy them.

I nod and then browse the catalog while Kacey patiently waits nearby. When I announce I'm done, Kacey places her hand in mine and leads me through another set of black doors.

The area is like walking into any fitting room in a department store, but darker, with purple lighting and soft music playing low. "Shit." The sounds of moans and grunts fill my ears and desire floods through my entire body. It happens quickly before I can attempt to gain any control over my impulses. It's too soon for me to fail my mission of self-discovery, to be more than what she taught me to be. I keep telling myself this even as I feel the thin fabric between my thighs become damp, sliding against me the more I walk and yearning to be touched, the more sounds I hear.

Kacey first leads me to a small circular locker room. It reminds me of a changing area at the spa. "First," Kacey slides her hands underneath my shirt. "We have to get you undressed."

Perhaps at some point Chasity and some of the other girls discussed pushiness being a part of the training curriculum at BED. I'm not offended. It's just the unapologetic way that Kacey issues her rationale as a command, reminds me of someone else. And that person, surprisingly, isn't Gabriella.

Kacey pulls my shirt over my head before hooking her fingers into the waistband of my pants and sliding them down. I obediently untangle the pants from my ankles and stand only in my underwear. Kacey sketches my body with her hands, gliding her fingers over my thighs, butt, stomach and the tops of my breasts.

Her contact causes my skin to become inflamed into a nerve of tickles. I suppress the giggling.

"Your satisfaction is very important to us. We never send a customer home without first trying out the merchandise." There is no memory related to this policy that floats to the front of my brain. I try to recall who was in charge of toy experiences or using toys during practices, but come up blank.

I nod in understanding, going along with the process I don't understand at all. I do know I want Kacey to do a lot more touching than what she's doing now.

When deciding to come to BED, I made a promise to myself to find the desires of the real Taylor and not continue the behaviors she taught me, but how am I supposed to know the difference? My body is evidence that I want Kacey to touch me. My pounding heart, my soaked panties, my erect nipples. Doesn't all of that scream, *I want this now!?*

The promise I made to myself weakens the more steps I take down the hallway. Kacey stops at a door with a gold bolt lock. No sounds come from this room and the sign on top of the lock reads: vacant. Kacey turns to me and smiles while pulling out a key to unlock the door. The moment she lets go of my hand to allow me space to enter the room, I know I should leave. But the room itself is so enticing. With the door open, I can see one piece of furniture: a medium-sized S-shaped sofa. I know what it is immediately. I have dreamt of it in my fantasies. Two screams sound off inside of me simultaneously; an erotic *yes*! And a defeated *fuck*! There's no way real Taylor or manufactured Taylor, whoever was who, could walk away from this chair.

Kacey places one manicured finger onto my back, propelling me inside. After directing me to sit on the sofa, she produces a small black paper bag. The sadness etched on her face is dramatic. The pout is overdone. Her eyebrows arch and scrunch together in heightened disappointment. Her frown is so deep her top lip almost reaches her nose.

"This bag is empty. You picked nothing for us to play with."

I grin, trying hard to contain my smile. She's right. I selected random toys to place into my shopping cart, but didn't complete the order. I intended to leave the store after telling Kacey that I was done, but then she grabbed my hand and I found myself in this chair, half naked, with Kacey's gorgeous face inches from mine.

Kacey drops the empty paper bag before sitting down between my open thighs, gripping them with her fingers. "I should've known you'd be trouble."

She presses her lace-covered breasts against mine. I watch as she uses her teeth to pull down the cup of my bra, producing one erect nipple. I clasp my hand over it before she pulls it into her mouth. Her lips meet my knuckles and her eyes fling up to me and narrow.

I smile. It's not that I don't want what Kacey's offering. It's only I've never done this quite this way. Gabriella was practically a stranger when we met, but we had years-long conversations.

I didn't just walk into a bar and take her home with me. I'm not even sure I know how to do that. Even Elaine, I knew before she propositioned me. And she's never gotten me to take off all my clothes. Kyle and Monica just happened and luckily I've never been forced into a conversation with either of them since.

There's no way for me to explain all of this to Kacey, who still stares at me as if I have taken the cutest puppy from the litter.

"They warned us about you, you know." Her back arches with her chest pressed into me. The curve of the chair keeps my body steady. "You try to act sweet and innocent, but all you want is to be punished."

"That's only a little true." Hearing Chasity's words from Kacey's mouth is amusing to me. Of course, she would say that. Gabriella used to say something similar. She couldn't believe that I had grown up in the entertainment industry and somehow was a decent person. Let alone someone nice.

"I *am* sweet. I'm *not* innocent, but I only like to get into trouble after dinner. Preferably once a week after 9 p.m."

Kacey doesn't laugh at my joke. She growls at me. Her arms straighten to lift her body to tower over me. Her body pushes into me to push my hips back and spread my thighs further apart.

I used to think Gabriella was too beautiful to be scary, so I smirked instead of screaming and walked when I should have run.

Maybe I upset Kacey on purpose, knowing what it would lead to. Gabriella would say so. Oh, the things she would do if she were here. I open my mouth to explain it to Kacey. Pissing her off was an accident. My ex-girlfriend made me do it. It's faulty wiring left over from my heartbreak. The words don't escape in time.

Kacey's tongue slips between my lips and I meet her caress with mine. Her hands roam and I let them. First over my stomach and up to the band that keeps my breasts from completely spilling out. The once-freed nipple hides again behind the cup, but with the way she moves, it won't be for long.

A knock sounds at the door. Kacey groans. I instantly feel a sense of loss when she pulls away from me. She makes no move to answer it. Only stares in defiance. The door to the fitting room cracks open. Her head disappears to the other side of the wall. My clothes, neatly folded, return to her arms. I feel confused and a little rejected.

At my expression, Kacey responds, "Don't worry. Turns out you're not the only one who likes to get into trouble." She lays my clothes at the end of the sofa, takes one last look at me, and leaves.

Chapter Six
Gabriella

IF EVERYONE JUST DID as I said, the world would be a better place. Shay's bedroom floor is a black and gold tile. I have a love/hate relationship with tile. I like how customizable it can be, but hate how difficult it is to clean. Shay solved that problem by requesting the gold grout. It blends beautifully with the black and gold mosaic. How Shay convinced Chasity to increase the budget for it, I've never asked.

Shay's bedroom does not look like the most comfortable place to sleep. It's built more for torture than for rejuvenation. Usually, if I'm looking for Shay during daytime hours, I find her in other places around the hotel. The only reason I'm here now, sitting on her sleek, black bedroom floor, is because of Kacey.

Kacey was one of the first people hired by Chasity. She was fine at first, but then she was keyed by a rich gold member, propelling her status to the top. She's been insufferable ever since. Kacey likes to push buttons and not in a cute way like Taylor. Not where you can pretend she's just naïve and doesn't know any better. Kacey's a bad bitch that knows she's a bad bitch. And bad bitches are way more trouble. I think that's why Chasity keeps her around, some bad bitch code of conduct and respect. She could easily fire her and just let her wander around the hotel like the rest of the Reserves, but she won't.

And now Kacey's my problem. Or, I should say, Shay's problem. What good is having an evil best friend if she won't burn down the world for you? Or in Kacey's case, get chained to a St. Andrew's Cross.

Shay called me down here as soon as she knew of Kacey's ill deed, ignoring the order of her superior. It was simple. I pride myself on being direct and concise, especially when giving important instructions to staff. The message was clear: Don't touch her!

I even went through the trouble of listing the amenities she could receive service in, like the hair and nail salon. She could go to the pools, the garden, most of the restaurants, and even to Embrace—after I had my meeting with them, of course. Under no circumstance was she ever supposed to be undressed, especially not by Kacey.

I checked all the boxes and Kacey tried to erase them. I can't be too mad at Taylor about it. Like I said, Kacey is a bad bitch. She can be hard to resist, especially for someone like Taylor, filled with love and hope. The two things Kacey enjoys sucking out of people.

Kacey is doing a good job of looking unphased, naked with her arms and ankles spread and chained. Which means her punishment is only going to get worse.

"How long do you want her to stay like this for?" Shay asks, observing her handiwork.

My response is quick. "How many places did you touch her?"

Kacey pretends to think, tilting her chin upwards with her eyes toward the ceiling. "Hmm. I took off her clothes." She extends one finger. "I think I bit a nipple or two." She adds two more. "Do her thighs flying open for me count?" She wiggles the fourth finger before leaving it with the group. "I was hoping she'd bounce her ass on my face, but then there was an interruption."

Busy with her theatrics, Kacey doesn't notice when Shay

produces a special instrument for each finger she proudly holds up.

I stand to leave at the same time I hear Kacey muffle the scream she intended to conceal. I don't need to be here for the rest of it.

I know Kacey doesn't want Taylor as much as she wants to be amused, but that's the problem. Taylor isn't her toy to play with.

Chapter Seven
Taylor

I MAKE IT BACK to my suite without getting into any more BED trouble along the way and dress for lunch. Given the reputation that I have already earned, according to Kacey, I contemplate wearing my clothing instead of the outfit selected for me; a yellow backless maxi dress. Thinking there may be some sort of theme to the lunch, I forgo my plan of rebellion and put on the dress after taking a much-needed shower.

Grabbing my small purse on the way out, I head to the elevator. After failing to secure a map of the hotel earlier today, I do not know where I am supposed to be going. My first plan of action is to go to the lobby, where the breakfast restaurant is located, and then ask for directions. I step into the empty elevator just as I hear a yell from behind me.

"Wait! Taylor, wait!"

I look up, placing my hand against the door to keep the elevator from closing. The voice does not belong to Britney, and as the yellow-dressed figure comes barreling down the hallway to catch her ride, I curse a little inside.

Fuck. It's Shay.

Shay looks glorious as she runs toward the elevator, her dark hair blowing behind her. She looks annoyed—her usual expression. I imagine her critiquing me as I stand between the elevator doors, preventing them from closing.

"What are you doing?" She smoothes down her tousled hair. "You should've gotten off and waited. Now you've held the elevator up for other people."

Bitch!

I don't bother proclaiming my good deed. "It's nice to see you again, too, Shay." She doesn't return the greeting. Shay and I have always been more like frenemies than friends. We've never hung out with each other alone, and I've always had the slightest inkling she didn't like me. The feeling is mutual.

With a perplexed look on her face, Shay looks at the elevator control panel before pushing a button. "Where were you going? Decadent is on the eighth floor."

I shrug. I glance at Shay, noticing her necklace; gold chain, gold key, and gold tag. Just like mine.

"They didn't give me a map at member services and I didn't see one in the suite, either." Vegas hotels are notorious for their complicated landscapes. It's not uncommon to receive a map at check-in detailing where your room is located, so you don't get confused.

"Ugh. I forgot Chasity waived the usual membership protocol. Did you see the manual?" I nod and watch as Shay appears more agitated at the mere idea of being helpful. "You can use that, but there's also..." She stops talking to retrieve her cell phone from her purse.

The elevator doors open directly into the lobby of the restaurant. Shay exits the elevator and ends our one-sided conversation. She gains the attention of the hostess and informs her of our lunch appointment with Chasity. The hostess, dressed in a lacy black top with fitted black trousers, escorts us to the table. We are not the first to arrive. Sitting across from Britney is Leanna, who I am genuinely excited to see. Leanna shoots up from her seat to hug me. She's the friend who makes you tea when you are sick and leaves you a snack before a late night study session. I've missed her.

Shay waves to everyone else before sitting down at the table across from me. We chat idly for a few moments, waiting for Chasity to arrive. In her absence, the wait staff showers us with small appetizers and drinks.

"How is everyone liking the hotel?" Britney asks, right before taking a bite into her warm cheese roll.

Leanna is the only one to respond. "It's so pretty. We should explore it more after lunch."

"Can't," Shay says. "We have to go to the spa."

We all nod, suddenly remembering it's on the itinerary for this morning.

"We can do it after the spa, then."

I silently consider Britney's suggestion. I'm already in need of a nap and the spa just might do me in.

Britney continues, "I don't know why she has us taking a nap. It's not like we're toddlers."

Shay snorts, and Britney shoots me a look as if to say, *What the fuck is her problem?* Leanna looks equally annoyed at Shay's attitude. She likes it when everyone gets along.

We adjust in our chairs as Chasity approaches the table. Smiling at us all, she bends down to hug and kiss us on each cheek. "I'm so glad you're here!"

The waitstaff stands by until she takes her seat at the head. She shoos them away. "Just bring out everything that we've already selected." She then turns to us. "Don't worry. You'll love all of it." Waiters clear the table of our small empty plates to make way for herbed caesar salad, Peruvian scallop crudo and beef tartare crostino for each of us. This trip is going to be worth it for the food alone.

"We are all very impressed with what you've done to the place, Chasity." It's Britney again, returning to her quest of trying to figure out the secrets of the hotel.

Chasity smiles and thanks Britney. "You guys helped. You really did. All of those late nights talking about the hotel. You may have thought I was just high, but I was taking notes," she said while laughing. We laugh too. She's right.

"What about the necklaces? We never talked about these." I pull on my gold chain, dragging the key across back and forth.

"The necklaces are new. I needed to create a hierarchy within the memberships, something to encourage financial aspiration. For the party, I made you all top tier members. You'll be able to do anything you want here, with almost whoever you want." She winks, encouraging Britney to smile wider.

"Good to know I didn't break any rules earlier." She turns to the rest of us. "Did you guys know that Lavish offers private fittings? They want to make sure that everything fits just right and that you receive the visual reaction that you're looking for."

My eyes shift around the table, noting everyone's reaction to Britney's confession. Expectedly, Shay is in the middle of an eye roll.

Leanna slides her phone closer to the edge of the table before asking, "What floor is Lavish on again?"

Britney huffs, not immediately answering Leanna's question. "I am a little sad that I didn't break any rules. Now, it doesn't seem as hot."

"What are the rules?" I ask, thinking of my private meeting with a staff member.

Chasity shrugs. "For members? It depends. There are limits to what members can do based on their status. You are top tier status, therefore you have very few limits. I trust you ladies to not do anything to anyone who wants nothing to do with you, though I couldn't imagine that. There are more rules for employees than there are for members. Employees are everywhere, but that doesn't mean they get to experience everything. There's an entire behind-the-scenes process that permits their participation in any scene or party."

Her eyes land on Britney and then swing in my direction.

"Where there are rules, there are consequences. Don't think just because of your top tier status you can do whatever you want," Britney gasps in mock innocence. I stare back in defiance. Anything Chasity has heard about me and my relationship to rule breaking is second-hand information, delivered to her by the woman who broke me.

She can take her rule book and shove it up her ass. I'm not here to be controlled by her or be reminded of my other lifetime when rules were titillating appetizers before the main event.

"There is a similar behind-the-scenes process for members, depending on what event you're interested in participating in. You won't be here long enough to meet the requirements to join our most popular clubs, but there may be others with fewer requirements that you can experience. When in doubt, consult the manual. If you're still unsure, contact my assistant."

A disapproving sound rumbles in Britney's throat. It's uncharacteristic of her to show any displeasure. She usually laughs everything off with a smile and a giggle.

"What? *We* have to prove that we can meet *their* expectations? Do they not know who we are?" Britney's open palm waves about in the air. Still staring at Chasity with a look of disbelief across her face, she misses the way Shay's eye cut at her from the side. Chasity takes her time chewing her food and then sipping her glass of wine. Leanna and I trade glances from across the table.

I understand what Britney means. Our prior experiences serve as the blueprint for this hotel. While I didn't expect there to be monuments of us lining the halls, I think Britney expected some level of recognition. Restricted access feels like rejection. The hotel is Chasity's baby. We would've never come together that summer if it wasn't for her dream.

"The requirements are an issue of safety, not privilege. I thought you, of all people, would understand that."

Britney's breath catches in her throat. She opens her mouth to respond, but Leanna interrupts her. "I noticed some of them have necklaces as well," Leanna says. I nod along to Leanna's observation, thrilled that someone else is paying as much attention as I am.

"Yes," Chasity confirms. "I thought real long and hard about how to set the employees apart, but also have them blend into the environment. Can you imagine having those plastic lanyards hanging from their necks?" She cringes. "The thing that sets the employees apart is the tag. It is always silver. No matter what the status of the employee is."

Leanna, Britney, and I all "Oh" in response. Chasity appears pleased with our reactions. Britney, having had time to adjust to the change in topic, is back to her usual level of excitement.

Leanna continues, "So what are the tiers? Did you keep them the same?"

"I changed the name of the top tiers to sound less juvenile." She scrunches up her face, apologizing for referring to our twenty-one-year-old selves as immature.

"Girlfriends and Boyfriends are now just called Partners, with Husbands and Wives changed to Significants."

I can tell by the looks on Leanna and Britney's faces that they approve of the changes. The new titles are more adult and inclusive. We never would have thought of it back then.

"Friends...with Benefits are now simply Friends. Employees can't be members of that tier. From a business perspective, it would be too messy. Friends also wear silver chains, but their keys are bare, not covered in diamonds like the keys of the higher tiers. You haven't seen too many of them around here. They don't stay Friends for long after they realize the limitations. The lowest tier an employee can be is a Lover. Lovers have platinum necklaces with platinum keys covered in diamonds. Remember, employees always have silver tags, but an unmatched employee will never have a key. So if you see an employee with a silver tag and a silver key, then they are also someone's Lover. The same can be said for Partners, who have rose gold keys and tags, and Significants, who wear gold keys and tags."

The information Chasity is feeding us logs into my brain as the waiters deliver the entrees: slow-roasted lamb, grilled duck, sea bass, asparagus, and chantenay carrots.

Kacey is someone's Significant. That must be the rule she was breaking. Lunch continues, with Chasity detailing the amenities, based on our status, that the hotel offers. I make note of a few of them before the waiters clear the table for the last time.

Britney pouts. "No dessert?"

"Desserts are later." Chasity takes a pair of sunglasses from the top of her head and slides them over her eyes. "You're going to need them."

As a group, we follow Chasity out of the dining room area, and across the hall to Embrace. Chasity guides us to the locker room. True to its promise of relaxation, Embrace has low lighting, soothing music and smells divine. I listen closely, but I don't hear any sounds of extreme pleasure. Chasity introduces us to Wendy, a cute small girl dressed in a deep v-neck black lace jumpsuit. I catch Shay staring at her breasts before we follow her down the rest of the hallway. Another employee whisks Chasity away.

My masseuse, Leo, is a woman with a glorious stretched-out mane. My massage with Leo is nice. She sets the temperature of my bed to high, just how I like it. Before she begins, she rubs an oil between her palms and tells me to breathe in deeply. I comply, inhaling the sweet scent into my lungs before exhaling again. I fall asleep shortly after she applies the hot stones, and don't wake again until it's time for me to turn over onto my back. My eyes close again after she gives me a tender foot massage.

The soft tone of a chime wakes me completely. Leo lays the warm robe at my feet before leading me out to the lounge area to enjoy dessert.

There, I sit and talk with the group about our spa experiences with Chasity. After Britney's massage, her masseuse immediately became her superior, punishing her for receiving a bad review. She then taught her how to properly give a massage, which involved a lot of spanking and hair pulling.

Leanna's masseuse sustained an injury during her massage, causing Leanna to do everything she could to make the pain go away.

Shay's massage was like Britney's, except instead of being punished, Shay punished her masseuse after she failed to inquire about her allergies, and then again when she dropped the oil, and for the last time after Shay's robe was not warm enough. Britney squirms while Shay details the events of her session. I can't fault her. She isn't the only one heating up.

I keep quiet about my massage, a proven outlier amongst the others. Leo didn't touch any part of me that a regular non-BED masseuse wouldn't touch.

We finish enjoying our desserts and cocktails. Another Embrace staff member pulls open a curtain to reveal a gigantic bed. We all gasp.

"It's an Alaska King!" Chasity shuffles onto it and settles herself in the middle. I crawl onto the bed myself and head to the edge of the right side. Leanna follows behind me, with Chasity on the left of us. Britney claims the position between Chasity and Shay.

"Do we have to take a nap? I'm not even tired." Britney unties her robe. The coverage falls away.

"Nope," says Chasity, as they chatter.

As the lights dim, I turn over to my side and close my eyes. I'm more tired than I thought. Feeling a slight tug on my robe, I look down to see Leanna's hands untying my belt, and then slip inside.

"I've missed you," she whispers in my ear as she cups my breast.

I think I may have missed her, too. It was a complicated time. And our relationship didn't help clear up any of my confusion. It was only a year after everything happened with Gabriella. I wasn't over it then. I'm still not. Leanna pinches and rolls my nipples between her fingers. I grind against her. The move is instinctual. I regret it as soon as it's done.

Leanna isn't a part of my plan for this week. She's in the past. Right where I want to leave Gabriella. I turn to tell her. It would only be fair for her to know my expectations for the rest of this trip. I look back at her, expecting her eyes to stare into my own. Instead, I find her eyes shuttered. Her hand still moves slowly against me. I change my mind, settling back into a comfortable position.

"Ouch! You fucking bitch, that hurt!"

Two seconds. I fell asleep for approximately two seconds and now the Alaska King is in the middle of a war zone.

Britney, red-faced and enraged, shouts from one side of the

room.

"You told me I could slap you!" Shay yells back.

"That was too hard, you crazy, dominating bitch!"

Old habits. We all have our limits, but Shay's limits have always been more on the extreme side of things. Britney forgets that the most. Drawn to Shay's dominating persona, Britney melts against her time and time again, only to be left angry and disappointed every time.

I reach for my phone, only to remember I left it in my locker. I bid the group farewell on my way back to change my clothes. "See you all at dinner." Chasity's mediation voice grows fainter and fainter as I leave them behind. I am nearly dressed when Leanna comes rounding the corner.

"Am I naïve to be surprised?" I shut the matte black door to my locker. It barely makes a sound. I thought everyone was mostly pretending that what had happened in college hadn't happened at all. Sure, there were some past references made, and I was suspicious of the nap, but a part of me had also hoped I would be wrong.

Leanna answers my question with a curious look on her face. "Why does it bother you so much now? It never did before." I instantly regret having this conversation. Leanna clearly will not understand.

"I guess I just thought that after three years, we'd have more in common. Are you telling me that my vagina is the only thing about me that's interesting?"

Leanna snorts, "No. I just think that you're looking at things through a distorted lens. It's been three years since we were all together. Chasity runs a freaking sex hotel and nothing about Britney has changed. When we were at lunch earlier, she asked me if I thought she would get into trouble for not tipping. And Shay is more dangerous than before. I'm pretty sure she works here."

"Why do you think that?" We walk out of the front doors of Embrace together.

"I'm not sure if it's her only job, but she already knows a lot about this place."

I think back to the elevator when Shay scolded me for not going to the correct floor and how uninterested she was when Chasity was filling us in on the membership details. But then I remember, "She doesn't have a silver tag."

Leanna shrugs. "I thought about that too, but it's the only thing that makes sense." We continue to walk in silence to the elevator. "I chose a Lover room. They bring you fresh rose petals every day." When the elevator doors open on the fourth floor, Leanna exits, "See you at dinner."

Chapter Eight
Gabriella

I BELIEVE SEX IS a very natural thing. I have few limits and when annoyed, the goal to satisfy my partner becomes what I need to accomplish. Taylor loved pushing my buttons before sex. She got off on it and I got off on making her pay for it.

That she still does it, even subconsciously, doesn't surprise me. I know the only reason she's allowing Chasity's friend to touch her like that is because she's secretly thinking of me coming in and dragging her away. It's one of her favorite games. I could do it. I'd be completely justified.

There's something that's missing from her body. Although the sight of her bare nipples without their jewelry is upsetting, I try not to obsess about it too much. I expected the jewelry to be missing from her fingers, but not from her nipples. I bite down on my lip at the memory of me tugging them with my teeth and her squirming underneath me, in front of me, on top of me. There were so many options.

Shay and the other girl are easy to ignore. They're still bickering about their sexual mishap. Chasity sits watching them while massaging her temples in irritation. Her robe is back on, but hanging open. We've been best friends since childhood and fully informed of each other's firsts, but we've never just gawked at each other's naked bodies like it was no big deal. We are not those types of best friends. Once I started working here, though, it was obvious things had changed.

"Will you just get over it already? You're fine. There's nothing even there," Shay snaps.

The redhead has streaks of blonde in her hair—or she's blonde with streaks of red—my eyes can't seem to decide. She pokes at her face in the mirror an employee brought for her. "I'm all red," she says, slamming the mirror onto the bed.

Shay stares at her incredulously, with an amused expression on her face. "You've always looked like that."

I snicker to myself at her tone. Because it's Shay, it comes off more condescending than it should. Shay doesn't boast about her light brown skin or the benefits of melanin. She could. She has in the past and is known for educating people about her Filipino heritage, especially if they get it wrong.

"Thank you, Shay, for that enlightening piece of information." Not bothering to cover herself with her robe, she shoves Shay on the way out.

"Did you think about waiting to have your lovers' spat?" Chasity looks at Shay with a disappointed scowl. This isn't unusual. There's a misconception at the hotel that because we are friends, Shay and I receive special privileges. It's less true for me since I very much enjoy the space I've carved out for myself. I know my strengths and I stick to them. Shay is always pushing the boundaries—and Chasity's last nerve.

"Lover? Please. She's fun to play with, but that's a very coveted position." Shay retrieves the tray of strawberries and settles herself down, cross-legged, on the bed. She takes a bite into one and then looks up at me. "What are you doing here? You just missed your lover." Her eyes roll pointedly at Chasity.

My body stays planted against the door frame I've been leaning against since Taylor's massage ended. "Didn't miss her. She left with someone else. Unauthorized." By the time the ruckus started, I hadn't decided on a course of action. Knowing Taylor, she would have wanted every option I had to give her. If everyone had slept, she would have loved for me to dip my hands into her robe. The other girl is inexperienced in the pleasures of Taylor. She needed to go lower. She needed to have done it without hesitation, filled with force and possession. That's what Taylor really likes.

"I thought you were done with sex for a while," I tease. Vows of celibacy aren't Shay's thing. She doesn't do self-reflections or spiritual journeys.

"I didn't have sex with her." She's technically right, but I'm pretty sure that's where everything was going. Taylor had just shut her eyes when the redhead freed herself from her robe and flung it to the floor. Her hands roamed over her body. Sandwiched in between the two, she put on a deliberate show. Chasity had responded to her immediately by sliding her tongue into her waiting mouth.

Although the basis of our relationship with Chasity is the same, the functions of Shay's and my friendship with Chasity are different. I've never facilitated or encouraged any of Chasity's hookups. I've rooted for one, but that's been long over.

I'm pretty sure the girl expected Shay to take over when Chasity withdrew. The first few slaps were light. Her cheeks shook at the impact that barely made a sound. The girl smiled with each swat. Shay started with small taps on her cheeks and then moved downward. Even when her moans grew louder, Taylor didn't stir awake. The hand dipped into her robe only moved slightly.

Once at the bottom, Shay had gripped the girl's hips to steady her, drew back her hand, and hit her harder than she had any of the other times. The move had interrupted the momentum and robbed Chasity of her snack. She doesn't indulge as often as she used to, thus the migraine.

"Okay. Is that how you're getting off? Facilitating sexual acts?"

"Are you feeling bad for her or something? She's fine. She was just being dramatic." Shay plucks the green stem off the next strawberry and then dips it into her mouth.

"Who was the girl?" I jut my chin toward the side of the bed Taylor was on.

Shay looks back. "Oh, Leanna? Ah, that's why you're all moody," she teases.

"Neither one of you thought to tell me about her?"

Shay shrugs. Chasity finds her discarded robe to slide her arms through. "It's not a big deal. I think they barely had a thing. Leanna was the best at always tending to her clients." Chastity looks at Shay, pointedly.

"My clients loved me," Shay defends, tearing off the end of another strawberry.

"Whatever." Chastity ties the front of her robe. "Don't cause any drama with Leanna, Gabby. Taylor's a big girl, whether you love her, or not."

I walk away without responding. Chastity and Shay's bickering voices follow me to the back door I use to escape back to my sanctuary. The theater should have my full attention. Not Taylor. Not at this moment. Something called me to the spa. I told myself I would only receive the report from Leo to ensure everything went as planned. I leave without it. If something went wrong, I'll hear about it later.

Chasity's words echo in the back of my mind with each step. I love Taylor. It's just times like these when I question whether having her is for the best. For both of us.

Chapter Nine
Taylor

THE BLINDS AND CURTAINS are open when I return to the suite. I shimmy out of my yellow dress before crawling into the bed. Coming to BED may have been a mistake. So far, the only thing this hotel has offered me is good food and terrible memories. The best chance I have of accomplishing my goal is to stay away from these girls as much as possible.

After my nap, as I change into the black pleated shoulder pencil dress, I strategize on ways I can avoid opportunities for group sex with old friends. I check the itinerary for tomorrow: breakfast, lunch in the casino, and then dinner at Play for Fantasy Night. While I struggle to imagine sex happening in the casino, something happening during fantasy night, while we are all in lingerie, is a definite possibility. Maybe I can be sick. No, that won't work with Leanna.

I scan the area to make sure no one is racing down the hallway before pressing the button on the elevator. I am escorted to the same candle-lit table we sat at for lunch. Shay's face is as sour as always, but she laughs and smiles occasionally. I notice throughout dinner that Chasity keeps looking at me strangely. She must know that I'm planning my escape.

Leaning forward on her forearms, Chasity asks, "What are you planning on doing after dinner, Taylor?"

"Uh...the show!" I blurt out.

Before the lover's spat at Embrace, I had been planning to watch tonight's performance at Masque, the hotel's theater. I don't know what it's about, but it might be a nice way to pass the time before bed.

Leanna claps her hands together. "Me too! Me too!"

Britney also perks up. "A show. I want to go."

Shay waves her hand dismissively. "The Monday show is always just for testing. It's better to go at the end of the week when they've ironed out all the kinks."

Britney looks slightly deflated until Shay mentions another show that she could go to.

After dessert, Leanna loops her arm in mine. As we walk to the elevator, Leanna explains the show on the way. "I read the theater has multiple entrances. The higher your status, the closer to the stage. There's also some difference in the level of interaction, but I'm not sure what."

At the entrance to Masque, the staff reminds us to download the hotel app to interact with the performers.

This information is not a surprise to Leanna. "No wonder you never know where you're going."

Once the download is complete, I press the tab for the live show and wait as a five-minute countdown begins on my screen.

As gold chain-wearing members, we sit in the first few rows of the theater, closest to the stage. Partners sit behind us, closest to the theater doors. I can only make out a few people in balcony seating. "Lovers, probably," Leanna whispers. Another balcony is higher up. "Friends?"

I nod at Leanna's raised eyebrows.

The timer strikes, and the theater grows silent, signaling the start of the show. The stage lights up to reveal three people on a circular bed. A young woman sitting in between an older couple. The young woman bites her lip in uncertainty, moving her head from side to side, and looking back and forth between them. Both the man and the woman softly caress the young woman's breasts. She moans through pursed lips. My phone vibrates with a notification. It displays a question with two categories, four options each. The first category lists kiss, bite, lick and touch. The second category reads lips, breasts, thighs, and throat.

My mouth drops open. *This is the interaction?* With only five seconds to respond, I mash my finger against my selections. I look over at Leanna. Her eyes are glued to the stage.

The woman leans forward. Her tongue slides across the young woman's nipple. The man follows behind, sucking in as much of her flesh as he can. The young woman calls out, sliding her nails against the sheets. The more their tongues trace her skin, the more excited she becomes; throwing her head back when they simultaneously tug at her with their mouths. I bite down on my knuckle and cross my legs, squeezing my thighs together.

Another notification. The options display on my screen: open, kiss, lick and touch. The 5-second countdown begins again. I don't hesitate with my selections and watch, seconds later, as the couple separates the young woman's thighs, revealing how glistening she has become. They continue to feast on her breasts while hooking her knees around their bodies, not giving her any opportunity to conceal herself.

I jump at the next vibration. Suck, kiss, lick, touch. There's only one other option left to consider. With the couple keeping the young woman spread apart, they reach down, one hand each, and roll their palms over her wet flesh. She jumps and bucks, stretching out her toes and gathering fistfuls of her hair into her hands.

Leanna's hands snake up the side of my thigh. She pulls at the outline of my panties. Soft at first, and then rough enough for the fabric to tighten around my damp middle.

My phone clatters to the floor. I dive for it, dislodging Leanna's grip. "No!" My outrage at watching the countdown light up on my screen is louder than I intend it to be. I'm on my knees, arm stretched, fingertips blocked by the secured bar bolting the chair to the surface, keeping me from my device. The screen goes black. I turn, my chest pains with regret, as they each transition their flat palms into two bonded fingers.

The woman is the first to circle the entrance, encasing her fingers in the young woman's warmth. The young woman bites her lip. Her hips bounce off the bed while her hips rotate in sync with the older woman's movements.

I dart toward my phone again, fitting as much of my upper body as I can under the seat. The pressure is suffocating. The space is too small for me to look ahead. I pound my hand on top of the carpet, searching in the place I last remember my phone to be. My fingertips graze against the end. I bend my finger downwards and lodge my nail in a tiny space above a button, dragging it back to me.

The countdown begins again just as the young woman lets out a throaty, "Fuck!"

"Shit!" Frantic, I release my hold, now able to grip it at a shorter distance. Options have changed. The first category lists a set of numbers from one to four. The second category only gives two options now. Finger or tongue.

With no time to think, I submit my response.

Two of the woman's fingers are already pumping deep inside. She twists, then exists before pushing in again. The young woman is uncontrollable. Her mouth hangs open wide. Every sound she makes echoes throughout the theater.

The man joins with two more fingers, matching the rhythm of the older woman. The young woman's breath hitches. She's forgotten how to breathe. I haven't returned to my seat. My knees prickle against the carpet and my shoulders tense in anticipation. My body yearns with need.

The screen glows as my hand vibrates. Wording precedes the options for the first time: for her.

Two words are in the first category. Touch or kiss. The next option reads her or him. These are not the options I wanted. My mouth can't possibly be the only one watering, craving for a small piece of flesh to nestle in between my lips and against my tongue.

The older woman inches closer to the young woman's face, her wrist never stopping to pause its movement. The young woman's pleasure drips down onto the sheet, covering them both. She's barely holding on. Her tongue swipes out at the older ones.

A new message. Lick, rub, flick and suck. And only one other option: clit.

I know exactly what I would do. The man ducks his head closer to where his hand rests inside and wiggles his tongue against her. The young woman shakes and shudders, panting out shallow breaths and clawing at her skin. Her muscles tighten. The pumping inside of her slows until her legs loosen, and her arms fall at her sides.

She can breathe fully again.

My phone alerts me to one last message: Goodnight. There are no options left.

The theater lights glow. I will myself to relax the building tension in my shoulders and look around at the other members. Shirts and skirts adjust back to an appropriate appearance. The sound of rattling buckles and zippers fills the air amongst the shuffling.

Leanna grabs her purse before taking me by the hand. "Come on!"

I follow behind, trying not to trip over my heels. The stickiness between my thighs makes walking more difficult. Before we make it completely out of our aisle, a side door opens.

And I see her.

Gabriella Flores looks the same as the day I met her. She radiates with mischievous confidence. Assuming she's shy or quiet is always a mistake. She knows exactly what she's doing. That's what made it hard to leave. When I left, she was wild and desperate. I hesitate to say that she was sorry. I waited for her to say those exact words. She never did. Her big brown eyes sweep past me with no recognition. Even so, I feel her. Somehow, her lips plant kisses on my skin from dozens of feet away. Demanding words burned into my brain make their way through my ears, looping through like a sweet melody. The type that lulls you to sleep without you realizing you won't wake up again. I've felt poisoned since our last day. This is the first time since then her face has graced my eyes. Now I feel alive.

I pull back at Leanna's furious tug, digging my heels into the carpet.

Gabby.

I can't ignore the ache in my chest. I've never loved someone so much that I needed to run so far. A chorus of sadness and anger swirls inside of me, mixing with tonight's pleasure, memories of hope and a promise of more. She's out of my sight before I can decide what to do about any of it.

Leanna steers us toward the stairs at the first sight of the crowded elevator lines. She pounds down the steps. I shout after her, "Leanna!" No response.

We fly through the door, steps away from my suite. "Which one is yours?"

I lead us the rest of the way before turning to her, asking, "Did you know?" Leanna looks confused. "Did you know Gabby was here?"

Her forehead creases, her upper lip raises and she blows out a breath. "Really, Taylor? Who cares? Weren't you just talking about us leaving the past behind?"

"This isn't about the past. No one told me she would be here."

Her ankles twist in place and her eyes close for a moment before she opens them again. "I received the same invite you did. I didn't ask about who else would be here."

Neither had I. I lean my back up against the door, earning a glare from Leanna.

"Goodbye, Taylor."

Chapter Ten
Gabriella

IT TAKES EVERYTHING IN me to keep moving. *One foot in front of the other.* When she left, I constantly had to remind myself how to complete the most basic of tasks. If I didn't tell myself to pick up the sponge, I'd stare at it. The volume of my stereo had to blast through the speakers for my mind to stay focused on the road. Otherwise, I'd wander to her and end up in places I'd never intended to go.

Sleeping was hard. The first couple of nights, I sat with my back against the wall closest to the front door, convinced she was going to come back. I had fucked up, but she would forgive me and she would come back. So, I waited. I gulped down cups of coffee because alcohol makes me sleepy. Besides, if she returned, I needed to be alert. She'd want to talk and I owed her that conversation. No matter how long.

When the coffee stopped working, I convinced myself that sleep was best because at least then I got to hold her. Staring at her pictures wasn't the same. I binged her TV shows until her lines looped through my brain like a song on repeat, except I didn't want it to go away.

Mom didn't text as much as she does now, and I didn't ignore her as much. Not then. That's how they knew something was wrong. They muscled their way to the apartment we shared and wouldn't stop banging on the door until I answered it. I looked as crazy as they behaved.

I refused to leave. The clothes they attempted to throw into bags ended up on the floor.

"Mija, you need to come home!" Mom yelled at me. I can count on one hand how many times I've seen her cry. That day was the fourth. I wouldn't leave, so they sat with me. The couch had stopped being a source of comfort. It held too many memories. Even the floor was dangerous. I couldn't stop my mind from imagining her everywhere. I even swore I heard her humming in the shower, so I sat there, too.

My dad sat next to me in his usual quiet. Now and then he'd clear his throat or run his hands up his arms as either a minor act of entertainment or comfort. I slapped my hand on top of his watch to keep the band from rattling. He shifted from his position to reveal his wallet. His face dipped low while he shuffled through it to retrieve the card he'd folded to fit inside. I only grabbed it because he kept poking me with its bent edges. There was nothing about it that was unique.

The end of her name in neat, cursive handwriting sparked something urgent inside of me. Fury rose in my chest at my dad for concealing something from me that was so important. I peeled back the layers to read the lost words of my first love. "*Please accept this gift for every hour, minute and second you spent taking care of your daughter until I could find her. Every tick of time is a reminder that the feelings we have for each other grow every day. While we're not guaranteed forever, I'll make every second count for as long as she'll have me.*"

That's when they took me away. When the tears leaked out of me, my body was too limp to fight them and force them to leave me there, alone.

My feet move with that memory. I kept waiting for her to come back to me. She was going to realize we had both made mistakes. If she had let me, I could've fixed it. Instead, she ran, and I waited, but now I'm running, too.

Chapter Eleven
Taylor

I WAKE UP THE next morning to the sound of talking and laughter. I take a few seconds to remember where I am.

Chasity. The hotel. Sex. Gabriella.

I hop up, pressing my ear to the bedroom door. I hear nothing but muffled noise. The doorknob turns slowly in my hands before I push out, widening the crack. A group of people huddle around in the living room. My eyes roam over them. I recognize the couple and the young woman from the night before. Fully clothed now, they laugh and chat, eating from a tray of bagels.

And then I hear her laugh. I lose my breath at the sound of it. My heart pounds at the memory of her most hidden expression. I can't move. I don't need to be reminded of what she looks like when she's happy. Remembering her as a cold-hearted bitch after these years helped me survive our nightmare. I don't want to think about her smile or the splatter of freckles just beneath her eyes. And how I hate it when she covers them with makeup. I don't want to wonder about what she might be wearing.

She looks good in everything.

Our eyes meet when she turns her head away from the person she's speaking to. Black t-shirt. Black jeans and a gold necklace hanging around her neck. *Gold chain, gold key, gold tag.*

The frame shakes and I know it means I lack the subtlety

necessary to be discreet. My response was an announcement to the world that Gabriella had hurt me.

It's another half an hour before I hear the door to the suite shut and silence follow. "You can come out now." Her voice sends a shiver down my spine. *No, I can't.* I try my best to steady my breathing.

All hopes of escaping the hotel room without having to see Gabriella again are dashed. Running will not work this time. I exit the bedroom to see her cleaning up the leftover breakfast. She stops when she notices me and completely ignores my attempt at a scowl. She's still beautiful. Her long dark wavy hair and big brown eyes tame my brewing anger and prevent me from lashing out like I have always imagined. She eyes the cute and cozy romper pajama set from Lavish before giving an approving nod.

She walks into the other bedroom—the door that has always remained closed—and retrieves a jacket. "We should go down to breakfast before it gets too crowded."

I dart my eyes towards the sink, now filled with dishes.

"That was crew food." She wrinkles her face in disapproval.

Gabriella acts as if nothing has ever gone wrong. As if she has never broken my heart, broken my trust—me. Is this how our relationship has always been? Has she always ignored my feelings? No, she just never asked.

"I'll pass," I turn to re-enter the room. Before I can make it past the threshold, her arms wrap around my waist. Startled, I freeze.

Her lips press against my earlobe. My eyes flutter, uncontrollably. She whispers, "I'm glad you came. I was worried you wouldn't."

I say nothing. After a few heartbeats, she releases me. I don't move again until I hear the door to the suite close.

I tear across the room and throw my belongings into my

carry-on. I can't stay here anymore. My feet kick off the romper. I dress in the practical clothing needed to outrun a Pitbull: a t-shirt, jeans, and laced-up sneakers.

A sense of déjà vu washes over me as a memory explodes in my brain. There's nothing I can do to stop the tears from forming. The last time I ran from Gabriella, I ran from the apartment we shared. Leaving was hard. I loved her. And even now, I miss her. Pretending my heart hadn't leapt at the first sight of her would be lying, but my mind knows the truth. My memories are not lies. I love and hate her all at the same time.

With a deep breath, I grip the knob and turn. I leave the room, choosing to take the stairs down to reception.

"I need to check out." My lips twitch out the smile I present.

The receptionist smiles and swipes my ID. Just as quickly, her smile falters. "One minute, please." She picks up the phone. Internal alarm bells fly off the hook. I wait a few minutes and listen to the woman tell someone on the other end that she has received an alert during checkout.

The young woman nods in understanding and ends the call. "My apologies for the wait. Ms. Coleman is requesting you check out with her directly."

"Oh." I guess this makes sense. A part of me felt slightly guilty for leaving the party without saying goodbye.

I arrive on the thirteenth floor to be met by yet another receptionist. She doesn't ask me to explain myself before allowing me inside. I'm taken aback to see Chasity's office is not designed in dark colors, as most of the hotel has been. The walls of her office are white, with every shade of purple and gold that she could make sense of. Chasity sits on the couch next to one of her assistants, who takes notes as she talks. I wait patiently. It takes only a few extra minutes for the assistant to leave and for Chasity to throw me her dazzling smile.

"Taylor, what's going on? I'm getting calls about you leaving early. Is there anything I can do to help?"

I roll my eyes, purposefully exaggerating the gesture. "You mean like get me a new room? You know, since you had me move in with Gabriella?"

Chasity shakes her head slowly. "I wish you wouldn't hold on to things. What happened to you, Taylor? You've changed. You're nothing like the friend I once knew."

I can feel myself losing my temper.

Friends. I think before shouting, "Friends!? Let's be honest, Chasity, we were never friends. She was your friend and when she decided to not be your friend anymore, I did you a fucking favor. And now you're fucking me over. You knew she was here, and you said nothing. You said nothing when you know everything. I don't have to tell you about what happened. You were there! So yes, I'm leaving, because I'm done with 'friends' who conspire behind my back to hurt me."

Chasity's face displays a multitude of expressions in the beginning. Shock, anger and a twinge of sadness, just for a second.

"I understand that you're hurt by the past, Taylor, but I think you should stay. The hotel has a lot to offer. If you don't want to take part in the events, then that's fine, but at least take this time to heal yourself."

Anger flares up inside of me. I take a few seconds to breathe and contemplate my next words.

"Good luck with everything, Chasity." My feet turn to the door without waiting to hear her response.

Chasity sucks her teeth. "That's one hefty bill you're going to be leaving with."

I pause.

"When you agreed to accept all the benefits of becoming a member here, you agreed to the contract. What do actresses make these days? Do you have the money to settle the debt? Trust me, it's much higher than what we thought it'd be back then."

Furious, I charge. I barely make it a few feet before security tackles me from the side. "You fucking, bitch!" They secure my hands behind my back. I kick everything I come into contact with. A vase smashes to the floor. I secure a small statue between my ankles and bring it to the ground as they drag me. I attempt to kick down an expensive-looking painting before security grabs onto my feet. They carry me out of Chasity's office like a criminal.

I put blind trust in Chasity and now I'm paying the price. On principle, I scream back to my hotel room. Admittedly, yelling out, "I fucking hate you, Chasity!" is probably doing more harm to my reputation than it is hers, but I don't care.

Fuck Chasity Coleman, forever.

To their credit, security is rather nice during my escort. They allow me to scream freely down the halls of the hotel and when they open the door to the suite; they place me down on both feet, wave and lock me inside. I expect more and am a little disappointed when there isn't.

A tapping noise pauses my steps to the bedroom. It doesn't stop when I freeze. Humming joins in. Whoever is in here is awfully chipper. It can't be Gabriella. I peer around the corner of the door frame to see a blue-haired girl humming and tapping her palms against her thighs. Black lace top, flirty apron skirt, silver chain with pendant. She stops when she notices me, and a large smile spreads across her face.

"Who the fuck are you?" Not being nice is a quick decision. Chasity has trapped me inside of her castle while her best friend makes plans to torture me. I don't know what's coming, but I know Gabriella.

It'll be brutal.

"I'm Trice. I'm kind of your fucking babysitter." The statement feels strange coming from her. She erupts into a giggle. The undertones of her light brown skin are more yellow than red. She has one of those big, puffy-cheeked faces that makes her look younger than she probably really is.

Deciding it best to ignore the fucking babysitter, I kick off my shoes and reach toward the closet for a change of clothes. I might as well unpack now that I won't be able to leave. Damn it. I forgot my carry-on. I'll have to wait until Queen Chasity blesses me with my clothing.

With nothing else to occupy my time, I stop ignoring Trice. "So, what does this mean? Having a babysitter?"

Trice sits up in her seat. "It means I have to travel with you and snitch on you if you misbehave. Usually, I only get assigned this role on days when members may invite their friends to experience the hotel, but apparently, you're an exception."

Trice appears disappointed at my lack of response. "You're so moody! What are you even upset about? You live with Gabriella. You know how many people would love to find a way in here?"

This piques my interest. I could use Trice to my advantage. She works at the hotel and her job requires her to know a lot of information. I change my mood, mirroring Trice's more upbeat personality, and ask her to tell me more about Gabriella. She is eager to oblige.

From Trice, I learn Gabriella is the head of live performances. Trice refers to her as "The Drama Queen." The live shows are the most talked about aspect of BED and consistently rank at the top of the list of reasons people decide to upgrade their memberships. Participation in the live shows depends heavily on membership status and Gabriella solely handpicks the participants.

Chasity and Gabriella have a long history. They were friends before I met them, but had a falling out shortly before Gabriella and I ended our relationship. And then I ran away.

Gabriella is coveted throughout the hotel, even more popular than Chasity. She is well-liked, but also mysterious. Only participants and production crew ever get to spend time with her. She's rarely seen in any part of the hotel that isn't the theater and when she is, people flock to her, starving for her attention and dying to be noticed in hopes of one day being chosen by her.

I can understand their admiration. That had been me once. Someone should probably send a warning—her attention comes at a premium.

Chapter Twelve
Gabriella

"She wasn't supposed to be there last night." I stare angrily at Chasity from the corner of her office. A second was the only time I gave myself to see her. It was nothing like I had imagined it to be. I didn't expect my heart to leap out of my chest or my breath to suddenly vanish.

I had imagined something much more logical for our reunion. The old me would just show up at her house in Santa Monica. I knew where she'd moved to pretty early on after following her best friend there once. Knowing was enough. I didn't need to bang on her front door, force my way in and demand that she listen to my apology. I could have, but I didn't.

Time was the alternative. A phone call was supposed to follow when everything was ready and maybe an email if she had a difficult time getting back to me. I was going to use my phone number and everything to give her plenty of time to recognize it was me who was calling to claim her again.

Last night wasn't a part of the plan. Although I hadn't decided when this apology was going to take place, it wasn't when I was most likely going to find her holding hands with another woman.

I had a sneaking suspicion after I left the suite that Taylor was going to do *something*. I didn't know if she was going to switch rooms or leave, neither of which was an option. Hearing her curse

Chasity's name down the hall was confirmation of everything I already knew.

"Why did you invite Leanna?"

Chasity throws her head back. "Why not? Leanna's my friend. So what if she and Taylor have a little history?" She spaces her index finger and thumb millimeters apart from one another. "I haven't fired anyone you have a history with."

She's being dramatic. I have a strict rule of not sleeping with anyone at the hotel. There are plenty of members and staff that I have seen in the nude, but they don't have a key to my suite, nor seen my ex-girlfriend naked.

"You should have told me." I am only mildly concerned about Leanna, so maybe I'm being a little dramatic, too. Chasity thrust this situation with Taylor upon me, and now it feels like she's sabotaging me on the way.

"And what would you have said?"

I'm trying to give myself the best shot before revisiting old habits. "I would have told you to not fucking invite her. And you would've listened to me because you love me."

Chasity's only response is to release a deep sigh. "Well, I can't ask her to leave now."

No, she can't. If Taylor finds out I orchestrated Leanna's exit, she'll be pissed.

"Don't worry. I have a plan."

I pass by the cleaning staff working to fix the state of Chasity's office after Taylor self-destructed. I hope the suite is still in one piece when I get back. Showing this amount of anger is new for her. Hopefully, she can forgive as good as she kicks.

I don't rush back to the suite. Taylor can wait. Once I realized she had every intention of abandoning me, I called for a babysitter. My first mistake was probably touching her. It was too fast, too soon. And too much of a reminder of what was. I have to give her time to understand how things have changed. She will still pay for leaving me, but she will beg me to stop knowing that I truly have her best interests at heart. If, by the end of this, she wants nothing to do with me, I'll accept it.

I stop at the theater to check on the production team. Our meeting this morning to iron out the kinks from last night went smoothly. Typically, the audience is so captivated by what's happening on stage that they don't notice when there are screw-ups, but it's my job to correct them throughout the week. Usually, by the time we reach Friday night, everything is perfect.

I travel down the one flight of stairs to my suite to see Leanna standing at the door. I know a love-struck puppy when I see one, and I have no interest in allowing Leanna to get any closer to what is already mine.

"May I help you?" I ask her as I approach, feigning complete innocence and civility. She looks at me with wide eyes before narrowing them. We've never met before, but she seems to know we're destined to become enemies.

"No, you can't," she replies, shaking her head before turning to raise her fist to the door.

I grab her wrist. It's swift. I don't realize I'm doing it until my nails are digging into her skin.

Her narrowed eyes bulge in fury. "Let go of me!" she yells, struggling to release herself. "Taylor doesn't want you here!"

I hold on to her. How dare she tell me what Taylor wants? The thought of her believing she knows Taylor well enough to relay that kind of message is maddening to me. They had a summer. I dedicated two years of my life to her — to us. And I would've given more if she had let me.

Pulling her arm closer into the valley of my breasts, I whisper,

"You're making a big mistake." She twists to escape.

"Yeah? What's that?" She grits her teeth.

"You're looking for a new playmate, but this is a losing game. Taylor has always belonged to me. Even if she's not mine by the end of the week, I'll make sure she'll never be yours." I release her, sending her crashing to the floor. She starts to stand, but changes her mind. "Your mask is slipping." I step over her and scan my pendant against the upper lock. "Don't come back here. There's only one person I enjoy punishing. Everyone else I destroy."

Leanna stares at me for a few seconds before picking her body up from the floor and turning to leave.

"And Leanna."

She stops moving but doesn't face me.

"Taylor will be fine. I always repair what I break."

I don't bother knocking on Taylor's bedroom door before entering. Knowing she was in the other bedroom, just a few feet away, had softened me up to be nice to her, but that changed once she left me again this morning. She's going to have to learn the hard way.

Once I realized I was going to have more trouble with Taylor than I thought, I assigned Trice. She's cute and likable. Her soft and joyful personality is a good fit for the fiery ones. I like her because she's proven herself to be pretty unshakeable. When she first came on board, her hair was pink. It's been blue for a few months now. I like blue the best.

I dismiss Trice from the room with one look. She doesn't hesitate to go. She knows better. Taylor will remember soon. At first, she ignores my presence; laid out with her arms spread wide from corner to corner. When I attempt to walk into her line of sight, she turns her neck in the other direction, staring at the headboard of her king-sized bed. The bed that I help pay for. Big mistake.

At the sight of the dark beauty mark etched on her neck, I inaudibly groan, keeping the tingling in my stomach a secret. Images form of the times that I used to slide my tongue across that very spot. I once latched my teeth onto that entire area every night, trapping that mark in between. I love all of her, but her neck is one of my favorite places.

I walk closer to her, tracing one finger up her neck to the base of her earlobe. She jumps, releases a low moan, and then shivers. "I missed you too."

Silence is her reply. As I allow my fingers to continue to explore her, up her neck, across her jaw and down her collarbone, her silence angers me. I probably shouldn't be touching her. I already made that mistake this morning, but she needs to know I'm serious.

"We need to talk." As painful as it is to remove them, I pull my fingers away and force them into my jacket pockets.

"I don't wanna talk to you." She already is. I crawl onto the bed next to her, our faces inches from each other. She doesn't look away this time. I'm almost disappointed. If she had, it would have given me the perfect excuse to touch her.

"You already are." Her jet-black coils cover one side of her face. If I touch them, they'll stretch before springing back into place. It's one of my favorite games.

"Chasity tricked me."

"Yeah." There's no reason to lie about it. "She was worried that if you knew I was here, you wouldn't come."

"She was right." Her response is cold with minimal expression.

"Do you hate me?" It's an honest question. After everything that happened, I don't hate her. I don't think I ever could. There were more good times between us than bad.

"Is there any way we can go this entire week without having to see each other again?" Anger is absent from her words. Her body has remained unmoving, but I'm grateful for any time I have her attention. I could go about my usual schedule and skip all the events, dinners included. I usually eat breakfast alone or with the crew. Shay is more of a night owl and Chasity is usually always busy.

Yes, is the answer.

"No," is my response.

"Then yes, I hate you." She leaves me with enough skepticism to display a smile I don't hide. It happens so quickly that I doubt she means to do it at all. Taylor swings her arms out to pinch my cheeks between her fingers. Her hand is warm. Her skin is soft. My body is alive. Her finger grazes my puckered lips. I pull back enough to capture it between my teeth before sucking it in fully.

Her breath hitches, "No." The word is small and shallow. She says it more to herself than to me. This was the part of her I knew so well. The part that likes to be chased—and caught.

Chapter Thirteen
Taylor

STUPID FUCKING FRECKLES. STUPID fucking beautiful face. Gabriella's freckles fill many of the memories that haunt my dreams at night. I should've never touched her. I should've never allowed her to remind me why I love her. Now here I am, trapped between the intoxicating smell of her perfume and luxuriously soft sheets.

They were the first I had ever loved. I had imagined this faceless girl with an amazing body and a dangerous attitude. I didn't know the girl of my dreams was her until she caught me. Then she became the girl of my nightmares. And it's been so hard to escape.

She wastes no time mounting me. My hand finds its way to her hip, I swear to it. Why that same force hasn't pulled my finger from between her lips, I don't know. It might be because of the feel of her tongue gliding against my skin, reminding me of the other things it likes to do. The things it does very well. It could be the view of her from where I'm lying; trapped and unmoving. Her hair is down, which is the way I prefer it. It brushes up against my skin with every movement she makes. I don't even attempt to buck. The force is faulty.

She stares down at me, smirking, fingering the hem of my sweatshirt, inching it up from around the top of my jeans and past my belly button. She's teasing me and I let her. I hate how much

I'm enjoying it. I hate expecting her next move, waiting for her to touch more of me. With her on top of me, it's hard to hide the way my hips adjust. I don't want her to know that she's winning.

"Emmy." I flinch at the sound of the nickname. I haven't heard it in a very long time. The shock is the force I need to finally free my finger from her hold.

As I attempt to keep my body from melting, Gabriella slides her hands underneath, tracing the outside of my bra, before pushing it out of her way. I arch my back when her hands make contact. She remains steady. I try not to moan when she grinds herself into me. My eyes close shut the moment she pinches and pulls at my nipples. My hands grip the top of the comforter. I don't scurry away when she hikes the sweatshirt higher, exposing my skin. My lungs stop expelling my breath. My teeth press into my lips when she licks and sucks me, pulling new flesh into her mouth.

The force does nothing to help.

"Stop," I speak barely above a whisper. She pauses for a while, her mouth wide with me inside, before sliding off of me and onto the bed. I pull down my sweatshirt. Bright red lipstick smudges decorate my skin.

"I'll see you tonight." No apologies linger behind. Only red-painted scars.

Her behavior confuses me. Mean and commanding one moment and cooperative the next. She's not done with making me miserable.

Before leaving, Gabriella lays out a yellow dress she pulls from the closet. "I'm not sorry Chasity lied." And then she's gone.

Chasity lied. Again.

Trice buzzes through the door to help me get ready for lunch in the casino. I refuse. Trice meets every excuse with, "She'll send someone to come and get you if she doesn't come and get you herself." I can't tell if *she* is referring to Chasity or Gabriella, but it doesn't matter. *Fuck them both.*

Despite the threat, I do not move. If they have to come to drag me off of this bed themselves, then so be it. Trice mumbles and stutters through reasons I should comply. I don't listen. Her job security isn't my problem. I've allowed Gabriella and Chasity to control me enough. I'm not going anywhere.

Soon all I hear is the sound of Trice's footsteps pacing back and forth. Occasionally she bends over me, speaks, and then stops herself, shaking her head as she backs away again. I chuckle at her actions. She's cute in an annoying little sister way. The type you'd ditch at the mall to hang out with your friends, but then bribe with sweets when you feel guilty afterward. I try not to laugh at a volume she can hear. Trice is trying. None of this is her fault.

"What's your kink?"

Her question catches me off guard. I've never thought about my sexual interests in that way. I have things that I like and things that I don't like. There are even things I'm unsure if I like at all. Thanks to Gabriella.

When I don't answer, she shakes her head. "No guest of Chasity is kink-less."

She's probably right. I doubt Chasity knows anyone who doesn't have any non-conventional sexual habits, including me.

I think about it. Memories of every single sex act, solo and otherwise, stroll across my brain like a strip of film. "Exhibitionism."

Trice squeals in excitement. Her reaction is enough for me to prop myself up to look at her. I listen as she speaks. The deal she wants to make is enticing. If I agree to go to lunch at the casino, then afterward Trice will show me a section of the hotel she swears I'll love.

"It was practically made for you," she says. Trice's knees hit the carpet. Her hands rub together in prayer. Going to the casino would satisfy Gabriella, at least temporarily. I think back to my original mission before I had any knowledge of Gabriella working here. Maybe Trice can help me after all.

With a sigh, I sit up, undress, and slip into the outfit designated by my evil ex-girlfriend. It's a snug fit. Trice never leaves. She dances around the room, celebrating her victory.

Minutes later, I follow behind Trice as she leads me down the elevator, chatting and humming mostly to herself.

The brightly lit casino is packed. We weave through the different card tables as groups of people gather around to place their bets. Staff members, dressed in red lace tops and flirty black aprons, carry trays of drinks and snacks to guests, flowing through small spaces.

Conversation and laughter fill the air and lift my mood in this strange atmosphere. I hate casinos, especially casinos in Las Vegas, with their overpowering clouds of cigarette smoke. But not at BED. Instead, there's a heavy but pleasant aroma of sweet tobacco wafting through. It smells divine.

Chasity stands at the center in front of a table decorated in white with cascading crystals above her. She looks every bit beautiful and domineering in her white suit.

A smirk crosses her face when I pass her without speaking. Trice gives her proper respect to her boss, complimenting her endlessly on her wardrobe and makeup. Chasity smiles and nods before turning away, dismissing her.

Britney and Leanna arrive after me. Britney greets me with a hug. Leanna ignores me. Her behavior hurts. When I feel I have no one, I could use a friend. If I apologize, she won't understand. Gabriella was before Leanna's time. She wasn't there to witness our relationship. She didn't see how much I loved her.

My time with Leanna had been short, only lasting a summer. I hadn't run from her like I had from Gabriella, but when I left, I'd had no intention of going back.

A piece of bread comes flying at me, almost knocking over my water glass before I have the chance to catch it. Britney holds back a snicker. Chasity's mouth downturns into a frown. The intensity of my glare softens at the first sign of an apology, Britney's hands clasped together under her chin with one eye directed at me. Britney is often hard to hate. With both elbows on the table, she leans across, raising her voice over the chatter.

"How was the show?"

The smile on her face tells me she's waiting for me to say something exciting. I have no reason to disappoint her. She's not familiar with Gabriella either. It's illogical to think she could have warned me, but chose not to. And there's no reason for me to lie about the enjoyment of the show. I loved every second.

"Wet."

Britney fans her face at my response before explaining her plans to go to tonight's showing. I wonder if Gabriella will be there. If there's a possibility I won't have to hide out in my bedroom every night, I'd like to know.

From the corner of my eye, I see the two devils, Shay and Gabriella, approach the table. Chasity greets them both with a hug and a kiss on the cheek. I take a deep breath and look away. Britney eyes Gabriella thoughtfully. When Britney finds out Gabriella holds the keys to her fantasies, she'll become her new best friend. Chasity has given us the run of her palace, but outside of meals, we have seen little of her.

Leanna's scowl is obvious, though I can't detect who it's directed toward. Leanna has always been neutral towards Shay.

Shay doesn't scare her as much as she scares me and Gabriella is a stranger to her. Maybe Leanna is still an ally.

Gabriella also wears yellow, though hers is a yellow off-the-shoulder top with white fitted jeans she was betting I would salivate over. She hardly ever wore anything skin-tight when we were younger. I complained back then. I'm cursing her now.

Shay doesn't bother speaking to me. There's nothing either of us needs to say to the other anyway.

I release a heavy sigh when Gabriella sits next to me. A small laugh escapes from between her lips. She has on red lipstick again. It seems to be an addition to her everyday look. It looks good on her.

I hate that.

I look everywhere but directly at her. I've seen enough of her today to not have to look at her ever again.

I avert my eyes each time she tries to gain my attention. I suck my cheeks in, willing myself to remain strong. Her chin settles on my shoulder. Her laugh vibrates through my skin.

When her breath tickles my earlobe, I pause, my heart racing faster with each passing second.

"You've always looked so beautiful in yellow," she whispers.

My eyes close long enough for me to catch the emotions that flood my chest. I stuff them down into my stomach.

She told me enough times during our relationship that yellow and red were her favorite colors for me to wear. The two pigments glowed against my cinnamon-brown skin beautifully. Back then, Gabriella demanded I wear them. A reminder that some things never change.

When my eyes open, they stare straight into Britney, her eyes bright and unmoving. There's a story here, and she wants to know it. I offer no explanation. I have to survive here for three more days.

Chasity finally takes her seat at the head of the table, addressing us all. "I hope everyone has been enjoying themselves."

She doesn't spare me a glance. Britney praises the hotel for their commitment to hospitality. I roll my eyes. BED has a lot of bells and whistles, but the accommodations haven't been exceptional. Especially when they place a guest in a suite that's already occupied.

"Does everyone receive breakfast in bed or is that only reserved for certain members?" I tuned out some of Britney's earlier speech and missed when she began talking about breakfast. Thinking back, there wasn't anything planned on the itinerary for us to meet.

Chasity explains breakfast in bed is reserved for higher-tiered members, but isn't automatic. It has to be ordered special at least twenty-four hours in advance. She thought we would like it, so scheduled it for us to arrive at 7 a.m. this morning.

Confused, I look at Gabriella and ask, "Did you eat my breakfast?"

Shay laughs, spraying out the water she had been in the middle of drinking. It was past seven in the morning when I left the suite to leave Las Vegas forever, or at least stay away for the next few months.

I watch Gabriella suppress her grin, her suddenly thin cheeks making it obvious.

"Uh, Taylor." I turn my attention to Britney.

"It was sex. Breakfast in bed is sex," Britney explains. Shay laughs more, holding the napkin against her face. A dreamy look crosses over Britney's eyes. "It was a couple. Both in tiny white aprons with their asses out. I knew what Chasity was blessing us with as soon as I saw them. The little cart they pushed had all types of fruits. Some we used. Some we didn't." She winks. "Maybe you missed them."

Britney looks hopeful there had been a mistake.

I know better.

If she could control it, there was no way Gabriella was going to allow me to have a sexual experience that she hadn't dreamt up herself. I'm not upset that she deprived me of a breakfast treat. I'm mad that once again Gabriella has found a way to control me.

The table falls silent when I don't ask additional questions. Leanna has expressed no enjoyment about her morning gold tier perk. After how I treated her last night, I'm sure she did.

I eat my lunch in silence while they all engage in mild chit-chat. Leanna loosens up at the end. Although she doesn't address Gabriella directly, she speaks with Shay and Britney in a normal tone, making plans to meet up with them later.

As promised, Trice comes to my rescue while the waitstaff clears the dining table. I joyously hop out of my seat as soon as she taps my shoulder, eager to flee. Before I can taste freedom, Gabriella snatches Trice away. They have a tense, but quiet, conversation. From my view, Trice mostly nods through the exchange while Gabriella scowls and points. I'm relieved when she finally releases her.

Trice skips to the elevator. If Gabriella scares her, she doesn't show it. The elevator doors open to reveal a cobblestoned street in between two rows of homes. I follow Trice inside, holding back my shock. We've been transported from a glitzy glass tower to a romantic European neighborhood.

We walk alongside the homes. For a long time, Trice is quiet, allowing me to take in the sights for myself and draw my conclusions. It isn't too hard to do. Every home we pass has a large open window where someone stands naked. Some are alone, but not all. Sometimes there is one person. At times, half a dozen.

As we pass, lines form in small alleyways. There are so many windows, even those waiting in line can't miss the show. It reminds me of home.

Trice offers me further information. The park is centrally located down the middle of the street to provide additional places for comfortable viewing. We pass individuals and groups of people sitting on benches and having picnics while they watch the shows from the open windows. They are all fully clothed, which I think is impressive.

From Trice, I learn this section of the hotel, appropriately named Peek Street, meets the desires of voyeurs and exhibitionists. Members of all levels can take part, which is what makes it a popular destination within the hotel. Only Partners and Significants can book an experience.

There are limits to the type of experiences available to book, and upper tiers have more options than lower tiers, but everyone finds what they're looking for.

Booking experiences on Peek Street are not a given. Even gold members have to earn points to gain access to the schedule and then you have to have enough points to receive approval to calendar an event during months of high demand.

The street turns into a horror night in October, with the agenda filled with participation requests from members wanting to create their spooky fantasies. The spots for masked serial killers and home invaders fill up quickly. Peek Street becomes Candy Cane Lane during the holiday season and members who've gained enough points receive approval to reenact their dreams of coupling with St. Nick, his elves, or Mrs. Claus.

Trice makes a mention about reindeer, but isn't sure if they're allowed this year. "Chasity hates everything that has to do with animals. Real or not."

As Trice continues to lead me down the road of depravity, I

catch several window performances. One is of a man deep inside a woman bent over the arm of the couch in a maid outfit. There are some assumed couples having sex as normal, but in the view of a dozen witnesses.

The view of the homes changes depending on the scene. Some homes only have kitchens displayed, while others have bedrooms and living rooms. Trice explains this is on purpose. Some people only want to perform in one specific section of the house, therefore only that part of the home is shown while the others are hidden away. The homes themselves are moving sets.

Members sometimes take their experiences very seriously, and in order to fully become engrossed in the role, they'll book the home for the day, as long as their points allow, and then live in the home as normal until their participants join in.

I see some of this with homes occupied by naked members performing mundane tasks like making coffee, watching TV, or even sleeping.

The sound of a police cruiser comes from behind. Trice and I shuffle to the side, allowing it to pass. Everyone looks, with a few trailing the red and blue lights. Up ahead, another car stops in front of one home. From what I can see, they're the only two vehicles on the road.

"Gold members. It's one of their specialty perks. Along with firefighters. Anything that costs extra, you must pay extra, and that includes house calls."

I watch as the cruiser pulls up and stops behind the parked Subaru. I keep my eyes on the action, while listening to Trice continue to tell me about Peek Street.

"It's the only part of the hotel with a curfew, unless there's a special event scheduled, like hitchhiking fantasies and most of everything that's planned for Halloween. There's a list in the manual if you're curious. Otherwise, no one is allowed here past 11 p.m."

From Trice I learn Peek Street is only pitch black one hundred percent of the time during October when they need the extra hours to fulfill as many requests as possible.

I keep the flashing lights in my gaze, eager to get close and witness the scene. We cruise by a crowd huddled near a fence. It's the first side yard I've seen on the street since we arrived.

"Neighbor fantasy," Trice offers, not pausing her movement.

I crane my neck to see some action, but can only see the head of one neighbor, leaned back in ecstasy with her hands clenched onto the top of the wooden fence.

My imagination does the dirty work my eyesight can't capture. My mind tells me the wood fence that divides the two yards is in pristine condition, except for a small hole big enough for two fingers to slip through. And on the other side of that hole—spread thighs and a very bad neighbor. What ramps up my intrigue is the spouses of both neighbors, going about their daily lives, completely oblivious to what their other halves are getting into.

I almost giggle at the idea of titillating trouble. It wouldn't be too bad. Once caught, the spouses will exact revenge by tying up the offenders and forcing them to watch them explore each other. The neighbors will beg to be set free, only to be ignored and made to endure their arousal without release. That's until one or both of the spouses takes pity on them and rides them so hard they pass out from exhaustion.

At least, that's what Gabriella would do.

A member being pulled from the Subaru, handcuffed and lowered onto the hood of the cruiser, interrupts my daydream. My heart rate speeds up at the sight of both female officers searching the woman. Because the scene is taking place outside, there's enough space for everyone to take in the view. I glance around and observe as the scene distracts some away from their original shows. I feel for their performers. *Gold member perk, indeed.*

One officer riffles through the contents of the car, throwing belongings out onto the street. When one on-looker picks up one item and sniffs it, I pay better attention. I realize then everything being discarded is sexual. What they had sniffed and pocketed was a pair of underwear. Pocket-sized vibrators, ball gags, and multiple pairs of small, thonged panties fly. The treats do not induce a frenzy, which I would imagine would not be tolerated at BED. Instead, people bend down and gather whatever falls near them.

A black paddle is the last thing the officer pulls from the front seat. She doesn't throw that one. Instead, she walks back to the hood of the cruiser, sucking her teeth and shaking her head to the side, the paddle smacking the palm of her left hand.

"Well, Officer Avery. It looks like we have a bad girl on our hands."

Officer Avery gives a slight chuckle.

With her hands clasped on the arms of the cuffed woman, she uses her feet to spread her legs further apart. The woman's ass wiggles under her short skirt in response.

"It's always the bad ones with the dirtiest mouths." Officer Avery pulls the woman's hair. When she cries out, she covers her mouth with her own.

A few people adjust where they stand. One woman next to me slips her hands down the front of her partner's jeans, discreetly sliding down his zipper. Something tells me sex acts may not be permissible on Peek Street outside of approved locations.

With her free hand, Officer Avery grabs hold of the woman's skirt, jerking it upward. Her cheeks bounce to celebrate their freedom. More people in the audience shift. "I was going to suggest we take her into the station."

The first officer stops beside the woman before continuing, resting her free hand on the woman's hip. "But I think this one's too pretty for jail."

She turns the black paddle sideways before sliding it between the woman's thighs. The woman moans out, her mouth still preoccupied by Officer Avery's tongue. My groan joins several others. The sight of the glistening edge of the paddle increases the heat in my already wet panties.

"Time to go. As much as I admire Gabriella, I have no interest in being murdered by her." Trice grabs my arm and pulls me through the crowd despite my resounding protest. Pretty soon, I lose all sight of the officers and their motorist.

I etch this moment in my memory as another thing Gabriella has cost me.

I grumpily follow Trice further down the street until we reach a dead end. The building is several stories high, towering over all the homes on Peek Street. Trice makes no apologies as she leads me through the doors and past some shops.

To see another Lavish location on the main floor makes sense. Members must look the part to make the fantasy feel as real as possible. No wonder Lavish offers such a wide selection of fabrics. Indulgence is also present on the ground floor, along with a few other stores.

I raise my eyebrows at a small medical station, which Trice promptly explains is legitimate. Accidents happen on Peek Street and the other, bigger facility is on the other side of the hotel. The people before me are actual medical professionals, not members. At least not while they're on the clock.

Trice huddles us into an elevator, where we're surrounded by members who look like they stepped off of several television sets.

There are doctors, nurses and patients. Suits and pencil skirts fit around the bodies of different presenting genders. Some members dress casually and are hard to place. A menacing man in the back sports multiple piercings and tattoos. It's difficult for me to tell if he's in costume or not.

Trice reaches past me to press a button on the pad I'm too distracted to notice. Looking at the unique descriptions, I now understand.

The first chime from the elevator reveals a hospital waiting room. All members in the appropriate attire exit here. The floor displays the correct bustling atmosphere of a hospital, but above the beeping noises of the machines are other sounds.

The suits and pencil skirts exit at the tone of the second chime. I glimpse another waiting room, but this one is more formal and luxurious, like one you would expect to see in an office of a high-powered law firm.

A woman I mistook as a part of the office crowd exits on the third chime. On this floor, a receptionist sits at the entrance. Above her head on the beige-colored wall reads: Dean of Academic Instruction.

The police station the officer on Peek Street referenced is the fourth chime. The gentleman covered in tattoos and piercings exits here.

Once Trice and I are alone in the elevator, we pass several floors I'm not able to look into. When the chime sounds again, I walk forward at the first sign of the doors opening, only to be blinded by a naked, muscular chest. Shocked, I look up to see a man with a tab collar wrapped around his neck. I lean to the side to see a cathedral set behind him. I take a step back.

"Sorry, I'm heading down." He's still smiling when the doors close.

I stand in shock for several seconds.

"That was a priest."

"Yup."

"With pierced nipples."

"Looked that way."

"Half naked in a church."

"God said 'Come as you are'."

"No, he didn't. But that's okay because we're all going to Hell, anyway."

Trice laughs just as the elevator doors open to our correct floor. The chilly Vegas air hits me immediately. Trice criticizes me for shivering.

"Hey, I'm from L.A. Anything below seventy-two degrees is freezing to us."

The rooftop is covered in greenery. Brown sand crunches beneath my shoes as I trail Trice down the walking path. I'm grateful I possessed enough energy to defy Gabriella's order for me to wear heels at lunch and slipped on a pair of flats instead. My rebellious act went unnoticed by her earlier.

Fewer people wander around on the roof than were present on the street. The weather probably has something to do with that. There are small tables scattered throughout, where people assemble to drink coffee and enjoy small meals. There seem to be no experiences taking place up here. As we approach the greenhouse doors, my eyes settle on a computer screen attached to the front. Trice waits next to it while I jog to catch up.

"I think this would be a good place for you to start." Despite my look of confusion, she continues. "You'll scan your pendant here, and then you can accumulate points. The more tasks you complete, the more points you'll earn. You get bonus points when members come to view you. You receive one point per viewing minute. If they stay for 10 minutes, the points double. Watch, like this."

Trice grabs onto her silver pendant and scans it. An image of the greenhouse populates with a star placed on a section of the map. Trice walks around and sits at a table pressed against the greenhouse walls. I occupy the seat across.

"Look."

At first, I see nothing. Frost blocks my view, but slowly, the frost clears until a sizable section of the greenhouse can be visible. I gasp. Inside is a naked woman. The watering can she's holding momentarily hides her from view. She's covered in dirt, wearing only green rain boots.

I look around and realize there are several small greenhouses on the rooftop, each with its seating attached to the sides. They aren't random at all.

I turn back to a smiling Trice.

"Welcome home."

Chapter Fourteen
Gabriella

THERE WAS ONCE A time when I enjoyed stripping privileges away from people. They may have earned them fair and square, but I was the one who got to decide whether they received the opportunity to experience them.

I stopped doing that for Taylor. I loved her and she didn't like me hurting people. Back then, she told me she didn't need me to protect her. I believed it then because she did a good job of avoiding the cameras. She's been a star almost her entire life, and she's mastered how to appear normal in most social settings. People stare and gawk, but they hardly ever bother her. Some even wonder if she's who they think she is at all.

I put the no-camera rule into place for her. Yes, it's a practical policy to have in today's social environment when everyone is looking for information to destroy someone else. But I don't care about those people. I care about Taylor.

Even though I thought I would need more time before seeking her out again, I knew that day would come, eventually, and the members would need to be ready. No pictures. No recordings. No autographs.

It's a shame I'll have to break my promise to her about not hurting other people. To be fair, this isn't like before when my goal was to ensure her success. No, this is to maintain her right to privacy and punish the people who dare try to jeopardize her sense of safety and peace. Not here, they don't. Not when I've worked my ass off to ensure she has everything she needs to no longer feel like she has to hide herself from people who seek an opportunity to take advantage of her.

The hammer comes down hard on the tiny SIM card. Its shattered pieces fly across the wrecked hotel room.

The Rose Gold couple has been here long enough to know the rules. No cameras allowed. I search their other electronic devices for additional material. Not one photo of her at this hotel will escape from this building.

"It's clean." The Link who gives me the information is one I don't know well. She's shorter and thicker than Trice. Links make up a portion of the staff who are without a manager. They exist to serve whoever needs them. They answer to all of us and sometimes none of us.

The badge on her shirt reminds me her name is Nyla. I mentally repeat it to myself, though I don't say it aloud.

She adjusts her glasses on her face and hands me the two new cell phone boxes. I hand her the others, the ones that used to be owned by the Lover couple, our new ex-members.

"If I find out that you have uttered any rumor about Taylor Townes being at this hotel, I'll find you and I'll finish ruining your lives." Chasity wouldn't like it, but there would be no way for her to know that I'm the one who revealed that this nice, respected, youth soccer coach is having an affair with her couples' therapist. "Do you understand me?" They both nod without speaking. "I can't fucking hear you."

"Y-yes, we're so s-s-sorry we didn't mean–" The woman's hands are shaking so badly that her necklace smacks against her chest. It annoys me.

"Shut up! Taylor Townes does not exist here. Do you understand?"

"Yes!" they shout in unison.

"Your membership is terminated. You are to vacate the premises immediately and never return. If I see you again, the last thing you'll need to be worried about is a cell phone."

Security marches them away with the Link carrying what remains of their belongings.

"I don't remember Chasity giving us the authority to terminate anyone's memberships," Shay smirks from the doorway. She was on my heels from the moment I spotted the perpetrators. I didn't need her help. I had it all under control.

"If we'd told you, there'd be no members left." I kick a shredded pillow to the side. It lands on the pile of glass from the mirror I smashed when I threw the phone across the room.

"That's true." Shay moves to the side to allow housekeeping to enter.

I walk around them to the hall.

"I'm still not convinced she's worth all this trouble," Shay announces behind me as distance grows between us.

"You don't need to," I shout back, pausing in my steps. I glance back at Shay leaning against the wall. "She's mine." Three years of therapy later and I know now I was in fear of her abandoning me. I'd do anything to keep her, even betray myself.

Some things change with time. Others remain.

Chapter Fifteen
Taylor

MY FIRST EXPERIENCE IN the greenhouse will be after dinner. As my fucking babysitter, Trice agrees to complete the booking on my behalf. I tell myself I have no reason to be nervous. Being naked in front of people is normal for me, but I usually do so after a great deal of observation, sly conversation, a bit of flirtation, and a great deal of instinct.

I return to the empty suite alone. It isn't until the door shuts and the quiet surrounds me that I hold no fear about returning to where Gabriella might be.

According to Trice, I don't need to know anything about gardening to have a successful experience. If I want, I can ignore all tasks and freely walk around the greenhouse until my booking time is over. If I do this, I'll be forfeiting some of my points, but will still be able to gain bonus points from voyeurs.

I look at the screen of my vibrating cell phone and groan. It's Nicole. I can't tell Nicole the truth about where I am. She knows Gabriella and Chasity and still hates Gabriella. My time with Shay, Leanna, and Britney remains a mystery to her.

My phone shakes, alerting me to the voicemail. I breathe a sigh of relief. It'll be easier to lie about where I was when I am no longer sharing a hotel suite with my ex-girlfriend, who my best friend despises.

The phone vibrates again. I answer.

"I've been calling you for two days. Where are you?"

"Vegas."

Las Vegas is a commonplace for us Angelenos to travel to on a whim. She shouldn't be at all suspicious.

"You hate Vegas."

Fact.

I notice my carry-on tucked into a corner of my bedroom. Placing Nicole on speaker, I sit my phone down on the nightstand and start the unpacking process for the second time.

"Yeah but, I decided to treat myself to a low key hotel stay to relax before they make the final decision about the pilot."

"Which hotel?"

"Uh..." I refold the shirt I had tossed inside without a second thought. "... the Venetian."

"What about the Venetian is low key? Are you with Christina?" She doesn't even give me a chance to answer the first question. I guess there's nothing low-key about the Venetian. It's not the most glamorous. That honor probably belongs to the Bellagio, but perhaps the hotel that has a section modeled after an Italian city is low key.

"What? Why would you think I'm here with Christina?"

Nicole's voice raises enough for her to try to get a point across. She's pissed. About nothing. I could piss her off about something, if I was stupid enough to tell her where I was, why, and with who.

"Because she's conveniently in Las Vegas with you at the same time. Her, I knew about. You are a surprise. Since you didn't know she told us she wouldn't be able to record the podcast this week, I'll let you off easy. Come home now before any damage is done."

My eyes roll to the side of my head until my body is rolling on Chasity's carpet to keep up. Nicole makes it sound so easy. She has linked Christina and Gabriella together simply because of their shared ethnic background, with no context.

What town in Mexico is Christina's family from? Do they make their tortillas from flour or corn? If Selena Quintanilla's murderer is granted parole, does Christina's family expect me to riot in the streets of L.A. or fly to Texas? I know Gabriella's grandma expects me to be in Texas. If Christina disagrees, there could be a problem.

And I don't want those problems.

"Nicole, for the last time, I'm not sleeping with Christina or anyone else you know. I'm in Vegas because I needed a break and I already live on the beach."

Nicole's silent. I can hear the faint clicking of her nails in the background. I hang my clothes back in the closet and stack what needs to go inside the drawers.

"Ok. Christina promises, too. Now I can tell you about my argument with Joshua."

I listen and apply the amount of "mm-hmm" necessary for support. I transition from unpacking to scrolling through the hotel app. It's fairly easy to navigate through. I locate the Peek Street ads under the Experiences tab.

Ad pages are organized by membership tiers. I filter the results by gender.

House 5428

Seeking one WLW for blindfolded bedroom experience.

House 9597

Seeking WLW for happy couple role play with U-Haul.

House 5683

Seeking a group of 3 female movers. Must come strapped and prepared to lift 200 pounds. Established groups only.

There is a reminder at the top of each page to check your total points before attempting to schedule an event. Ads within the

Tower, the tall building at the end of Peek Street, are listed on a separate page.

Office #11

Printer in need of repair by female tech.

Dean of Administration

Disciplinary action for low-performing students will take place between 8 am-10 am, 3 pm-5 pm, and 7 pm-10 pm.

WANTED

A gang of 4 men seeking revenge on 2 female officers.

Worship Service

We will offer private confessions between 9 am and 12 pm and then again from 4 pm to 8 pm. Warning: The priest is in a very forgiving mood.

My shiver lowers the volume of Nicole's voice and replaces it with an X-rated image. Some listings are for floors I wasn't able to peek inside of.

My eyes land on a listing for a "Member locked in a *DREAM* with a desire to reveal her true self" in Greenhouse 4. I cringe at her use of my moniker, unsure if we're supposed to be advertising my celebrity status. I understand the hotel has rules in place, but those can be broken. I know that more than anyone. Seeing my invitation listed on the app, where other members are going to read it and possibly even attend, causes my nerves to shoot up.

I think about contacting Trice to remove the post. The thought vanishes quickly when images of my enjoyment push away my panic. I can do this. This is child's play.

I maybe should have waited until the morning to walk around nude on the rooftop. It has only gotten colder since earlier. And yet seems much busier than it should.

Dinner is a blur. Britney and the rest of the girls talk about spending the day at one of the indoor pools. There are multiple pools available at BED, each with its own unique rules. I smile and nod, feigning interest while counting down the courses until I am finally free. Even Gabriella can't bring down my excitement. She once again sits next to me to taunt me.

I don't twitch when her arm slides across mine to reach for the salt or when her knuckles tap against my own, holding her glass too close to mine.

After dinner, I don't tell anyone where I'm going or what I'm doing. I stand, ignore when they pause their discussion, and walk out of Decadent. There's no shouting. No questions. No aggression. I'm surprised and also relieved.

Trice follows me to the suite to change, but passes the door while I enter. She knows I'll behave my way through the hotel and up to the greenhouses. This is exactly what I want to be doing. The only reason I came. There's no need for a special costume I'm only going to remove later.

My walk through Peek Street is as eventful as the first time. It's more crowded than it was before. The lights are dim to mimic the evening sky. Even faint stars grace the ceiling. They illuminate scenes on display in the darkness. The experiences seem more erotic and enticing in this setting. There are other scenes, too, that I didn't think to stop and notice before.

Two women sit and eat dinner at a dining table. They're fully clothed, with no props. Some members sit and casually watch them, like viewers watching a TV show. They talk and they laugh, trading small but intimate touches. One tucks the other's hair behind her ears. In return, she dances her fingers on her partner's arm. They kiss. Small and slow and deliberate. It's a sweet act that clouds my memory even after I walk away. Each step produces an old memory of me I thought I convinced myself I no longer wanted.

My hand folded into someone else's.

My breath caught in my throat. And not because I was lost in orgasmic bliss, but because I was lost in her. Her, sitting on the couch sketching with a pencil and then later with a stylus. Her, running her fingers through my hair. The way she laughs, discreet and tight-lipped and the challenge I would silently accept to hear it more often. Burned into my memory. She is.

For a long time, I thought I didn't want her there.

Maybe I lied.

When the painful ones set in, I hurry. My steps pound on the cobblestone harder. I greet the members on the elevator with a forced smile. A shield. I need it to continue with my mission. There's a life without Gabriella. I've been living it for the past four years. The memories are only reminders of the pieces of me she took. Now's my chance to reclaim them.

Greenhouse Four isn't where I think it should be. The numbers on the greenhouses are etched in gold on the ground in front of the door. I stop at three. It's the last greenhouse, exactly like the one Trice took me to earlier. I continue down the path until gravel crunches underneath my feet.

The large greenhouse is situated across from the smaller ones. The exterior is lit up with bright lights. Potted plants and flowers outline the walkway. I step from the gravel to the pavers leading to the front door. The number four shines on the last square. I lift my chain from my skin and scan the pendant on the screen of Greenhouse Four.

I wait as the screen lights up with a welcome message and the door clicks open. I step inside, shivering in gratitude for the much warmer climate. Moss fills in the gaps of the stone floor. The room resembles a small house. There's a black cast-iron stove in the kitchen and a cast-iron fireplace in the living room. In the center of the room is a clawfoot tub. It's not a greenhouse. It's a conservatory.

Strawberries drip down from baskets hung from the ceiling. Other pots of green line the walls with the only glow from the room coming from small lamps. I run my hand across the cushions on the couch. My eyes wander up the spiraling staircase that leads somewhere I can't see. I imagine the landing stocked with more greenery, pots, and dirt to complete the fantasy of what this place is meant to be.

It's not a garden. It's an oasis. A fairytale.

There's a basket to place my clothes into on a shelf that also holds an assortment of shoes. The shoes are optional. I know because the sign attached to the shelf tells me so. I strip completely naked before slipping on a pair. The satin flats remind me of an old movie. The scene plays out in my head of a young woman slipping out of bed when she isn't supposed to. Imagine if Gabriella caught her. The heels of her feet scrape against the floor in a helpless struggle. She has no chance.

I glance back at the door I trust to be locked into place. It is, but I'm no longer alone. Faces shine through the glass walls of the conservatory. One woman whispers to a friend when our eyes meet. At least I think she whispers it. The inside of the conservatory is dead silent. I can see them, but I can't hear them. I watch her excited expression and focus on her lips. "It's Piper Paige!" I think she says, before clamping her hand over her mouth.

For a moment, I feel self-conscious and unsure. My hands move to cover my breasts I'd revealed so easily and shield the hairless triangle with the other. Dream Daniels and Piper Paige were a big part of my life. Still are. I wouldn't be where I am today without them. I am Piper Paige. I'm also Taylor Townes. At 19 I fell in love with a girl who showed me what it felt like to live a fantasy off screen. She broke my heart at 21, but that lesson didn't die because our relationship didn't survive. I didn't stop being Taylor because Gabriella lied to me.

The muscles in my arm relax to allow my hand to slip from its protective position back down to my side. My breasts bounce out freely. I take a deep breath and exhale, moving my lower hand away from my middle. I hold both hands behind my back and survey the scatter of faces coming into view. They're all smiling and waiting for my next move.

This is easier back at home where I know Kyle and Monica are simultaneously watching me, but also lost in their activities. If public sex is only permissible in specific situations, then these people have only me as their entertainment.

I turn away from their eyes to face the cast-iron stove. There's a three-ringed binder sitting on the counter beside it, wedged between the stove and the fridge. From this angle, everyone in attendance has a full view of my ass. I'm okay with that. My ass is one of my best assets. Gabriella never said it, but she claimed it for herself many, many times. Especially when I upset her and she'd force my head onto the bed or the couch, rip away my panties, and...punish me. Any way she wanted. It didn't matter. I took it. Every invasion of her tongue, fingers or delectable toy—attached or detached — was a victory for me. Her being angry meant I had played my role.

Tonight I can be a good girl for all these people, who barely know me, especially the ones who think they do. I can be sweet and innocent and walk around this place as if I don't know that they're there.

Gabriella would hate that. If she knew what I was doing right now, she'd barge in here, drag me out by my hair and show them who I really am. All of her favorite places are already here. The dining room table. The couch. The floor. We're only missing the bed, but I'm sure that won't matter to her.

They'd see who she is, too. Their precious Drama Queen. They'd watch her be moody, controlling and aggressive. The way she grips my skin would frighten them. They wouldn't believe how she forces me open to serve her and the words she makes me say—oh—they'd be dismayed.

It feels like she's here with me. The image of their shocked expressions while Gabriella claims me replays in my head with every turn of the page in the recipe book. Gabriella's hands clasp my neck when I stop on the baking instructions for the quiche. Her fingers attempt to pry my lips open when the page displaying an oyster dish flips into view. When my mouth refuses to open for her, she smacks my pussy, not commenting on the fact that it's already wet. Just how she likes. How she demands it always is. The brownie recipe is accompanied by invisible bite marks on my shoulder.

I flip the page again and take a deeper breath than her assault has been allowing me and stare down at the hot chocolate recipe. The fridge has the milk I need. The cupboards hold the cocoa powder, sugar and vanilla. I bend to retrieve the saucepan, slowly, so everyone who's watching enjoys the view. My legs part slightly to reveal what's been gathering there since Gabriella barged into the conservatory.

I whisk the ingredients together and grab the coffee cup on the lowest shelf. I stand on the tips of my toes to search for the bag of small marshmallows. My lips form the shape necessary to blow the steam away and cool the liquid to my desired temperature. I want it hot. Not scalding. They all watch me walk from the kitchen and pause at the dining room table, my feet kept warm by the satin slippers. If I sit here, they won't be able to see me. The edge of the table will conceal some of the best parts of me. I keep moving. By the nods of their heads, they agree. I place the cup on an end table and drag a chair to the corner of the room. From the buttons on the side, I'm sure it's one that reclines.

The members closest to the corner clap. I smile and wink with the knowledge that I've made them happy. Knuckles tap on the window from the other side. I turn to look, noticing as their eyes travel from my nipples up to my face. They form one hand into a letter c and make a swirling motion with the other. I look back at my hot chocolate. They nod. When I pick it up, they make the swirling hand motion again. I think I get it. I get up to open the fridge again and find the canister of whipped cream in the door. I hold it up and see an array of affirming thumbs and pleased expressions.

The whipped cream conceals the top of my cup like a fluffy, white volcano. I balance it as best as I can to sit again. The leather chair is comfortable and provides a slight coolness to my skin in contrast to the warm air. My tongue darts out to taste the tip of the swirled whipped cream. Others do the same. They lick as I lick in encouragement. One woman's teeth sink into her lip.

I lick slower in response.

They mouth words I cannot hear. Sometimes to each other. Other times to themselves. A flash of a cell phone screen fills my chest with panic. I remember the rules and calm my nerves. Even when my senses tell me to flee, I stay. I think it's what Gabriella would tell me to do. She wouldn't want me to be afraid.

There is barely any space for any other faces to appear. They're all here for me. I continue to leisurely clear away the whipped cream until I have enough space to consume the hot chocolate. I pull my knees apart to create room for my hand to slide through the tiny crack. A tiny trace of my wetness kisses the skin of my fingers.

My wrist lowers to settle the cup down to the end table beside me. I can feel the froth of the whipped cream, bubbly and sticky on my lips. I refrain from licking it away. It's something I know I wouldn't be allowed to do. If not by them, then certainly by *her*.

My head tilts back to rest. I start slowly at first, tickling the curve my lower lips create together. The tip of my finger is slick and slides easily. I groan with my eyes closed and breathe, aware of the excitement building inside of me. My arm brushes against the side of my breast with every swipe I take. I grip one breast in my hand and separate two fingers for the nipple to slip through. It's what they would want.

And then I hear her voice.

Look at me. My eyes spring open to nothing but the view of the kitchen. Gabriella isn't here. The door isn't hanging from its hinges. The conservatory still stands in pristine condition.

Still, I grip my neck and squeeze. My thighs pull back as far as I know she'd want them to be. Dozens of eyes stay glued on me. There's no going back now. They see all of me.

My heart thuds in anticipation. She's bound to find out what I've done, eventually. Every face here is a witness to my crime, which means they're also liabilities. When they deliver the news to her of what they've seen, they'll be in just as much trouble as me.

Better make it good.

The armrests do a good job of keeping my feet planted right where she would want them. My fingers delve into the stickiness and disappear between my folds to create the music she wrote for me to perform. They can't hear it, but they can see the effect it has on me.

The air that was once a welcoming warmth is now causing me to sweat. There's not enough of it or I wouldn't be losing my breath. Even with the force of her wrapped around my throat, I should be able to breathe easier. Her presence has stained me for four years.

For her, this is punishment for everything I've done since the last time she touched me. I come for her. Not for Monica. Not for Kyle. Not for Elaine. Only for her. I tailor my performance to her lessons. In the hours upon hours that we spent melted into each other's skin, I learned everything.

I come for her.

I scream for myself.

I shake her free from my mind with every pass over my clit. Sometimes it hurts to touch it. The pain keeps me going. I rub faster with four fingers pressed against me, completely out of control of my body's muscles and bones. My thighs ache and cramp. My toes curl and uncurl at a pace I'm unable to keep up with. The hand that grips my neck loses all strength and my nails dig into the leather instead.

I see foreheads pressed against glass, hungry mouths and wide eyes by the time my hips rise for the last time to finish. I pant out the last of it and squeeze my thighs together to stop the charge that's shocking every vulnerable place on my body.

No one's whispering anything now. Not to themselves and not to each other.

If I could talk to them, I'd tell them I tried to be a good girl, but she wouldn't let me.

And it'd be the truth.

The ten-minute warning sounds—a melody of chirping birds. It's so adorably not Chasity that I giggle. I use the remaining time to rinse myself off with the type of small shower I've only ever seen at the beach. I do this delicately and slowly, knowing it'll be my last performance.

At the sound of more chirping birds, the faces disappear from view. I dry off with towels placed next to the basket that holds my clothes. The night air is even colder than it was before. I keep my head down on the way to the elevators. The gravel is no help with concealing my whereabouts. People fill the rooftop, strolling about and talking. I make no eye contact.

Multiple members join me to wait for the elevator doors to open. I hope everyone remains silent. The ride down is excruciatingly long. In the real world, I would look at my phone as a distraction, but looking at my phone now would reveal details about my performance I'm not sure I'm ready to see. I pretend to study my nails, play with the zipper of my coat and pull at invisible pieces of lint.

When the bell chimes for the ground floor, relief floods through me before I hear the words, "Don't forget to check your messages, Gold."

I'm halfway down Peek Street when I spot an empty bench and sit. The notification symbol for the app is bright red. One hundred and forty-two notifications. The number repeats in my head over and over.

One hundred and forty-two.

One hundred and forty-two.

One hundred and forty-two notifications.

I click. Eighty-eight members watched me in the greenhouse. And no one left until the end of the show. My original booking had been for sixty minutes, but was extended by an additional thirty minutes because of acute interest.

I scroll through the chat, laughing to myself at a few of the comments. Most of the viewers were extremely encouraging, even taking down a few trolls who left comments that weren't so nice. Happiness spreads through my chest. I can't believe it.

An echo of studded footsteps interrupts my temporary bliss. My head whips to the side at the sound of the connected acoustics.

Chasity, Trice, and one of Chasity's assistants walk towards me. Chasity smiles, waves, and greets members she passes on her way. She is still in the same outfit she wore to dinner.

My back stiffens. I tense and close my eyes as the echo of their footsteps becomes louder. The sound stops. I hesitate, squeezing my eyes shut before I hear, "You know we can still see you, right?" It's Chasity, dashing away all my hopes and dreams, that this time, she wouldn't notice me.

"I know. I've decided to pretend you're a mirage."

"Your eyes have to be open to see mirages."

Shit.

I crack one eye open to see Trice silently laughing to herself. Chasity's assistant also looks slightly amused. Chasity looks impatient. She huffs and sits next to me on the bench. She looks tired. Despite her invitation to help with BED's business plan, we were never close. Chasity was always my girlfriend's best friend. I got along more with Krystal, who I haven't seen for years.

"Everything okay?" I ask. Chasity's eyes brighten at my question. Her back strengthens and a smile forms on her perfectly painted lips.

"Perfect." She leans closer to me. "You were perfect." She reaches out an arm to her assistant, who hands her a black tablet in return. "We built the garden a year ago. It's supposed to be a part of the live performances, but Gabriella hasn't been able to get around to training the performers on it yet. Members have used it from time to time and it has a pretty good usage rate, but what you did tonight—Taylor, we've never seen numbers like this at any of the greenhouses before."

Chasity hands me the tablet to show me a chart. The numbers mean nothing to me, but Chasity is excited. "At the end of every show, we ask about expectations and whether the member would want to see the show or the performer again." She scrolls down to another number. "100% said they would watch the show again, and they wanted to see you in it."

"That's great." I'm unsure if I should say anything else. While Gabriella has a knack for getting me to feel things I wouldn't, Chasity has always been good at getting me to agree to things I shouldn't. I say nothing more. Chasity looks frustrated.

"Taylor." She clasps her hands together tightly. "This could be an amazing opportunity."

"For who?" I ask. I have a job and a dream. Neither of which involves being a performer for Chasity. BED was her dream and she's living in it. Acting is mine.

"We need your help." I roll my eyes at Chasity's attempt to sway me. Gabriella has never needed me for anything.

Chasity stands, shoving the tablet back into the hands of her assistant, who, caught by surprise, holds the device close to her chest.

"Come with me." She walks before I even stretch my knees to stand. Her assistant follows. Trice waits for me in silence, not complaining when I take a few more seconds before standing up. Chasity doesn't wait for us. She's in the elevator while Trice and I are only halfway down the quad.

"Was it fun?" Trice isn't looking at me when she asks the question. I think about it for a moment. Being in the greenhouse had been fun. It had also been liberating.

"Yeah, it was. Thanks." A genuine smile spreads across my face in gratitude for Trice's unlikely friendship. She still doesn't look at me.

"Good. It's almost as if it was meant to be."

She turns to me and grins just as we reach the elevator Chasity's assistant keeps open for us. I don't know what Trice's last words mean. And in the presence of Chasity, I don't ask.

I don't pay attention to which button is pressed. I don't know the hotel well enough to guess our destination. The chime of the elevator seems louder than usual given the silence between us. Chasity's assistant stands to the side to wait for Chasity to exit. With a nod of her head, Trice motions for me to exit next, subtly reminding me of her position here. I forgot she was my babysitter.

I recognize the theater's doors ahead and though I don't see anyone near them, they pull open for Chasity, allowing her to walk through without delay.

I hear her before I see her. Gabriella's standing in front of the stage, speaking to the performers. Her hair's up in a topknot, instead of in its usual loose curls. Unlike Chasity, she changed her clothes after dinner, discarding her dress for a pair of gray joggers and a simple black t-shirt.

The performers are all dressed in casual clothing while they listen to her instructions.

One performer points directly at our group heading down the aisle. Gabriella's head turns to look at us. Her brows scrunch together and her lips turn down into a frown. "What did she do this time?" She asks as she approaches us.

Her insult calms my pounding heart and chills the warmth that was growing in my chest. I turn to Trice. "Is this how all guests are treated at this hotel?" She doesn't respond. Trice is more alert now that Gabriella joins the group. She stands up straight with her shoulders squared and pushed back.

Traitor.

Chasity doesn't answer Gabriella's question and she doesn't respond to my comment before she turns to lead the group back out of the theater. Gabriella follows behind our grade school line in silence. The entrance remains empty once we exit. There must not be a show on the schedule tonight.

"You're still recruiting tonight, right?"

Gabriella shakes her head. "Tomorrow night."

Chasity's head jerks in my direction. "Take her with you."

Gabriella's facial expression bears a mixture of offense and annoyance. "Why?"

Chasity takes the tablet from her assistant and places it into Gabriella's hands. "These are the numbers from tonight's performance."

Gabriella looks confused while scrolling through the pages.

Chasity continues, "She was in the garden."

Gabriella's fingers still on the screen.

I watch as her eyelids close tightly for a few seconds, before she releases the tension in her face. She looks up at Chasity. "What does this have to do with the recruitment?"

Chasity shrugs, aware Gabriella is now angry with her. "She's a natural. Let her show them what to do." Gabriella shakes her head, handing the device back to Chasity. Her assistant takes it instead. "Gabby, you throw a fit anytime I even suggest hiring someone to help you run the shows. If she does this, it will help lighten your load."

Gabriella turns and walks off down the hallway. Chasity follows. I make to move as well, but I'm held back by Trice. "No, stay. This isn't for us."

Chapter Sixteen
Gabriella

BESIDES THE THEATER, DELICACY is one of my favorite places at BED. As one of the few restaurants that stays open late into the night, it's always crowded with members munching on their evening treats.

I twirl my plastic spoon around the chunk of cookies and cream ice cream before sliding it into my mouth and down my tongue. Taylor hasn't touched hers yet. Her double scoop of frozen hot chocolate sits melting in its small sized cup, in danger of spilling off the side and onto the white tabletop. I've made my mind up about Taylor. I have never doubted my love for her, but I won't allow myself to pine for someone who won't bother to look me in the eye or flinch anytime I touch them. I haven't decided how I'm going to let her go yet, but she won't leave quietly.

I sit my now-empty cup to the side. "Are you going to have that?"

Taylor doesn't respond. Her chin rests on her palm, her eyes stare across the room at nothing of interest to me. I slide my hand across the table, wrapping my fingers around the small cup before pulling it towards me. Taylor's hand springs from her lap, latching onto my wrist.

"Let go."

I tug again, trying to keep the smile from forming on my lips.

Breath expels from her chest. She turns toward me.

"Let. Go."

There's no fire behind her eyes. And I know her well enough to detect the emptiness behind her threat. I release the cup from my grip, using the back of my fingers to push it towards her.

"Congratulations on your performance." It's not what I want to say, but it might be the one thing I can say to prompt her to use more words.

"Thanks."

She twirls the tip of the spoon into the middle of the ice cream, forging a deep hole before scooping it out and sliding the first chocolate chunk in between her lips.

"Did you watch?" Her eyes stay planted on her treat.

"Did you want me to?"

The corners of her lips turn down and she shrugs. "Are you angry I did it without you?" She looks at me then, awaiting my response. I'm not. She's always happy when she is in the spotlight.

"Why are you here?" I know the superficial answer. *Chasity invited me to her birthday.* I want the truth.

"Chasity invited me. If I had known you would be here, I would've said 'No' for the twentieth time."

If she hadn't come, I would've followed through on my original plan and found her at a later time. She was never supposed to come to BED. At least not yet.

"Stripping in the garden was not on today's itinerary."

"So you *are* angry." She leans in close, pushing away the half eaten cup of ice cream. "You're mad I did something without you."

I lean in, too, my elbows sliding against the smooth surface until my forearms rest against hers. "It's been four years. I'm sure there's a lot we've done without each other." Taylor's forehead crinkles into a frown. She slides her arms further away. "Is that why you're here, then? You flew to Las Vegas for sex?"

"No!" she shoots back, whispering in a hushed tone. I look around the room at the many occupied tables and chairs.

"Why are you whispering about sex in a hotel that has a floor dedicated to orgies?"

"Can we go now?" She's up from her seat before I can answer fully, tossing both of our cups in the trash can on the way out.

I walk to the counter to retrieve my to-go order. I'm surprised to see Taylor standing at the entrance, waiting for me. The walk back to the suite is quiet. When we enter, she sits on the couch instead of immediately going to her room and closing the door behind her. I uncover the plate of freshly baked churros coated in cinnamon sugar and place them on the coffee table. I watch Taylor's eyes fall on them before she looks away.

"Do you want one?" She shakes her head. I pluck one for myself, biting into the crispy surface, and savor the sweetness.

"You're so disrespectful."

I respond to her accusation by licking what's left of the cinnamon sugar from my lips.

"Why the fuck did you buy those?"

"Because they're good. You used to love them."

"I used to love a lot of things." The last part is supposed to hurt me. It doesn't.

"It's getting late and I'm going to bed soon. Will you just tell me what we're supposed to be doing in the morning?"

"Recruiting. We've had a few show ideas for a while now, but it has been difficult for me to break away and cast for them."

"I thought the members were cast."

"I cast members for specific shows like Choose Your Own Fantasy. The theater runs three different showings. We want to expand the performances to the other parts of the hotel. The garden is one of them."

"Chasity said earlier you won't let her hire anyone to help you."

I stand to brush the remaining crumbs of the churro off the couch and onto the floor. Housekeeping will clean it in the morning.

"You've always had a hard time not being in control. You controlled me during our entire relationship."

I pause to look at her face. She's not looking at me, her eyes face up towards the ceiling.

"What are you saying?"

It's silent for a while. I watch her open her mouth to close it again before speaking.

"Nothing." She stands and walks to her bedroom door.

"Goodnight, "I sing out. The click of the door closing into the frame is the only response.

If I were big on alcohol, I'd have a drink. And I'd deserve it. I would've told her I watched her show today. And that she was beautiful, but every word I say to her comes off as an attack.

I built the garden for her to do exactly what she did tonight. I could never be mad at her for expressing herself. No one could touch her from behind the glass. That was the point. This is how I keep her safe.

Chapter Seventeen
Taylor

ANOTHER HOUR PASSES BY before I feel safe enough to sneak back out into the living room. The plate of churros is no longer on the coffee table. I find them on the counter near the microwave, covered with a paper towel. They're cold. I locate a separate plate in a cupboard, sliding one churro on top while attempting to silently open the door of the microwave.

Reheating a churro is tricky business. If you leave it in for too long, it becomes too hard and crunchy to eat. Five to seven seconds tops. I flinch at the whirling of the machine, hoping Gabriella won't hear the noise and catch me.

She knew what she was doing ordering these. She was right about them being my favorite. The churros at amusement parks are the best. They're extremely long with just the right amount of crunch, kept warm at a comfortable taste bud pleasing temperature and coated in cinnamon sugary goodness.

Gabriella would argue they weren't the best churros, but I don't care. Churros are easily accessible in L.A. these days on dessert shop menus. I prefer my churro neat and plain, but that's not the only option. I've tried churro sundaes, covered in fruit, like a crepe, drizzled with chocolate syrup and caramel. But the original is always the best.

I pulled open the door to the microwave before it sounds

its finishing *ding*. With as little pressure as possible, I push the microwave door close and scurry back behind the safety of my bedroom door.

I hover the churro over the plate before I bite into it. Perfect.

I should have grabbed two.

I choose to dump the plate into my bedroom trash can instead of the living room. Can't leave any evidence behind.

Sleep claims me quickly. The click of the bedroom door startles me. I realize in my rush to not get caught I forgot to lock it. Gabriella enters slowly, not bothering to close the door behind her. I feel her hand slide across my stomach and travel down to my panties.

"You didn't say goodnight." She whispers the threat, knowing I can hear her every word. It isn't about the churros. She doesn't know about those, yet.

Against my will, my back arches and my thighs spread further apart. One touch from her and I am already wet. My arousal seeps through the thin material below me. She grabs at it. I expect her to tear it away, but she grips it, pulling it tighter against my skin until only my inner lips and clit are covered, freeing my outer, thicker folds.

She slaps her fingers in between them. I cry out at the mixed sensation of pleasure and pain. My hips move in rhythm with her hand as she slides against the now drenched fabric.

"See, Emmy? You like it when I punish you."

I moan in response. The tension at the base of my belly is building. My mind tells me to fight, but I can't contain the breath that escapes from my chest. I can't stop my hips from rising and falling to the rhythm she created. She stops, removing my panties from me completely.

My thighs spread apart as far as they can go once she releases my ankles from her grip. She smiles down at me. "You kept it just the way I like it."

Bare. A hairless pussy meant the moisture she coaxed out of me would not be absorbed by the strands growing there for protection. There is no protection from Gabriella.

I fight the urge to moan, and instead pull my knees closer to the sides of my breast, groaning at the strain the move puts on my inner thigh muscles. She wiggles three fingers slightly above me before gliding them down my newly freed lower lips. My nails dig into the skin of my knees. I try to remain steady.

"You still haven't said goodnight to me."

And I still don't. I close my eyes, relishing the pleasurable pressure she adds to my clit. I feel her push back the hood, using one fingertip to test my sensitivity. I lose it.

"Oh, God!" A gushy slap sounds in the bedroom's silence. She slaps her fingers against me again, each blow harder than the one before. I bite my bottom lip in compliance.

"You are such a bad girl. Even after I try so hard to teach you to be a good girl." She runs three fingertips across my opening, teasing me as she enters and exits one at a time. I bit down on my lip harder. "A bad girl with a soaking wet pussy."

I force my legs into a deeper stretch. She enters one finger. And then another. Her eyes flick to mine. She is not smiling. Her two fingers are not moving inside of me. I shift my hips forward in an attempt to entice her. It doesn't work.

"You still haven't said goodnight."

I shift my hips again. I feel her fingers slowly slide out of me.

"No, baby," I repeat the word no over and over. I feel her fingers pause before leaving my entrance. I squeeze my muscles around them. Gabriella pushes them forward, allowing them to fill me.

"You still haven't said goodnight." She curls the two fingers inside of me, moving her thumb against my clit.

"Oh G–" I bite down. The tension in my belly continues to rise.

"This is your last chance." Her knuckles uncurl and the rhythm slows.

"Goodnight." I'm breathless and yearning.

"Goodnight, what?" Her thumb traces across my clit once more. Slow. And then fast. And slow again. I know what she wants me to say. The words race across my mind like a train barrelling down a set of train tracks. She moves her fingers inside me again, increasing the pressure she applies to my clit.

I moan out, dropping my knees beside me, my arms no longer strong enough to hold them up. Gabriella leans one arm across my thighs, keeping them spread apart.

"Goodnight, what?"

"Goodnight...I love you."

She slides her fingers out of me completely. I reach for her only for her to push me away.

My heart sinks. I don't want her to leave me ever again. She turns to straddle me in reverse, her ass resting just below my chin. I raise my hand to smack it and grip the meat against my palm in gratitude. She inserts her fingers again, three this time. I moan out at the fullness.

She leans forward, gently kissing my clit while her hands move through me. My hands travel up to her breasts and squeeze. Her tongue sweeps across, lapping up the juice she helps to create.

"Be a good girl, Emmy. Come."

I jump up at the sound of a knock on the door. My scream caught in my throat, my heart pounding against my chest.

"Hey, are you ready?" I look down at my half-naked body. My t-shirt, underwear and pajama pants are missing. My bra is still securely strapped in place. My right hand is sticky with my own excitement.

Shit.

It was a dream.

A knock sounds again.

"Taylor?" She attempts to turn the knob, but nothing happens. It's locked.

"I just woke up. Go without me." I crawl across the messy bed to head to the bathroom to shower. I run each finger through the steamy water, cleansing what was left over from what should've felt more like a nightmare and less of a fantasy.

Damn this hotel.

I fully dress to leave for breakfast only to see Trice seated on the couch in the living room. I look around, not spotting any sign of Gabriella.

"Am I so untrustworthy that I can't walk myself to breakfast?" Trice shrugs at my question, not offering any information as to why she's here. Nothing about her hair has changed since I saw her last. Her demeanor differs from the night before. Chasity's stoic soldier has vanished. The Trice I know, an energetic bunny bouncing on the heels of her toes, has returned.

A thought crosses my mind and tumbles out before I have time to fully think about it. "I think I need your help."

A smile spreads across Trice's lips before quickly vanishing. "With?" Her eyes narrow. "I can't get you out of your date with Gabriella." Her right hand stretches across her chest, landing on her heart. "Boss' orders."

I haven't forgotten about going recruiting with Gabriella tonight, though I would hardly call it a date. If anything, my dream from the night before serves as a reminder of why I need to refocus on my plan. I can't keep allowing her to control me.

"It's not that. You helped me last night with the show at the garden." Trice pats herself on the shoulder, nodding along to my compliment.

"Now I need you to help me with something else. I don't know what I'm looking for, but I need something new to try. Last night proved how much I love being an exhibitionist." Saying the wording out loud sends an uneasy feeling down into my belly, but I know the words to be true.

Trice's eyes shift from side to side. She paces, walking around in a small circle. "You don't have specifics?"

I shake my head. I only know the words of things I've done with Gabriella. Everything else is basically a mystery. "No."

"How about age play?"

The image that pops into my mind is too absurd to be what Trice means, but I can't take any chances. "What? No, I don't think so."

"Electrostimulation?"

My eyes nearly cross in confusion. "I don't know what that is."

"Do you have a foot fetish?" She stops her rounded trek and moves to approach me. Her sweet, innocent eyes suddenly become so wildly hopeful.

My feet shuffle backward to put some distance between Trice and me. "Absolutely not."

"Do you want one?"

She pauses and awaits my answer. I turn away from Trice and take the time to envision my tongue sliding over a set of toes and sucking each one into my mouth. I mentally swat away at the image of the owner of the foot I'm servicing, a girl with long, dark curly hair. She doesn't budge.

I reverse the image in my mind and try to feel the same sensations. I turn back.

"My feet are very ticklish. I already have to focus extremely hard when I'm getting a foot massage or a pedicure. I'm always afraid I'll end up kicking them in the face. That sounds more like torture."

"Well, there's a lot more to having a foot fetish than that. I once had to babysit a guy who was obsessed with anyone who polished their toenails blue. It was the worst! I had to stay with him to make sure he didn't launch himself at members. The day Chasity revoked his membership was one of the happiest days of my life."

I shake my head at Trice. "That wasn't helpful."

"Yeah, sorry. It really wouldn't have been a problem if he'd had self-control. There's a pretty sizable group of members who share that fetish though, and they're cool. I can introduce you and then you can make an informed decision."

"No, thanks." I mentally cross *foot fetish* off of my list of possible sexual interests. Trice stops forming a circle in the middle of the living room.

"Don't worry. I'll think of something while you're at breakfast and have it ready for you before the end of lunch."

I nod in confidence, following her from the suite, to the elevator. My mind floats to Gabriella.

"Last night, Gabriella said there was an entire floor dedicated to orgies." I don't look at Trice when I say it. I don't see her facial expression to my announced interest.

"Can you take me there?"

"No." The answer is immediate. I try not to display my shock to her, but I'm sure she notices when my shoulders shake and my feet shuffle backward.

"That's not how it works. They aren't free for anyone to just join." I turn to her now, willing to listen to her explanation. "They are established groups, dedicated to specific kinks. Each one has its own set of requirements. Some require prerequisites and proof of class completion."

"Class completion?" It all sounds ridiculous. Not at all how it happens in my fantasies.

"Yes. Serious members only. Not everyone wants a newbie just walking in to 'try something new.' You have to show you know what you're doing and that you enjoy it. It would be a miracle to get you into one in two days."

I huff in exasperation.

Wednesdays already look busier than Mondays. There are more staff walking the hallways, greeting members and more luggage being wheeled down the hotel's purple carpeting.

Trice leads me to Delight, the smaller bistro-style restaurant I met Britney at on the first day. Britney and Leanna are already here, sipping on glasses filled with mimosas. When Britney spots me, she clasps her hands in excitement. Leanna gives me a small smile, scooting her chair closer to the window. I take the hint and occupy the seat next to her. I turn around to glance at Trice. She's gone.

"I heard a rumor about you."

The waiter interrupts to take my drink order. I accept the offer of a strawberry mimosa. I rarely drink and hate the taste of most alcoholic beverages, but Britney and Leanna's drinks look too appetizing to pass up. I follow up my mimosa order with a request for an avocado toast with an over-easy egg on top. Britney's acai bowl is half empty and Leanna's stack of pancakes sits untouched. I direct my attention back to Britney once the waiter's gone.

"So, when were you going to tell us?" I look to Leanna for some sort of clue as to what Britney is referring to.

"Your performance." I shrink internally and try to navigate the complicated feelings of knowing someone close to me knows such intimate information about me. My stomach settles when I remind myself there are already a lot of sexual details Leanna and Britney know about me, especially Leanna, whose information rivals Gabriella's. I quickly say a silent prayer that she never finds out about that.

"Trice showed me and I wanted to try it. I've never done it to that scale before. Not in front of so many people."

"Well, you killed it. Heard a couple talking about you at the pool. Said they were going to contact Gabriella to request another show. I wasn't sure they were talking about you at first, but when they caught me eavesdropping, they asked if we were friends. Turns out they saw us sitting at dinner with Chasity earlier. I claimed you to the fullest, of course. Told them I taught you everything you know." I laugh along with her joke. It's hard to find reasons to dislike Britney.

"Funny how they said they were going to contact Gabriella, though. Shouldn't they be contacting Chasity?" Leanna doesn't laugh along with us. Her mimosa glass is almost empty. She takes one last sip before sitting it down again. Britney doesn't explain and neither do I.

The waiter returns with my order, placing a glass filled with blended strawberries and a small bottle of champagne on the table. The food follows shortly after. We eat our breakfast in silence, with Leanna cutting into her stack and stuffing half a dozen small pancake squares into her mouth.

I stand, ready to excuse myself, only for my arm to be looped into Britney's. "Oh, no you don't. You keep disappearing and not sharing all the fun places. This time, we're going, too." The smile she gives me portrays innocence, but I know better.

Leanna joins at my other side and slides her hand through mine. I pause for a second before folding my fingers into hers. We move as a group out of the increasingly bustling activity of Delight.

Chapter Eighteen
Gabriella

MY BREAKFAST THIS MORNING is a simple bagel with cream cheese. I grabbed it off the cart meant for the managers' meeting, one I rarely attend. Usually, I would go straight to the theater and talk with the crew about the show schedule and stage preparations. Wednesday is the start of the busy week. All shows will be filled to capacity. There can be no mistakes. Everything has to be perfect.

I don't talk to many other managers besides Shay. There is Xuan, the manager of private parties, who I semi-like because she knows how to follow instructions. I only had to tell her "no" once when a member requested a private performance. She has been smart enough to never ask me again.

I am staying at the meeting because of Trice. Since Taylor's arrival, I've been using her more often than usual. As a Link, she doesn't have a dedicated manager. Links are only held accountable by Chasity, though they help to serve the managers by completing minor tasks. Tasks that are harder to define under an establishment like this one.

"There you are. I went all the way to your office looking for you." I'm surprised to see Shay. While I rarely attend, Shay is very vocal about having never attended a managers' meeting.

"What the hell possessed you to come here with these losers?"

I hold up one-half of my bagel. Shay doesn't look convinced.

She takes a seat next to me, trading menacing facial expressions with anyone who meets her eye. They all look away. She laughs softly to herself at their defeat.

I choose not to deal with most people. People are exhausting and serve more as a hindrance than as an advantage. Shay has the same understanding, but where I can be intentionally standoffish and mildly cruel, Shay is intentionally distant. I don't care if people like me. Shay makes sure they don't like her.

She figured out on her own who I was to Chasity and then from there connected the dots to Taylor. She is how I found out Taylor spent that entire summer crying every night. Because of me.

"So?" She turns to me when she asks.

I shake my head in response. "No."

"I'm not. I promise." Shay lowers her voice down to a whisper, not wanting anyone else to hear the pleading behind her words.

I have a strict No Taylor rule with Shay. When we first met, she would bash Taylor whenever she was brought up. I stayed quiet at first, but as we grew closer, I stopped her completely.

She's done her best to listen this week by staying away from the girls during the day except for mealtimes, when Chasity is present. Shay's department runs from evening to early morning. She usually sleeps in, not making an appearance outside of her office until close to lunch.

Shay sighs, leaning in closer to me. "How are you doing?"

"It's hard."

She nods in understanding. "She can be..."

I cut my eyes towards her in warning.

"... difficult. She can be difficult."

Having Taylor here while also working has been harder than I thought it would be. She has completely thrown me off my game.

"I skipped a show last night to watch her in the garden." I

expect her to comment on my unlikely behavior. In the past, I wouldn't skip a show for anything. I thought Taylor would stick to the group, but since she's arrived at the hotel, she's gone rogue, choosing to go off on her own instead of sticking to the planned activities, giving me less time to complete my actual job.

"Everyone's talking about that, you know. People think you planned it."

I know. I have already read more than one message requesting a repeat performance by the newest addition to the crew.

"How did it feel?"

I contemplate Shay's question. "Good. She was happy."

"Does she know?"

I shake my head.

"I hope when she finds out, she appreciates it."

Shay's words imply she knows Taylor won't. I look up at her face and I know instantly she's not sorry for what she said.

Taking the last bite of my bagel, I lean back into the chair and prop my feet up in front of me. The meeting hasn't started yet. We're going to be here for a while.

A group of Links pile into the room. I'm not surprised to see Trice standing on the tips of her toes and craning her neck around like an ostrich. She spots me and runs over, sitting in the empty seat to my left.

"So happy I found you. I went to the theater, but you weren't there and then I went back to the suite, but no one answered. I almost went to Chasity's office, but something told me to check here first even though I never see you at these meetings. Do you have a phone number by any chance? This was really exhausting." She stops her tirade long enough to hand me her phone.

I hesitate. "Promise you'll only call me if it has something to do with your assignment."

Trice holds up her three middle fingers, crossing her thumb over to press down on the tip of her pinky.

I barely hold in my laughter as I take her phone and enter my contact information. I give it back to her. "Here you are, Girl Scout." A glance at Shay's scrunched-up eyebrows, raised lip and narrowed eyes tells me all I need to know about how Trice makes her feel.

"So Taylor wants me to get her into one of the groups upstairs." She points her index finger up, indicating the floor right above us. The floor that the hotel dubs the *party floor* where all the large playrooms are located. The floor dedicated to orgies. The exact floor I told Taylor about last night. I don't dare look at Shay, who makes an exasperated noise as soon as Trice reveals Taylor's request.

"Did she say why?"

"She said she wants to try new things." I'm taken aback by Trice's response.

Shay looks at me with bright eyes and a grin. "Don't tell me you've never given your teenage girlfriend a sex party for her birthday."

I kick her, aiming for her ankle, but only catch the heel of her foot.

She laughs harder, placing her hand over her heart and belly, wiping at the tears that leak from her eyes. "I'm sorry." Her breathing slows while she attempts to catch her breath.

Taylor and I had plenty of sex. It's one of my regrets. Not the sex, but how the sex started. It's almost like she's trying to erase our beginning with new experiences. As much as I'm not proud of how we came to be, those times are a part of our memories. There is no erasing us.

I haven't spent the last four years trying to forget us. I've spent the last four years trying to forgive myself for everything that happened between us. The good times were amazing and the dark times were unfortunate, but those weeks don't define who we were as a couple and who we could become again.

I close my eyes to think of my options. I can instruct Trice to tell Taylor she couldn't find anything, which no doubt would just propel Taylor in another direction, or I can call in a favor.

"Ok. This is what you're gonna do."

Chapter Nineteen
Taylor

PEEK STREET IS BUZZING this morning. Street carts I'm sure weren't present before make small coffees and pastries available to members sitting and observing at the park. There are plenty of performances happening in the windows of the various houses.

Britney becomes distracted by a shower scene between two women and stands directly in front of the window. Leanna and I sit on an adjacent park bench. We have a view of a few of the shows taking place all at the same time. Leanna releases my fingers and places her hand on my thigh.

"It's weird to meet her."

"Who?"

"Gabriella, the girl who made you cry every night."

I don't know what to say to her about the summer we spent together with Chasity, when we first met. Leanna was the only one who heard me. If anyone else did, they said nothing about it.

"I hate her."

Leanna's words shock me. A bit of something roars out of my chest, right where my heart is supposed to be. "You don't know her."

"I know what she did to you."

"No, you don't."

Only Nicole knows the reason I left Gabriella. She was there with me the day I walked out of our apartment, determined to never see her again. She was also there when I refused to exit the elevator and when I almost turned the car around.

"I read about this," she'd said to me, after she engaged the child locks on the doors and shoved me into the back seat. "The first time a girl gets her heart broken by another girl is the worst. They say it's beyond any heartbreak you'll ever experience with a guy. You will survive this, Taylor. I'll make sure of it." All I could do was cry.

She'd stayed with me at my parents' house for a few days. My phone stayed in her possession the entire time. We practiced writing out my words on a notes app, instead of sending them to Gabriella. Pretty soon, *I miss yous* became *I hate yous*. I couldn't stop crying, even when my sadness morphed into anger.

There was no one else I could express this to. My parents figured out we had broken up on their own, but I never told them why. They adored her and would be heartbroken. I also didn't want to jeopardize my relationship with her family. I can't imagine never speaking with them again.

"Why do you still love her?" Leanna's hands grip my jean-covered thigh.

"I don't know."

Opening my sacred box of tender moments with Gabriella would make no difference to Leanna. How am I supposed to explain that even the darkest times have moments of sparkle? A moment stuck in time tugs at my memory. *Does it matter? I'm going to spend the rest of my life with you.*

"She's good at it."

I snap my attention back to the conversation, stuffing secret envelopes back into the corner of my mind.

"Everyone here loves her. She barely speaks to anyone. No one knows anything about her, but they all sing her praises. There's a portrait of her in the hall by the theater. Did you notice it?"

I hadn't. I shake my head.

"I don't need to know what happened. I know she hurt you. That's enough." Leanna returns her hand to mine and squeezes. I squeeze back, grateful for her words.

Leanna looks around the park. "We should do one." She winks at me. I smile and shrug.

"Can't. We're just guests here. We won't be here long enough to earn enough points." I watch as Britney parts through the crowd, spots us on the bench and walks over.

"I like this place. I wonder what else Chasity is hiding around here." Before Britney can move to explore more of Peek Street, Trice appears with three black bags hanging from her wrists.

"You," she passes one bag to me, "are in luck." Britney and Leanna both accept their gifts without complaint. "Don't open them yet. You're supposed to wait until you get to class."

"Class?" I ask cautiously, remembering our earlier conversation about prerequisites.

"Yup! I got you an audition for the Kitten Club."

I know I'm supposed to be excited. Leanna also doesn't react, but her expression is neutral and calm. Britney squeals.

"I know them! We were at the pools, remember Leanna? They came in with those long tails. Oh! Is there a tail in here?" She shakes her bag around, expecting to hear a noise. A bell sounds. Britney gasps, "I think there's a collar in here!"

I try not to show my apprehension at Trice's news. I have never thought about being collared before or doing anything sexual that involved any type of tail. I look at Leanna.

"Relax. At least it's something new to try. Isn't that what you wanted?"

It is. It's exactly what I want.

We all follow behind Trice as she leads us from Peek Street several floors down to the classrooms. Britney peppers her with questions about the club along the way.

"The club is run by Kat, and yes, that's her real name. She has a pretty strict reputation. Kittens are never to be seen without their collars. I'm sure you've seen more of them than you think. You just haven't noticed. They have a group party every Friday night called The Litter. Today's class will determine if you can attend that party. I have to warn you, though, it takes place during Chasity's birthday dinner. If you're late to The Litter, you're automatically out. Don't even bother knocking on the door, they won't let you in. And remember, be respectful. There's no penalty for ending the class if you realize it's not your thing. Just say, 'I'm not a good fit for this experience' and then you can leave."

Trice opens the door to a waiting room area. The woman behind the counter seems to already know who we are. "Potential kittens?" she asks. We all nod.

The kitten classroom is a lifesize version of a kitten playroom. A few cages line the sides. There is a row of drinking bowls on the floor towards the back of the room. Large cat beds hang from the ceiling. And in the corner, a human-sized cat tree.

I take several deep breaths to calm my nerves. Leanna settles herself on the floor of the room behind a fluffy cat bed. Britney attempts to jump inside of one of the hanging beds, but is unsuccessful. When she lands on her ass the third time, the instructor calls out, "Get undressed, please."

Getting undressed is the simple part. I strip myself completely naked and place my clothing in the box she provides for each of us.

My eyes catch the vibrancy of Leanna's tattoo. When I first saw it years ago, it was incomplete. The bold lines used to create the image on her spine are stark. Flowers weave between pieces of bone. Poinsettias are easy for me to recognize, but the other flower I'm less sure of.

Britney's tattoo seems so unlike her; a dagger balancing two scales, placed on her upper arm. The dagger is adorned with flowers. Something I can't make out sits in the lightest weight. Script flows down the dagger's blade: Honor Thy Heart. I'm sure it wasn't there the summer we met.

I wonder how much Gabriella's body has changed. When we were together, she'd had exactly one tattoo. After what happened, it might not be there anymore. I shake my head, ridding myself of the memories in time for the next instructions.

"Ms. Kat likes her kittens playful. You do not have to meow at all times, but you do need to be in proper cat form. Down. Now. On all fours." With trepidation, I lean forward on the palm of my hands.

"Crawl."

I follow behind Leanna, doing my best cat impersonation. I can't quite decide if cats have arched or straight backs. I alternate between the two, admiring how great Leanna's ass looks hiked up into the air, her back arched deep. I fight the urge to ask if knee pads are going to be made available for future practice sessions. If I can sit on my knees in anticipation of a mouth-watering and delicious treat, surely I can withstand a cat walk.

I shake my head to rid myself of that memory, too. There's only one woman who I've sat on my knees for and sometimes that included filling my mouth with an added accessory.

"Good. Good." I deepen my arch at the praise. No straight back for this cat. "Now roll onto your sides and give me a good purr." I watch Leanna gracefully stretch out and roll to her side in one swift movement. I attempt to do the same, but when it's time for me to roll, I lean too far in and feel a muscle in my hip ache. The pain is brief and doesn't last. My pause causes me to miss my purr, which I don't realize until Britney lets hers out. The instructor comes around our half circle and pulls a black feather tickler out from her apron.

"Here, kitty kitty." She runs the tickler across Britney's face and neck. Britney first giggles, then purrs out, playfully swatting the tickler away. "Such a good kitty." She runs the tickler over Britney's belly. Britney continues to purr and swat, lifting her arms and feet. "Good."

The instructor moves on to me. The feather tickler brushes against my neck and I laugh out. She pulls the tickler away, her brow arched and her lips thin. I take several deep breaths, ridding myself of my giggles. I nod to her to try again. The tickler runs down my side. I hold back my laugh and attempt to purr instead. The sound that comes out of my mouth is one of a dying engine. Britney blows out a laugh before slapping her hand over her mouth.

I laugh, too. This time completely unable to contain myself. "I am so sorry." She shakes her head at me before moving on to Leanna.

I tilt my head upwards to watch her swat away at the tickler; her purr deep and sensual. I look down at Britney and mouth. *How the fuck is she doing that?* She shrugs.

"Very good girl."

I turn to see Leanna has caught a few of the feathers between her toes, her knees now spread apart, fully exposing herself. I look at the instructor, her eyes suddenly bright behind her hooded gaze. She licks her lips before lowering the tickler down to Leanna's vulva. Leanna's toes curl around the gripped feathers. She doesn't stop purring.

"Good kitty. Pretty kitty." Leanna's hips rise as she moves the tickler out of her reach. She lowers them back down in an exasperated plop.

"Time to get dressed, kittens." Each bowtie-style collar comes with a bell attached. She fastens the collars around our necks. I stay perfectly still as she tightens mine and try to mentally shake the anxiety buzzing beneath my skin.

She next pulls the ears from our bags. Each set of ears sits atop a thin black headband. Britney's ears are black and blue. Leanna's, black and white and mine, black and gray. Small bow ties are pinned to the side of each ear. There are no mirrors in the kitten room for me to see how ridiculous we all look once they're placed.

Britney keeps moving her body from side to side to force the bell to sound. Leanna's hands stroke the faux fur of her fluffy new ears. There's something about the way the instructor smiles and coos at us in her thick accent that ramps up my annoyance.

When she extracts a pair of paws from our bags, the protest almost jumps out of me. I calm myself enough to listen to her words. "These are optional." We nod in understanding, the bells around our necks ring as we move our heads. I sigh in relief. Too loudly, I think. The instructor's eyes cut at me and her movements pause until I look away to study a display case across the room that holds collars that look far more ridiculous than the one we have on.

The last items she pulls out of the bags are thick, black, fluffy tails. They look soft and playful. I imagine us each biting at each other's asses. It seems like something cats might do. I expect the instructor to pull at a string, but instead, at the end of the tail, she presents a plug.

"Have you all had your anal training yet?" My eyes grow wide. No one looks as concerned as I do. I shake my head. "Well, then."

She steps toward me. "Usually we would start small and then increase the size of the plug over time. No worries though, people start big all the time. You just need to relax."

She pulls a bottle of lube out of her apron and approaches us with all 3 tails in one hand. From the corner of my eye, I see Britney, back on all fours, wiggling her hips in anticipation. The instructor stands behind me.

"Up, kitty." Her voice is commanding. I don't move.

"Uh, I think I'll wait for another time."

"Another time? The Litter is in two days. If you don't pass today, and you won't without a proper tail fitting, there's no way you'll make it into the club." I lean forward on my palms to push to a stand.

"I think I'm okay with that." I savor the way her eyes narrow. Her agitation fuels me to say more. "I'm gonna go find a club that involves less fur and stupid costumes to feel exclusive. You–" I point my finger at the instructor. "Should tell the head kitten in charge–"

"Kat," Britney interjects. "Her name is Kat."

"You should tell Kat," I continue. "All of this is unnecessary. The imagination is a wonderful tool. If she wants to pretend to be a cat, then do it. No one needs to hurt their knees from crawling on the floor or have stupid ears put on their head." I snatch off the headband and throw it on the carpet. "The feathers I can get behind, but the ears serve no purpose. And this–" I reach out and grab a thick, black, fluffy tail out of the instructor's hand. "Cats don't have tails stuck up their asses. Their asses are plug-free." I throw the tail to the side and turn back to my basket of clothes. No one speaks while I dress. I do so with a triumphant look on my face while Leanna and Britney continue with the rest of the class.

The instructor stands behind Britney now, cleaning the shiny metal plug before applying a generous amount of lube. As she positions it at Britney's back entrance, Britney purrs.

Chapter Twenty
Gabriella

"So, how'd it go?" The first show of the day is in a few hours. I'm confident things will go well. We've been running the same show for months and nearly all the kinks have been ironed out, literally. Our major female star couldn't decide on hers. She was specifically selected after developing a reputation within the hotel for trying and mastering different kinks. She held the record for most classes taken. She was a member of several private clubs and had gained a loyal following.

However, when it came to performing, she was suddenly never comfortable. After each show she'd proclaim not to like the showcased kink at all, causing us to switch course.

Turns out her preference was the one thing BED didn't offer a class on: older adults. Once I saw her batting her fake eyelashes at Larry, our 75-year-old theater usher, I knew I had cracked the code. Larry was happy for the promotion and I rearranged her show to the 4 pm slot, right before the dinner rush for the older hotel population. It's been a sold-out house ever since.

Trice doesn't respond right away. She looks at her phone, types away a text message, and sighs. "Not good. She failed. Vanya says she wouldn't accept her tail." I knew she wouldn't.

"She's on her way to Chasity now. Vanya reported her."

I snort out a laugh. I didn't expect or plan for Taylor to get into any more trouble. I knew she'd hate kitten training. Her refusal to have the anal plug inserted provides me with a tiny piece of information about her four year absence from me.

The problem with Taylor has always been her refusal to be honest with herself. She knows exactly what she wants. She knows exactly what she likes. But she won't admit it. Lucky for her, kitten play is not a kink that interests me. She doesn't have to worry about me sliding a tail up her ass anytime soon.

"Looks like Britney's the only one who made the cut. Leanna did well, but walked out after Taylor."

More reason for me to not like Leanna. I'm not particularly worried about her. She doesn't have the history with Taylor that I have. The time she spent with Taylor was superficial. She doesn't see it that way yet, but it would be in her best interest to start.

"Chasity's calling. I have to go." Trice leaves out the back door entrance just as Shay descends the theater aisle.

"Did you hear from Vanya? She said she was going to call you. She's pissed." I called in a favor to Vanya on her day off. Kitten Club classes aren't usually held two days before a big party.

"Not directly, but I'll handle it later." I'm not worried about anything Vanya has to say. I motion for Shay to follow me from the front of the stage to my office. She gives me a look filled with questions, but follows anyway. My office is at the back of the balcony, attached to the production room. I sit on the couch, pulling my hair from the clip holding it in place. Relief washes over me when it tumbles down around my shoulders.

"See. She's exhausting."

I hold back a smile. As annoying as it is to police Shay's words against Taylor, the banter is appreciated.

"Tell me about that summer."

Shay's eyebrows lift to hide behind her layered bangs. "How will this help you?"

"I don't know, yet." I'm honest. That summer wasn't much different from the others that followed the breakup.

Not wanting to move back home to San Diego, I stayed at our apartment in Santa Monica. I did my best to stay away from her, and to follow the rules. I worked during the day and went to school at night and on Saturday mornings, just so she wouldn't have to see me on campus. Every day hurt, but I pushed myself through it. It was temporary anyway.

But that summer, Chasity called with news about her new business. She wanted Taylor to be a part of it, and she needed my help. I refused. Taylor needed time, and I couldn't be a part of something so secretive. Not again. Plus, I was still pissed off with Chasity about how much she hurt our other friend, Krystal. When the summer was over, I didn't ask any specifics about what had happened. It was better that way.

"I remember she was the last one to show up. Chasity was freaking out about it. We already had our assignments, the invoices were paid and one of us was missing." She dragged the gold key back and forth down the chain.

"She was different back then. When she walked in, she looked like a scared cat. I argued with Chasity a lot about her being there. She wasn't like Leanna. Leanna looks like she crawled out of a true crime episode. She looks sweet and innocent, but you can tell she's trouble."

I nodded along to Shay's assessment of Leanna. There's something about her that feels familiar. She has everyone else fooled. She's probably gone through life with no one noticing the menace lying behind her smile and cute little girl persona, but not me.

"I thought for sure Taylor was gonna lose it. She cried a lot. Once

I heard her in her room. I went to tell her to get over whatever it was already, but Leanna beat me there. Should've seen her face when I knocked on the door."

From the moment I saw them together in the theater, I knew something had happened between them. I can't be upset about the past. It won't ever happen again.

"I don't know who her clients were. We never saw who the others were with, and Chasity was always super secretive about what population we each were serving."

She looks at me with her elbows resting on her knees, her hair falling to frame her face. "Are you worried?"

I shake my head no just as Trice returns with Taylor following slowly behind. Instead of walking at a normal pace, Taylor drags each foot behind the other as if she's being dragged into my office by an invisible rope.

"She is to receive a strict punishment from you. Chasity's orders." Trice throws up another scout salute before patting Taylor on the shoulder and closing the office door behind her.

"I can take her off your hands if you want."

I know Shay means it. It would be her absolute pleasure to punish Taylor for her perceived misdeeds.

Taylor huffs out a breath, plopping herself in an empty seat. Her shiny coils let me know she washed her hair this morning after oversleeping. They are springer than they were yesterday, responding to the added moisture of her hour-long hair routine.

"She doesn't need your help. This" —Taylor points to her chest—"is all her fault."

Shay sneers at her before standing. She stops at the door and turns to me. "I don't think your lessons are working."

I disagree. Taylor's attitude is proof that my lessons worked a little too well. The good and the bad ones.

"What's all my fault?" I ask.

Taylor doesn't respond. She leans back on the couch, hooking her knees over the armchair.

"I'm pretty sure you were crazy before I met you." Taylor's not crazy. She's headstrong and defiant. I love that about her. We sit in silence for several more minutes before she finally speaks.

"I was nice before I met you. Only your grandma still sees me as the sweet girl I used to be." She repeats my grandmother's compliments in Spanish. Her pronunciation is perfect. My grandma has always liked Taylor because Taylor would sit with her to watch her novelas. Sara, my ex-girlfriend, she hated.

"That's not true. You're nice now," I say. It doesn't surprise me that Taylor thinks she's somehow a bad seed. Her best friend, Nicole, is the epitome of holiness. She comes from a church family, has only had one boyfriend and is saving herself for marriage. Or at least she was.

"Did Nicole get married?" Her type usually marries young. She hesitates to answer, pulling at a few loose couch strings. I make a mental note to punish her for that later.

"Not yet. He proposed, but they're in couple's counseling...for his porn addiction."

I try not to smirk. "Lovely."

"It's not like we've never watched it before."

We did more than watch it; she performed it. The memories of those times cause heat to build between us. I have no choice but to ignore my urges and focus on Taylor's. I promised I wouldn't do that anymore, but hey, this is a special circumstance. One I'm partially responsible for creating.

I think back to Shay's departing words about my punishments. Taylor was already a defiant shit-talker before I met her. Her mouth got her into trouble with me. And her imagination.

Listening to her moan because of me lit a fire within my chest, I have yet to figure out how to extinguish. And then she came back for more. For me. I have to disagree with Shay. I think I did too good of a job.

Chapter Twenty-One
Taylor

APPARENTLY LAUGHING DURING KITTEN play class is an egregious sin punishable by torture, executed by your ex-girlfriend. I had only managed to enjoy two spoonfuls of ice cream when Chasity's assistant approached me in Decadent, read me a list of broken rules, and passed me off to Trice.

Now I'm back in the kitten play classroom, watching Gabriella have a conversation with the instructor who snitched on me.

"Disrespectful and rude behaviors (including verbal remarks or insults) towards another group or club within the premises will not be tolerated. All violators will be punished."

Tough crowd. I had nothing to say when Chasity read the rule out to me. I fail to see what was so rude or disrespectful about my refusal to have a tail stuck up my ass. And so what if I laughed? Who tickles someone with a feather and doesn't expect them to react?

I can't make out what Gabriella and the instructor are talking about. They're a few feet away, with Gabriella's back facing me. The instructor hasn't looked at me once. I guess she's too upset by my disrespectful behavior to be polite.

I walk around the clean classroom. A few balls of yarn topple to the ground when I run my fingers across the pile. I freeze, wait and then slowly turn around for witnesses. They're both looking at me now. I conjure up a weak smile, as innocent as I can muster. The instructor glares at me, takes another look at Gabriella and leaves.

Gabriella says nothing as she walks across the room to gather a feeding bowl. She disappears with it for a few minutes before returning, setting it down on the carpet.

"Take off your clothes."

She says it with authority and I do it without complaint. In the span of our relationship, there isn't a moment in time when I've received a punishment that didn't involve me removing a piece of clothing. I strip down to my bra and panties and wait, secretly hoping Gabriella notices my minor act of defiance.

She attaches a collar to my neck. I search for the buzzing I felt earlier, but find none. My skin feels calm even as my heart races. This collar differs from the one I wore earlier. This one is thick and black, and instead of a bell, a gold heart dangles from the center. I expect it to be cold and hard against my skin, but the fabric stitched inside of the collar provides a surprising level of comfort.

I ignore the sting in my chest that always arises whenever I see a gold heart anywhere. It's a silly reaction that should have dissipated long ago. The key around my neck also resembles a heart, a fact I've tried to ignore.

Gabriella moves to kneel behind the bowl she sat down moments prior. With her index finger, she beckons me forward. "Here Kitty Kitty."

I'm unprepared for the electric shock that pulses between my thighs at her words. I will my knees and wrists to move against the carpet, remembering to arch my back low with my ass high in the air. Her eyes brighten and her lips stretch across her face. Pride soars across my chest. I raise my neck higher, pressing my breasts forward. I might look more like a wildcat than a domesticated one, but I don't care.

The bowl is filled with a white substance. The consistency isn't quite right for cows' milk. I bend my head, extend my tongue, and dip the tip inside the bowl before lapping up my first taste. I know right away it's not your typical cow's milk and is not thick enough to be almond milk. It is more watery, with a hint of sweetness. I continue to drink and as I drink Gabriella continues to give me praise.

"Good kitty. Such a thirsty kitty." Each word sends an extra wag down my tail-less hips. She knows exactly what she's doing to me. And I love every moment.

Reluctantly.

The trail of her fingers down my spine encourages me to drink faster. When she reaches the band of my panties, I hear the click of her sucking her teeth.

"Naughty kitty. You never learn."

She's right. If I were good at learning the lessons of a broken heart, then I wouldn't be here. I followed Chasity that summer for the same reasons I came to BED; because I can't get Gabriella out of my head.

So instead, I sit. For good measure, I place my two hands in front of me like the mental image of the cat I'm modeling my movements after.

She almost had me. For two years, I went willingly into her control and followed her every command. I was happy to do it. I love receiving pleasure just as much as she loves to use my pleasure as a punishment.

We were made for it. The constant push and pull of the chase served as our key ingredient. I loved how powerful I felt back then. And how powerless I'm about to make her feel now.

"What are you doing?" she breathes through my ear. The lace edges of my underwear dig into my skin with her tightening grip.

Her voice is low and threatening. It's rare for her to take that tone with me. By the end of this, I'd have earned it.

When I don't respond right away, she bends her head down and clenches a piece of skin on my neck between her teeth. I hold my breath instead of catching it and close my eyes to keep them from rolling off to the side in bliss.

I've always had trouble controlling the movement of my hips in desperate times such as this one. I hold them steady by pressing my ass down onto the balls of my feet. The additional weight adds both pressure and pain to my ankles. It hurts like a bitch.

I won't give in.

When I can no longer hold my breath, I allow small knots of air into my nostrils and press my lips tighter together.

No breaths will escape from me. If I have to struggle to breathe, it'll be to spite her instead of praising her for her efforts.

"I'm sitting." I finally answer when she pulls her neck back to focus on my gripped panties. Under a watchful eye, she pulls the center of them to tighten around my vulva. The dark coloring conceals the dampness, but the moment she touches me, she'll know.

"I didn't tell you to sit." Her body slightly shifts in place behind me. With one hand, she gathers the front of the fabric and pulls up while pressing the silky texture down on my clit.

I bite my lip to keep from saying what I really want to.

Shit.

Shit.

Shit.

The challenging sensations make me want to do things I shouldn't, like roll my legs from underneath me and spread them until she tells me to stop. She'll be nice then and remove my panties to punish me properly.

"Do you think naughty kitties get to tell me what to do?"

No, I keep to myself. Naughty kitties should be punished. They should be brought to the edge of an orgasm and then ignored, like when cats beg for their owners' touch and then dismiss them with sharp claws.

Because I can't say what I want, I say nothing. I lean a little farther back with my head resting on her shoulder. My lips part to allow in a little more air.

The wetter I get, the easier it becomes for my panties to aid in my punishment. My entrapped clit only knows what it feels like to be served by Gabriella, even when the method is torturous. It only swells for her. It doesn't scream in my head as I do now about how much we've missed her—missed this.

Her other hand stays just in the corner on top of my thigh. No doubt ready to take over at any minute. I try to arch my lower back to restrict access, but the position only forces the hold to tighten. Instead of pulling in quick bursts, her tugs become slow, long and deliberate.

No longer able to maintain my defiant kitten pose, my arms retreat to my sides to hold me steady.

"Good kitty."

Her approval is enough to motivate my body into a new position. I free my ankles from my jarring weight and spread my legs before us. Gabriella allows me space to lean further back into her. A glance up allows me to witness the hunger in her eyes. She loosens her hold on my panties and my clit is relieved of the building pressure she created.

If it could scream at me, it would. It would call me the biggest traitor in the history of sex for denying it its rightfully earned pulsating orgasm. It was sure to get one.

She always delivers.

Sacrificing my orgasm is necessary for the cause. I can't be defeated by Gabriella again. She can't believe that she's the only one that can get me this far.

Even if it's true.

So when she unhooks her fingers from my panties and the pleasure my clit was basking in dissipates, I run.

The key around my neck swishes wildly as I dash through the nearby cat tunnel. I lie flat on my back in the center and shift my eyes up and down to the two ends to check for her arrival.

There's not enough room for her to command my body to bend into any of her preferred positions, and there's no room for her to trap my body underneath hers.

"You know, you don't have to do this. I can cry to Chasity later about how mean of an ex-girlfriend you are. It's not like I don't have other evidence," I call out when she doesn't step into view.

"You broke the rules," she responds in the distance.

I use my feet to propel me upwards, towards the opening above my head. My view clears the plastic blue tunnel up to the white ceiling. My eyes travel across the room and I spot her at the exact place I left her behind.

She sits next to the bowl she fed me out of with her legs stretched out before her and her ankles crossed, propped up by her elbows.

"You like when I break the rules. You should be rewarding me, not punishing me. I was probably the most entertaining kitten that instructor has ever seen."

Her laugh makes no sound. Her slightly protruding cheeks are the only confirmation that her expression has even changed.

"Bad kitties don't get treats."

I watch her push herself to a stand and start over to me. I plant my feet deeper into the tunnel in preparation to use them to pull myself back to my previous position. The tunnel bunches when

I attempt to move, and the bottom of it lifts in non-compliance. I attempt more movements that don't get me very far. She steps into my peripheral vision at the same time she drops to her knees and her hand comes down to grip my neck. It happens in one swift movement.

"If you want a prize, you'll have to behave."

The muscles in my thighs tingle in exhaustion. I'm breathing deeper than I should. It's either because I restricted my lungs earlier or because she hasn't stopped staring down at me. And I haven't looked away.

"Purr, Emmy. You know you want to."

I do…and don't. Her hand slides up my throat to trace one finger over my bottom lip. The act doesn't make me purr. It causes my hips to lift and my breath to struggle, which is bad enough.

My lack of movement is not compliance. I have not given in. I mentally work out a new strategy for escape. The door to the classroom is close to the tunnel. She'll be angry that I've fled in my underwear, but what I choose to wear in front of others is none of her concern. Unless doing so is against her rules. And in that case, well, shit.

Her hand drops from my neck and dips into the valley of my breasts. I pull my bottom lip in between my teeth again and clench my fists atop the plastic tunnel.

"You're only bad because you want to be good. Isn't that right, Emmy? You want me to tell you how much of a good kitty you are when you stop trying so hard to fight against what you really want."

My right breast is pulled roughly from its cup and massaged in her hands while its nipple is pinched between her fingers. I don't bother with attempts to conceal my rotating hips. I do turn my head to the side, out of her intense gaze to allow myself more air to breathe.

She takes it as an invitation to press her lips to my cheek, jaw and earlobe. Her words sway through only seconds later. The dirty ones in Spanish I knew to never repeat aloud.

One moan escapes from me then. And then another. My lips part with more breaths than I intend to release and my knees push against the tunnel with no room to spread.

My lips graze against hers when I turn back to face her. The look in her eyes is one of arrogance. She thinks she's won. I open my mouth to tell her otherwise, only for the space to become occupied with her tongue, which I suck in welcome. Her fingers clasp around my nipples harder and stretch them for longer.

My moans hide behind our kisses. I'm hopeful they sound more like curses than gratification, but when she pulls away, I'm unable to disguise the guttural outrage. The result of my failure is her smirk with swollen lips from fervent kisses. Desperate kisses. Kisses lost in memories I might want to stay in for a little while longer.

"Are you ready to be a good kitty now?" she asks.

I purr.

Reluctantly.

The Las Vegas chill causes my whole body to shiver. Standing outside of BED is odd. It has only been a few days and the world outside feels unfamiliar. Gabriella declines the valet's offer to retrieve her car. "That's okay, Darnell. We can walk." A small smile spreads across her puckered lips. I shoot Darnell a look of irritation. His expression is resolute in my attempt to sway him.

My head hangs down and my eyes follow Gabriella's footsteps as I trail behind her down the driveway and onto the sidewalk of the strip. My cheeks are cold from the wind. The pockets of my sweatshirt give my hands some relief. As an L.A. girl, I am stocked on hoodies, but low on gloves and scarves. It's not until the wintertime that I remember there are articles of clothing in existence to keep us warm and shield us from the cold.

Gabriella's feet stop at the corner. I look up when I feel her hand slide inside my pocket, curl her fingers around mine and then slide out again, taking my hand along with her. Gabriella's pockets are warmer, lined with something better suited for cold weather than cotton.

Her hands are still soft. She's always kept her nails short. Easier to draw that way, she'd say. I picture her sketching with her pencil across the pages of her notebook, her nose close to the surface or her cheek resting on the outside of the page. A deep ache fills the bottom of my chest, right underneath my heart. Missing her has always been the hardest part.

When the light changes and the signal flashes for us to walk across, I keep my head up. With one hand still clasped between Gabriella's fingers, we continue our way past a few popular Vegas hotels.

Confusion etches across my face when Gabriella steers us toward the entrance of Excalibur. I expected a smoke-filled bar or loud nightclub for recruiting. Gabriella doesn't stop. She skips the slow-moving conveyor for guests with tired and aching knees and walks us alongside it.

The air in the hotel lobby isn't as suffocating as some others. It becomes worse as we walk through the casino floor, past rows of bars and people sitting at slot machines with their cigarettes and their drinks in hand. Gabriella leads us down the escalator to the

Fun Dungeon where we pass groups of families, with and without kids, playing various arcade games.

We come to a stop at the entrance of a Tournament of Kings. I'm confused, but also excited at the prospect of attending the show. If Chasity wants to feed me a large bowl of soup and a turkey leg, I won't complain.

I've been to Medieval Times, in Buena Park not too far from home, many times. The Tournament of Kings show in Las Vegas is very similar, but different countries instead of colors represent knights. My favorite Medieval Times knight is the black and white knight.

"Really, Gabriella? Do you ever take a night off?"

The man who approaches us looks friendly, with a slight smile on his face. I turn to glance at Gabby, who mirrors his expression. She gives him a one armed hug, still holding onto my hand in her pocket. She grips my fingers when I attempt to pull back.

"Oh, nice to see you finally have some company." He points to me, a mischievous grin on his face. "This one looks a little too pretty for you, though." He winks and then laughs, coaxing a smile out of me. Anyone teasing Gabriella is a friend of mine. Gabriella huffs dramatically. She knows he's full of shit. No one on this earth would think she wasn't gorgeous. I squeeze her hand in reassurance. I curse myself.

"Do you want me to tell her you're here?"

I miss who they're discussing. Gabriella shakes her head no just as another staff member opens the gates to the grounds. My hand is released in time for me to shimmy down the aisle to our seats. Waiting on our table is the crown displaying our country's colors and our country's flag. I proudly showcase the paper crown on my head. Tonight we represent Ireland. I assemble Gabriella's crown, sliding it down and entrapping her curls.

The soup comes first. Mouthfuls of delicious tomato bisque sail down my throat. I pass Gabriella my piece of garlic bread. She nods in gratitude and dips it into her bowl. Together we watch the tournament take place, cheering on our country's knight and booing all others. My vocal cords strain as I yell out my support and utter disdain. Gabriella sometimes joins in, chanting out 'Ireland' along with the rest of our section.

We eat our way through the Cornish hen, corn on the cob, and roasted potato comfortably. My muscles tense when she leans over to whisper in my ear about our knight's performance. He's doing terribly. Despite our group's encouraging efforts, he's lost every challenge, including a sword fight with France. It's embarrassing.

The black and white knight would never.

I take a sip of Gabriella's margarita. Alcohol gets along better with my body when it's blended with ice. I don't know if the heat that rises within me is from the tequila or the warmth of Gabriella's hand caressing my inner thigh. I squeeze my thighs together, eliminating the space she has to travel between. She turns to me with almost a smile; puckered lips not quite pulled at the corners of her mouth. The muscles in my thighs relax, allowing them to part. I barely catch her smirk when she turns away, her eyes landing on the performance in the arena.

I skip a breath when her hand settles in the space between my hips. These feelings are not my fault. If there's one thing I know for certain, I am absolutely one hundred percent without a doubt attracted to Gabriella. Fact.

My heart raced from the moment I saw her, when we were nothing but bitter enemies, playing a dirty game of chance and temptation. And then it ballooned into more. Lust. Love. Pain. She didn't belong to me then. Not at first.

I know the urge I have for me to kiss her shoulder is a genuine act of desire and not a yearning fantasy for me to untangle. As real as my heartbeat, I know I want to wrap my hands around her arm and lean so deeply into her. I feel the steadiness of confidence beneath my cheeks. This is not a dream. I love Gabriella Margarita Flores. Still. And that scares me.

Nicole is going to kill me once she finds out that I unfolded for my enemy with one bend of her finger. It's not my fault. If you think about it, she has conditioned my body to respond to her every need from the first time we met. I have no one to blame for my actions but the woman who broke my heart.

I unclench my thighs one last time, then take her hand and place it in her lap. I don't look at her after. She never turns her back to face me again.

The black cape of the Dragon Knight swoops past us. A fight ensues. As expected, our knight is left crumpled on the arena floor. The Dragon Knight celebrates with a victory lap, circling the arena on horseback. The crowd can't help but cheer and even I'm impressed with the knight's talent. Gabriella leans forward in her chair, her elbows propped on the table, her eyes following the Dragon Knight's every move. The knight performs several tricks. The act is new to me. I have never seen that happen at a dinner and tournament show.

It's when he passes us again, his back hanging off the horse with one foot tucked in the saddle, I realize what's different. He is not a he at all. The woman's long hair glides past us at the same time Gabriella reaches out. It happens quickly. Their fingers touch and something passes between them in a flash. I stare at Gabriella, but she doesn't return my questions with so much as a glance.

The rest of the Dragon Knight's performance confirms my suspicion. She dances and flexes on the back of her horse with ease, winning the crowd over. No matter which knight they were rooting for before, they belong to her now.

Dragon Knight chants fill the air. Feet bang against the floor and fists pound on the tables. There has never been a woman knight before. Some may argue historical accuracy for the lack of diversity. I don't have an argument myself. I went to the tournament for entertainment. Not for a history lesson, but I have to admit, seeing a woman dominate on the field is exciting. I feel pride watching her display her talents and almost tear up at the sound of everyone in the crowd rooting for her success.

My burgeoning tears dry up quickly when Gabriella's smile is wide and her eyes light bright. *Why did she bring me here?*

The story continues with an explanation for the Dragon Knight's traitorous cruelty. Once a joyful woman, her husband was taken, her children stolen, and she needed to exact revenge. Not solely on her own country, but the world. One day, maybe, the Dragon Knight can just be a bad bitch wanting to do bad bitch things without a justification of trauma and turmoil. But today, I'll count it as a win.

The Dragon Knight's reign doesn't go unchallenged and, true to form, good conquers all evil and she's taken out on the battlefield after the knights come together for the greater good. The dragon knight's body is carried away to a room filled with boos and hisses. Sometimes, the bad guys deserve to win.

Gabriella's silence continues all the way back to the hotel. We avoid most of the evening cold air by taking the indoor route from Excalibur through Luxor and Mandalay Bay. There's no reason to even attempt to hold my hand until we walk out the Mandalay Bay entrance. She doesn't move to do so, and I pretend it doesn't matter.

I walk out of the greenhouse after my second performance feeling on fire and completely alive. There's no doubt I love performing in front of other people. Continuing on my journey of exploration, I walk down a row of bars in a section of the hotel I have not traveled down before. After leaving Peek Street, my feet kept moving, turning random corners and peeking through shuttered windows until I found something interesting. I look up at the Paradise Row street sign. I might not remember how to get back to the suite tonight, but I'm also hoping that won't matter.

Gabriella and I parted ways as soon as we entered the iron doors of BED. Peek Street is the only route I have bothered to remember so far. The decision to go there after being shunned by Gabriella and replaced by a trick rider was an easy one.

The bar I stare into is busy. There's loud rap music playing and blue lights flashing through the windows. I can see multiple men inside enjoying drinks and laughing. They're all dressed similarly in long white or dark blue t-shirts and baggy jeans.

I notice eyes peering out of the different windows on the block. A few feet away is a different location, but these men wear suits with slicked back hair. I don't need to guess which bar caters to the biker gangs at the end of the one-way road. Their music is not as loud as the one I'm standing in front of, but the bikes are a dead giveaway.

Next to each bar is a dimly lit alleyway. I eye the one in front of me with trepidation. Blue lights from the bar flash onto the concrete walls like a portal in a gateway. It looks clean enough. There are no posters plastered on the concrete walls and no one seems to hang out in the shadows. The alley, which looks like it belongs to the mafia crew, is made of brick. It also looks clean, but is much darker, with no light to guide anyone through. The alley belonging to the bikers is also concrete, with posters and signs lining the walls.

I take a step towards the middle. The mafia hideout looks like it might also be a restaurant, and while my feast at the Tournament of Kings was plentiful, after my performance, I'm feeling hungry again.

"Oof. I wouldn't do that if I were you."

I turn, surprised to see Kacey standing behind me. I haven't seen her since that first day at Indulgence. It's late, but she's still dressed in her flirty black apron.

She takes her hand and waves it out in front of her. "Paradise Row is for good girls who like really bad men." Her eyes lock onto mine. She circles me, continuing her explanation. "Now, I was under the impression that you were a good girl who liked emotionally unavailable women."

I don't care much for her assertion that I'm a 'good girl', but it's the Gabriella slander I find difficult to tolerate. Gabriella isn't emotionally unavailable. She's...complicated.

Before I can respond, Kacey cuts me off.

"You can't walk down these alleys without a waiver stating you agree to participate in a role-playing exercise, which may involve activities that would be considered criminal outside of these walls. Do you understand what I'm saying?"

I nod because I think I do.

"There's a protocol. These things are very delicate. Participants are required to meet all members of the club. That way, no unsuspecting victim or nosey birthday guest, in your case, gets taken by surprise. They keep rotating the men out to make sure no one knows who you are. You won't make it within two feet of those doors."

She squeezes my shoulders between her open palms and steers me in the opposite direction, away from Paradise Row. We stop in front of a nondescript door. There are no flashing lights seeping through the windows. There's no loud music. "This is where we keep all the good girls. There are plenty of emotionally unavailable women here."

I watch her leave, noticing for the first time a slight limp in her step. The tips of my fingers press against the black door, prying it open. The music is the first thing I hear, not blaring obnoxiously, but low and mellow underneath the clatter of voices. The bar is packed with women in evening gowns, freshly done hair and makeup. I am severely underdressed in my usual T-shirt and jeans. I skipped dinner tonight with the girls since I was away with Gabriella and the greenhouse doesn't require me to dress up in nice clothes. It doesn't require me to dress up in any clothes at all.

I order a drink from the bar. I only know three from the top of my head; mimosa, margarita, martinis, and rum and coke. For this, I go for the martini, asking the bartender, whose shiny, sequined top sends a blinding reflection through the mirror behind the bar, to make it filthy. I have a small understanding of what this means. I know martinis are made with olive juice and if you ask for a dirty or filthy martini, then you're asking for more olive juice. At least that's what I hope it means. This night can't be a bust for me. I need to make sure I'm successful at exploring something new. And this damn martini better help.

The strength of the gin burns my throat as the liquid goes down. I keep my face as neutral as possible, not wanting anyone to see me struggle.

"Did you hear about what happened to Angela?" I shake my

head at the woman who sits on the barstool next to me. I raise the glass to take another idle sip. It goes down better the second time.

"No? Well, I heard Georgia finally caught her with Unique and Nova."

I choked on sip number three, causing the woman's smile to spread.

"You didn't read the script." I shake my head. I know nothing about a script. The only thing sitting atop the bar is a few napkins and drinks meant for the other patrons.

I follow when she grabs my hand. Following women around in bars is something new. For one, I don't go to bars on account that I barely drink and for two, not since Gabriella have I dated a woman. It's much easier for me to not fall in love with a man. Which is odd for me to think, really. I am bisexual after all. Maybe if I leaned into it a bit, I would find a guy to potentially fall in love with, except my mind just never seems to quite go there.

She leads me to a table surrounded by fancy gowns. Two women's noses smash up against each other. They aren't kissing, but having an extremely close conversation. I look around the rest of the bar and realize I've entered an updated, more modern version of a saloon, the one with a hotel attached on the second floor, where men would round up the "working girls" when riding into town.

Except The Kitchen is run fully by women. It is glitzy and glamorous, with bright lights and soft cushions instead of gritty, wooden, and rustic tables and chairs.

Yeah, I am definitely underdressed.

"Who do we have here, sister?"

I am both shocked and confused by the greeting from the woman with the green dress sitting in the booth. All the women are of different ethnicities.

"I brought us a new friend to play with and maybe a new sister to join." The look in her eyes sends heat across my hips. The tips of her fingers roam across the waistband of my jeans.

"And maybe, if she can play nice, we can take her back to Mama Mae."

It's the moment I realize the group is speaking with a Western accent. Images of Mama Mae race across my mind. I imagine Mama Mae tall with a gun belt around her waist. She doesn't take the belt off when she slides into me from behind, her movements causing the holster to slap against the back of my thigh.

And oh, Mama Mae is older. I don't know this for certain, but for my fantasy, an older, more mature woman with exquisite horseback riding skills will help me check a few boxes off my list. Most of these boxes I didn't even know I had, but still.

I try not to show how enticing meeting Mama Mae might be. I didn't know I had a fantasy involving the Wild West, cowgirls, or gun holsters. I especially never thought I would be heating up at the idea of being with a group of sisters, no matter how thin the branches on the tree.

The sister with the full cheeks and pale pink dress smiles at me. "Mama Mae likes when we bring home the good ones."

I fight the urge not to ask what happens to the bad ones, the ones that don't play nice. The ones who don't listen to commands. Will Mama Mae drag me across the room by my hair if I don't do what she says? Will she handcuff me to the bed? In the Wild West, everyone has handcuffs. Before I can go too far into my Mama Mae fantasy, I stop to ask the important questions.

"What is this place?"

"Role playing bar."

The voice comes from behind me, the Western accent still present. "We all have roles here, except for you, for now. But don't worry, little darlin', we'll be happy to rope you in." Her laugh does nothing to stop the pictures taking shape in my brain of my body in more sexual positions. It doesn't stop the electrifying feeling from racing down my spine.

I clear my throat and lean gently into the woman behind me, suddenly remembering I never caught her name. "And which sister are you?"

She presses her hand against her chest in mock modesty.

"I'm Destiny." Nude lipstick is perfectly applied to her beautiful, full lips. The sister in the pale pink dress is East Asian, though it becomes impossible for me to ask her name once she and the woman in green fully pull each other in for a kiss.

I ignore Destiny's fingers continuing to play with my clothing while I consider the opportunity before me. Do I like women? Yes. Do I enjoy having sex with women? Yes. Absolutely. Two years of sex with a woman would be hard to fake. And the years I spent pining for the affection of a woman—before and after Gabriella —are difficult to ignore. Not to mention the moment we had earlier in the kitten playroom when I wanted to tear her clothes off. It has never been just about my pleasure. I've always wanted her just as bad.

Role playing is not a new avenue for me. I've been there and done that plenty of times with Gabriella. I even got in trouble for it a few times. She hated when I did it without telling her first. Back then I blamed it on my acting. When Trice first asked me about my kinks, I thought about telling her about this one, but exhibitionism sticks out for me the most. For me, role playing is more about just having someone watch you. It's about having that one person watch you while everyone else is out of the loop. At least it was.

I've never done it with anyone else, and I've certainly never had sex with more than one person at a time. I don't even know what Gabriella's reaction would have been if I had ever proposed it, especially if I had sprung it on her during an impromptu role play. Being with the sisters will allow me to figure out for myself without needing to consider anyone else's feelings about it.

I drink more of my martini and consider asking for a second glass. All the surrounding women are attractive, but my panties have remained dry. I don't stop Destiny's fingers from dancing across my skin. I need their encouragement to get me to the next level.

"What is Mama Mae like?"

Destiny takes a moment to think before responding. Her eyes narrow and her nose scrunches up. "What do you mean?"

I rephrase my question to better reflect my interest in Mama Mae's personality and not her taste in movies.

"Oh, girl, I don't know." Her accent has disappeared, replaced with a more familiar tone. "She don't really be sayin' much at all. Except–" she leans closer, "When she starts hittin' it right, that's when you go from Mama Mae to Mother Mae. Get the timing right or she'll replace that ass real quick."

I absorb the information Destiny gives me. My visuals of me screaming out to Mother Mae help move my body along. I shift a bit in my seat. Destiny smiles down at me. She lifts the martini glass to my mouth, not stopping until it's empty. Her index finger swipes across my lips. My tongue darts out to catch it. I'm being both daring and bold. My body heats up.

"I'm gonna go and get you something a little stronger than this."

The two sisters don't stop kissing when she leaves. I turn and glance around the room, noticing they aren't the only ones engaged in public affection. I vaguely remember a rule about sexual interactions in public places being prohibited at BED. Kissing must be okay.

A soft squeeze of my ass forces me to look back. The sisters have navigated from their kissing spot to centering me between them. Pale Pink Dress tugs at my arm, sliding me back down in place. As their faces move closer in another kiss, I move mine backward, expecting to watch as their rose gold necklaces clash together in haste.

When their hands caress my neck and pull me forward, I slide out my tongue. Our three tongues join in movement. Moans pour from them, sending an erotic signal shooting between my thighs.

"Oh, hell yeah."

The two sisters part to make room for Destiny to place herself on my lap. In one swoop, she pushes my chin back and pours the clear contents of the small glass into my mouth. Whatever it is, it's strong. It takes me two tries to swallow all of it.

I've had sex under the influence once before, after naively eating a banana muffin at a study group. It wasn't foolish because you should never eat anything from anyone's home, ever. It was foolish because this group, in particular, were known weed heads. No one warned me about the muffins and it wasn't until I got home an hour later that I felt the effects. The feeling in my body was one I had never felt before. Like the world had completely turned upside down. My head was spinning, my thoughts were racing and time was missing from my brain. One minute I'd be standing in the bathroom and then the next, in the kitchen, with no memory of how I got there. When Gabriella found me, I was walking in circles in my room, unable to stop my legs from moving.

Finally, in exhaustion, I'd tossed myself onto the bed. Gabriella ran to get me water. I remember her repeating to me over and over that I needed to stay hydrated. The world kept spinning, even with my eyes closed. I had vivid dreams of me falling and obsessive worries that my brain would be stuck like that forever. And then I'd come up with the perfect idea to distract me.

Sex.

Gabriella had been hesitant, but I'd argued a solid, intoxicated point. My first experience of being high was awful. It was most likely never going to happen again, so we might as well make the best of it. And we did.

At the memory of our time together, the intense heat in my body rises to meet the demands of the sisters. Gabriella and I have never shared a three-way kiss. I consider this an experience I'm having completely separate from her, to be a win.

Destiny envelops my lips in a kiss. I return it, gripping her hips when she grinds into me. The sisters egg us on with one hand disappearing down my top and another up Destiny's dress.

"Sisters, I already warned you about doing too much before going into the bedroom. Everything is not meant to be seen. Stop right now or next time I'm going to report you to the Dun—"

The woman stops speaking when Destiny dislodges herself from my lap.

"Oh."

Her thin black eyebrows shoot up in surprise. She's kept close to the Western theme with a black cowgirl hat, little black gloves, a black patched sequined top and black detachable chaps.

"Is this..." She leans her body over the table to get a better look at me. I display a smile I hope is cute and awkward, symbolizing complete harmlessness. I don't know where this woman recognizes me from, but if it happens to be from a television show or a theater production, I hope she likes me enough to not say anything. "...Gabriella's pet?"

My smile drops. My throat lodges with my upcoming protest, but I don't know what to say. I'm not surprised that she knows

Gabriella. From her getup and the two lackeys flanking her at the side, I have already discerned that she was someone in a power position.

The sisters look away, staring down at their laps. "Oh, did you three not know? The Queen sent out a notice that no one was to touch her prized possession." She drags a coffin-shaped acrylic fingernail across my chin. Her silver chain pokes out from the collar of her shirt.

"And yet, look who we find in my house. That little bitch doesn't run anything in here." The sneer she gives me has the opposite effect of intimidation. Instead of fear, I grow angry at her implications. She doesn't like Gabriella. As the president of the I Hate Gabriella Club, I could admire that, but as the co-chair of the   Gabriella Flores-Is-Amazing-At-What-She-Does-And-Deserves-Nothing-But-Respect Committee, *fuck this lady*.

I haven't been in a physical fight in a long time. I spent a sizeable chunk of my childhood and adolescence in trailers and not in traditional classrooms. Still, kids in the entertainment industry were vicious and eventually, I learned I had to bite back.

I stand from my seat and lean into the crazed-eyed chihuahua. I maintain my peripherals on the other two. Knowing if they jumped, I had to be ready to handle all three.

"What did you call her?"

She laughs, tossing her head back and exaggeratedly shaking her head. She says her next words slowly and deliberately with eyes so narrow I can barely make out the wing of her eyeliner.

"La llamé puta perra."

"That's what I thought."

My fingertips find the edges of the cheese platter and I slam it across her face. Cheese crackers and small meats fly across the room, but I barely have enough time to register where they land before I fling myself over the back of the booth. It takes seconds too long for me to shake the dizziness from the gin and tequila when I land. I take off, rushing through the front door and making a sharp left turn, away from Paradise Row.

I hear screams and shouts behind me. I tell myself to focus on moving my muscles to run, despite my earlier alcohol intake. I have no idea where I should go. Ending up on Paradise Row was an accident, the result of aimless roaming.

I sprint through any opening I can, turning down half-empty aisles instead of crowded ones. My feet pound against the pavement of an alleyway I did not know I was heading into. She yells from behind to stop, but I will my legs to keep going forward. The alleyways zig and zag with no sign of an end. I hope for a doorway to slam into, but none appear.

I hear growing chatter on the other side of the concrete walls and I move faster. My breath is more ragged, the muscles in my thighs taunt. She doesn't sound any closer than she was before, but she also hasn't given up.

I see the trick rider off in the distance, and I know I'm almost to the end. For a second, I wonder why she's at BED at all, and when I see Gabriella striding next to her, I know the answer.

Anger fuels me now. Thoughts of barrelling into them charge my system enough that I take a chance with my aching lungs to scream out, "Gabriella!!"

Chapter Twenty-Two
Gabriella

I TENSE MY CORE and plant my feet in place before Taylor slams into me. She's out of breath, hunched over with her hands placed on her knees. "What the hell are you doing now?" My eyes follow to the place where she points. Vanessa and her two assistants, whose names I never bothered to learn, are walking towards us. Vanessa is pissed.

Oh shit.

Vanessa was one of Chasity's first hires. She manages the themed locations, different from the themed group parties. Brandi manages those. Vanessa has a background in theater and was gunning for my job before Chasity convinced me to come on. We've never gotten along.

"What's the problem here?" I let my annoyance show, but keep my attitude in check. This isn't just any job. It's Chasity's dream. I have to respect it. Or at least, try as hard as I can to not destroy it.

"You need to give her to me. She broke the rules. You can't shield her from punishment."

I laugh in her face. "That's not your fucking department." I don't deny that Taylor broke the rules. She probably did. She has a knack for that kind of thing. It was cuter when we were younger and I'm sure, outside of the walls of BED, not that bad. I have to be tougher with my punishments next time. My mistake was probably touching her earlier. I didn't mean to. The plan was just to force her through the entirety of kitten training, but then she disobeyed me and I couldn't resist the smell of her. She's even more delicious than I remember. And being inside of her again? Huge mistake. I was limited in the playroom, but if we'd been back in the suite, there's no way we would've made it in time to recruit Erica. Then I thought things were different, and we could move forward, but at dinner, she'd pulled away from me.

I whip out my phone to do the only thing I can before an all-out brawl ensues. There's no way Vanessa is getting her hands on Taylor. I don't care if she burned down one of the halls. Chasity has enough money to replace it. And besides, isn't that what insurance is for?

The negative thing about living in the hotel you own? You're practically on call 24-7. Dressed in pale blue silk pajamas, Chasity looks wide awake. She barely spares a glance at Vanessa, who's been talking nonstop since we entered the room.

Shay is here, laid out on Chasity's couch. The popcorn she's eating is a coincidence. Though she fancies herself as some kind of know-it-all. She's not that good.

"And then she hit me in the fucking face!" Vanessa ends her hysterical rant by pointing to the left side of her face. There's nothing there. Taylor didn't hit her hard enough, apparently. "This isn't fair, Chasity. She was in my area, causing disruptions. Her punishment should be at my discretion."

Chasity holds up a hand to stop Vanessa's blabbering. "Taylor's not just a member here. She's my guest and while she's here, she's Gabriella's responsibility. Not yours."

Vanessa's fists clench and her shoulders square. No words escape her pinched lips. She leaves Chasity's suite without uttering another word.

"Nothing from you?" Chasity directs her words to Taylor, who took a spot on the couch next to Shay. She thought she had been sneaking small handfuls of Shay's popcorn, but I know from the glare Shay sends me every time she does it, she isn't doing a good job.

"What? I was minding my own business. *She* attacked *me*." She says it with confidence mixed in with a tinge of arrogance, as if she's done Chasity some kind of favor. I try not to smile at that. If I encourage her, I'll pay for it later.

"You think you can find your way back to the suite without causing any more trouble? I need to speak to your handler." When Taylor's only response was shoveling a handful of popcorn in her mouth, Chasity loses her patience. "Alone!"

Taylor blows out an exasperated breath before pushing herself up from the couch. Her pace slows at the exact moment she passes by Erica, our new recruit. With everything that's happened, I forgot I was giving Erica a tour of the hotel.

I'd met Erica by chance. I was partaking in a personal exercise of reclaiming formerly beloved activities of mine when I visited the tournament. It was the first night of the new script change and the debut of the new Dragon Knight. I was so enamored with her skill that I'd begged Chasity to hire her. I didn't know what for but I knew at some point she would become a great asset to the team.

Taylor looks at Erica and then looks at Chasity with one eyebrow raised. "Alone?"

For a second time, I conceal my smile. It has been a long time since I have seen the jealous side of Taylor. It was at the beginning for us, when everything was new and forbidden. She'd tried to hide it then, but was being pretty blatant about it now. It's hard to know if she wants me or if she wants me to be miserable. Shay would say Erica is my type. And not because she's smart and driven. Shay takes the teasing part of her best friend job description seriously.

"I'll see you in the morning." Erica nods politely before wishing Shay and Chasity goodnight, which produces a frown on Taylor's face. Taylor doesn't say goodnight before pushing the door closed behind her.

"You've lost your touch. Your punishments don't seem to work if your girlfriend is causing havoc in my hotel again."

I know she uses the word girlfriend on purpose, and I let it slide. "This is Vanessa we're talking about here. You know she wanted her for more than just disciplinary action." What Vanessa said had been true. We, as the managers of our respective departments, report rule violations from members and other staff, but most of us report directly to a specific department instead of imposing the discipline ourselves. Vanessa, however, likes to inflict her own punishments.

"Yeah, I agree." Shay wipes her fingers on a nearby napkin, setting the now empty popcorn bowl aside. "She probably attacked Taylor first, not expecting an untrained baby dragon to come after her."

Chasity sighs before kicking off her fluffy slippers. "I need you more than I need Taylor, especially since I now have Erica. I need you focused, Gabby. Take care of her. Make sure she doesn't mess anything else up for the next two days." I promise I will, ignoring Shay's offer of assistance by booking a room for me to use in her office. I don't need Shay's help with this one.

My eyes settle on my best friend. I know she intentionally had her eyes on me instead of on Vanessa to send a message. I appreciate that and I know she'll understand the reason behind my words. "I never want to hear you raise your voice at her again." I leave before Chasity has the chance to respond. There's no need for me to stay. She knows how serious I am. And as far as Taylor goes, I know exactly what to do.

Chapter Twenty-Three
Taylor

I SHUFFLE AWAY FROM the door as fast as I can without making too much noise. After leaving the room, I'd left it open just enough to leave space for me to listen in. Holding the door with enough strength to keep it open while also creating the illusion that someone securely shut it had been difficult.

My action hasn't escaped the new recruit, who stops and stares at me before disappearing down the hall. Screw her. This is none of her business, anyway.

I'm fuming at the words sputtered by Chasity. Gabriella doesn't own me. Not anymore. She is not my *handler* and I don't need her to teach me how to behave in public. That woman attacked *me*. But if they want to pay a visit to the past, to help make Gabriella feel better about training me properly, I can help with that.

I find my way back to Paradise Row by asking staff members to point me in the right direction. If I'm going to be cooperative, then I can't be too late getting back to the suite. I enter the doors of The Kitchen quickly, planning to do a quick scan for the sisters before I'm caught by Vanessa or one of her assistants. Chasity hadn't bothered saying their names during the meeting. They must not be worth learning.

When I don't see any of the sisters at any of the occupied booths, I make my way upstairs. In true old Western saloon style, I have no cover here. There are no markings on the outside of the doors to show who might be in them. I'm going to have to do this guerilla style.

I open each door and peek in quickly before moving on to the next. Each view adds heat to my simmering fire. I pause for seconds too long when my eyes land on a group of four women, two of whom have tails as long as a horse's mane attached to them. One of them notices me watching, and instead of alerting the others, she speeds up her aggression, pulling the strap-on she's wearing in and out at a rate that sends her tail wildly swishing around. I offer a silent apology before I close the door, the image of her replaced by someone else.

When I find the three sisters together, they are no longer in their fancy gowns. And they now have one addition. My replacement is a brunette with pale skin. The type of pale that burns in the sun instead of tans. None of them are fully undressed. I'm right on time.

The foursome is more than willing to come back to the suite with me. The girl in the pale pink dress, whose name I finally learn is Aimi, gives me a small tap on my butt, admonishing me from running away from Vanessa. She promises being with Vanessa would've been one of the best experiences. I don't disagree. I smile and giggle, playing the innocent role. I learn Nisha's name when Aimi grabs her hand to follow me out of the room. Zoe, my replacement, pauses while Nisha quickly finishes zipping up her dress and then everyone heads out the door.

I expect to see Gabriella in the suite when we arrive and am disappointed when we're greeted by silent darkness. I alter my plan. Originally, I'd intended to not so subtly inform Gabriella of my proposal for a foursome — now fivesome—in my bedroom across the hall from her. I'd imagined her angry, yelling at me even. My mind went blank after that, but I have full confidence in my improvisation skills.

I tell the girls my idea of having a slumber party in the living room. Gabriella will have no way to escape us. They agree, oblivious to my revenge plot.

I run around the suite, looking for appropriate snacks for a slumber party. I throw the bag of popcorn I find in the cabinet into the microwave, but don't come across anything else. I try the door to Gabriella's bedroom and it opens with a click. I rush in searching for the drawer of snacks that should exist. Knowing she keeps them far away, I search the closet first, starting with the shoeboxes on top. Disappointment fills me when I realize they're all organized as described. I move to her closet drawers, only to find they are just as organized, separated by colors and styles. I search the nightstand to the left of the bed first. Gabriella sleeps on the right side of the bed, the closest to the door. The bottom drawer gives me nothing. The top is filled with stationery and performance drawings.

I scramble over to the right side. I don't manage to stop the anger that surges through me at the sight of multiple packs of condoms surrounded by silk drawstring pouches. Ignoring the condoms, I open each pouch to reveal hidden sex toys. I replace them as quickly as I uncover them. The drawer shuts louder than I intend, the images of the condoms dancing around in my brain. I can explain away the sex toys. The condoms, I can't.

I find the bags of chocolate candy and packs of licorice with less excitement than when I started.

Back in the living room, I empty the popcorn into a bowl and the bags of candy into two other bowls I am able to find in the kitchen.

I hear the door to the suite click open just as I sit the bowls atop the coffee table. Realizing I'm still fully dressed, I quickly unzip my jeans, grip the waistband on them in my fists, and pause. I act coy when Gabriella's eyes land on mine.

"Oh my God."

It's not me who says it. I look down to see Destiny's hands covering her mouth in shock, her eyes open as if she has just run into her favorite movie star. I look around to see the same shocked faces on the other girls. Trice's voice rolls through my brain. *You know how many people would love to find a way in here?* Shit.

The bag Gabriella is holding comes into view when she steps forward, pushing the door closed with her shoe. I recognize it from Indulgence. The idea of me spoiling her evening plans gives me some hope of success tonight.

"What's going on here?" The look she gives the group is open and curious, but also strained. It reminds me of the reaction of a parent when they find their child in the middle of wrongdoing. It's me. I'm the child.

Aimi is the first to speak. "Taylor invited us all over for a slumber party." She gets up and hugs me as if we're old friends, pressing her naked breasts against my t-shirt.

"Did she now?"

Everyone except me nods. The girls sit in place, waiting for further instructions. I stop holding onto the jeans and sit on the floor to discard them. Gabriella watches me slowly free each leg. I toss them at her feet before pulling my shirt over my head. The girls gather around me to join. I stare into Nisha's eyes, feeling the snap of my bra loosen from around me.

"Wait." Gabriella's eyes land on each woman in the room. Fingertips freeze onto my skin. I hold my breath. "Maybe you would all like to do this on stage." She offers a wide smile that's accepted by the whispered yeses throughout the group. "Great. Let me grab a few things and we'll head out." The click of her bedroom door breaks the silence.

Aimi sandwiches my face in the palm of her hands and says, "You didn't tell us you were with *the* Drama Queen."

The girls take turns squealing in silence, their facial expressions displaying pure excitement, with wide eyes and mouths gaping open. Zoe runs her fingers through her hair. Destiny plants her body in a different position, as if she's posing for a magazine cover and not having sex on carpeted flooring. Aimi flings herself towards her dress, producing lip gloss from a discreet pocket.

Nisha looks at me, stuck, "Do you know how many roles she's casting for?"

I shake my head slowly, thrown off by this latest development.

Nisha pulls Zoe onto the couch, spreading Zoe's legs apart before intertwining them with hers. She grinds against Zoe, moaning out with each point of contact. "How did that sound? Do you think it should be more like this?" she asks. She rubs herself against Zoe again, her moans at a higher pitch. "Did that one sound better?"

My nod is more subdued than Aimi's, who nods along vigorously. They take turns practicing, switching partners quickly, unsure of when Gabriella will return.

"Alright. All ready." Gabriella doesn't comment on the girls' actions. They spring up at the sound of her voice, gathering their dresses before heading out the door. I take longer to redress, wondering if I should skip this performance. I follow along anyway, trailing behind the group.

The women crowd around Gabriella at the base of the stage, glued to her every instruction. They nod in sync at her words before throwing their dresses to the ground and moving to take their places on set. The set is the same as the one I saw a few days earlier: one enormous bed. My eyes move from the stage to Gabriella and I immediately know she's not happy with me. My clothes come off slowly. I imagine her anger growing with each second I take to become completely nude. Finally done, I move towards the steps.

"Not you, Mrs. Friendly." The *Mrs.* comes out forced and long and I know she's emphasizing her possession of me. I yank my arm back when she grabs it, but it's not enough to keep her from dragging me up the stairs to the production room.

She bends me over the production booth, facing the glass window that looks out onto the stage. She stands behind me, her voice echoes across the room. "In position now, ladies." Destiny and Zoe both sit with their backs against the headboard. Nisha crawls into the space Destiny creates, her thighs open. Aimi occupies Zoe's space. Their backs lean up against Destiny's and Zoe's breasts. As Destiny runs her hands against Nisha's thighs, mine are pushed forward, stretching me further across the control panel, Gabriella's jeans pushed up against my bare ass. For the second time tonight, we find ourselves in this position.

"What part of stop causing drama don't you understand?"

There's no need for me to respond. Whatever is going to happen will happen, anyway. I've always been the one pleading and apologizing. Things have changed.

In my silence, she continues. "Did you think you could go off and play with Mama Mae's girls in Mama Mae's cabin?"

I offer a slight shrug. Enjoying the tickle on my skin created from her breath. Thoughts of Mama Mae have long been replaced by Gabriella. I'm *her* captive now.

"What do you think I would've done to Mama Mae if you had succeeded? Hmm?"

I want to yell out that this isn't about Mama Mae anymore and never really was. *Fuck, Mama Mae.*

"What do you want them to do?"

I don't understand the question. The girls below me continue to caress one another. Aimi's head rests on Zoe's shoulders, one arm thrown back to grip the headrest while Zoe bends her neck to fill her mouth with Aimi's breasts. Aimi's vagina is in full view. She's willing and ready for Zoe to do something more.

I think I understand what Gabriella is asking me. If this is at all like the show I watched before, I have options. "Zoe should touch Aimi more. She should put her hand down lower."

Gabriella says my command into the headset she picked up as soon as we entered the room. I watch Zoe move her hand down Aimi's stomach, and across her hips, weaving her fingers through Aimi's hair until reaching the spot that makes Aimi groan and shift her head from side to side. Zoe rotates her wrist, maintaining her hold on Aimi's breasts.

The sense of power I feel watching Zoe obey my command comes as a surprise, but not without consequence. I squirm, not being able to help the heat that rises within me.

"What else?"

I can't help but think Gabriella has something to do with Destiny and Nisha not progressing any further. I think for a second.

"Nisha should turn around to taste Destiny." The words are painful when they come out because I know I won't be receiving any of the pleasure Destiny is about to receive. Gabriella relays the message. Nisha turns almost at the same time that Destiny pushes her hips forward in preparation.

"She should grab her hair." Seconds later, Destiny does, gripping Nisha's dark strands with both hands, her hips grinding against the strokes of Nisha's tongue.

If Gabriella had allowed me to keep on my panties, they would be wet. I shift my weight from one leg to the other to create much needed friction. I hope she doesn't notice.

Nisha alternates rubbing Aimi fast and slow, trying her best to not allow her to cum too soon.

"Nisha should put in one finger. Just one. Aimi might be too close for anything more than that." Nisha does it, pulling her hand back to slide her index finger between Aimi's folds. Aimi's legs open wider. I know what she means. "Another one." The second finger slides in with ease. Nisha lifts one of Aimi's legs to further accommodate. I look at Gabriella, wondering if she's going to admonish Nisha for doing something she wasn't told to do. She says nothing.

I'm still bent over the control panel with Gabriella standing next to me. I rise to ease the ache building in my lower back.

"Don't you fucking dare."

I pause. I find a place between the dozens of buttons and switches where I can rest my forearms.

"This is exactly what you fucking wanted, isn't it? To be bent over and waiting for one of them to fuck you? For Mama Mae to fuck you?"

She's so angry I don't dare speak to defend myself. I orchestrated this entire thing, and it blew up in my face. The reason is now lost. The theater, with the collective moans of both women, does nothing to dampen my growing flame.

"More." Gabriella doesn't seem to feel anything. She hasn't

shifted or panted. She stands completely stable, like stone.

"Aimi should lick Zoe's fingers clean." She does. Aimi traces her tongue around the tips of Zoe's fingers, sliding each one between her lips and back again. "And then she should touch her, too."

Gabriella doesn't deliver my message. "Touch her how?"

I'm distracted by Destiny writhing in pleasure, Nisha's tongue flicking wildly at her clit. Shit. I exhale the deep breath caught in my lungs, my body quakes on its way out.

I hear Gabriella huff before my vision goes dark with the blindfold she uses to shield the group from my view. I'm almost relieved, except the pool between my thighs continues to grow.

"How?" Gabriella demands.

I recall the last position Zoe and Aimi were in. I change course. "Never mind. She should ride Zoe. Pull her down. Push one leg back and keep the other folded to the side." It's my favorite. One of them anyway. I loved looking up at Gabriella from that angle, her pussy rubbing against mine, her eyes closed, breasts shaking. Fuck!

There is a pause from the time I finish speaking to when Gabriella gives the order. Zoe's panting fills me in on what I can't see. She can barely catch her breath, gasping and moaning and begging.

"Can I see?" I ask as nicely as I can and hope I'm successful.

"You're asking me if you can watch a group of women have sex?"

I pout, turning my head to the side where Gabriella's voice comes from. "You're watching them."

"And I wouldn't have to, if it weren't for you." *Damn. She's right.*

"Will you touch me?" I quickly add, "It's not about them. I know you're not going to let me touch myself."

"I touched you earlier and it ended up costing me, so no. Take your consequences like a big girl."

There is nothing left to say. On a hunch, I rub the left side of my face against my forearm, pretending to have a scratch. Gabriella doesn't react. The left side of the blindfold slowly rises, enough for me to peek through a small slit. I'm too afraid to do more than that.

Nisha's face remains placed between Destiny's thighs. Her licks are slow and deliberate, her hair still captured by Destiny's balled fists. "Nisha should sit on Destiny's face now." Gabriella sends out the command. I put my head down, hoping she doesn't notice the position of the blindfold has changed.

Nisha straddles Destiny, her ass pointed to the headboard. It's not what I initially had in mind, but it'll do. From Destiny's neck and head movements and Nisha's heavy eyelids, it's working as intended.

Zoe's orgasm sends her into a stutter, gripping onto Aimi's leg. Aimi slows her pace and Zoe stills, releasing her hold on Aimi, her body limp in exhaustion. I almost tell Gabriella to send Aimi over to Destiny and Nisha, sealing my fate as a cheat and ending up in more trouble.

"Was that Zoe?"

Gabriella grunts in the affirmative.

"It sounds like she's done. Can Aimi join the other girls? Tell her to do the same to Destiny."

Gabriella sends the command, but she alters it to not disturb Destiny's position with Nisha.

Aimi pulls back both of Destiny's legs, using her body weight to keep her in place before grinding against her. Their moans join Nisha's, who reaches down for a kiss with Aimi, who happily obliges. They stay this way, rubbing and sucking and kissing each other until they all climax. Nisha goes first, yelling out a slew of expletives through shaky breaths. Destiny's moans are muffled, but her hands claw at Nisha's thighs and ass the harder Aimi rides her. Aimi collapses to the side of the bed, near Zoe's feet, out of breath. And I stay waiting.

"You have 15 minutes to get back to the room. Tell your friends goodbye. You shouldn't be seeing them again."

The door is left open after Gabriella departs. She doesn't stop to talk to the group. The bed that was so neatly made when we first entered is now a mess.

I allow my body to slide from the control panel down to the floor. My lower back really does ache. I gather enough strength to push myself up. My eyes land on the room I had entered earlier with Trice. I hadn't cared enough to look around Gabriella's office before. It looks no different from any other. Stacks of paper are neatly organized in a corner of the desk with different colored file folders sitting in the middle. An iPad sits off to the side.

A press of a button on the keyboard of her laptop reveals a photo I've never seen before. I spot her little face immediately. She looks the same, but with a much brighter smile and fuller cheeks. The screen changes and another photo takes its place. They're almost identical, but in this one, young Gabriella is looking up instead of straight at the camera. As the photos alternate, I follow her gaze. The group of kids are at a theater. What I assume is her class stands at the base of the stage, with another row of people of different ages standing behind them. I recognize each face until I land on mine.

"Oh my God," I can only whisper to myself. Because seven-year-old Gabriella was looking up at seven-year-old me with stars in her eyes. *"Maybe I've loved you before you ever knew my name."* She's said those words to me in many variations throughout our time together. I never realized she said them in truth.

It all comes seeping out of me. Every message I wrote and then deleted. Every whisper I said in my sleep. Every time I placed her name on a leaf and begged it to float down a river I couldn't convince my mind to move. As badly as I wanted to, I couldn't convince myself to forget her.

She's loved me almost her entire life, and I never knew. I crafted a beginning of us in my mind that I thought fit my fantasy better than the real one. This is our actual story. I wonder how Gabriella would phrase it. *We locked eyes while she sang to the tune of Silent Night in a Christmas play*. It was the only one I had ever been in. I've complained about it since. If only I had known the love of my life was staring at me in the audience.

Tears spill from my eyes and fall my cheeks in waves. When I think I'm done, they follow again. I cry for every lie and scheme, but with a different meaning than I ever did before. She was trying to make her way back to me. Maybe she went about it wrong, but you don't look at someone how Gabriella has always looked at me and want to hurt them.

We traveled down different paths after that night all those years ago, only to miraculously end up in the same place. Something tells me I should be more angry and more unforgiving, but I can't.

I make my way out of her office and down the steps to the theater. The tops of my thighs are sticky and warm, but that's the furthest thing from my mind. My bruised ego has replaced my quest for sexual independence.

The ladies roll out of bed as I pass. They walk slowly, gathering their clothes as they go. Zoe reminds me of a 70s stoner, her mind in the clouds, her body swaying from side to side. Aimi's walk is similar, her dress dragging on the floor from behind. "Oh my God." Her voice sounds dreamlike and hypnotic. "That was so much fun."

Chapter Twenty-Four
Gabriella

I KNOW I SAY this all the time, but things were supposed to be different. I had every intention of punishing Taylor last night as promised, but in private; tied to my bed with nowhere to run and no one to care enough to hear her scream, even if that's what she wanted.

But of course, Taylor had to be true to herself and find a way to earn more red marks on that perfectly tight ass of hers. I could have told the girls to leave, but letting them stay and knowing she wouldn't be able to touch them, made it worth it.

It's 7 a.m. on a breezy Las Vegas morning and Taylor insists on wearing sunglasses. I doubt she packed a pair of sunglasses when traveling to Las Vegas in the winter. She didn't even need them out in L.A. She leans back in a chair, her feet propped up on a padded stool. She's playing her role of the quintessential snotty Hollywood actress well. And it's not even her time to rehearse.

We haven't spoken since last night. I heard the door to the suite close 2 minutes before her deadline. Since no one has approached me about her destroying hotel property, I think she's learned her lesson.

After instructing the crew on the next step of the set-up, I take the empty lounge next to her. Outside performances here are rare. An additional amenity service Chasity wants to develop. We staged the set to resemble an outdoor bakery. The garden will eventually hold dozens of naked bodies, concealed by a large vine-covered pergola. We must maintain the feeling of being outdoors while protecting member privacy. And providing shade to the garden during the hot Nevada summers is a plus. When it's done, it's going to be even more beautiful than I imagined. She'll love it.

Danni arrives with the baked goods meant for the scene. They're not completely necessary for the rehearsal, but they'll feed the crew afterward. "For you." The tray of cookies they sit in my lap is warm. Danni has been sending me a tray of cookies a week since they started working here eight months ago. I like Danni. Everyone does. They never say a bad thing about anyone. They believe wholeheartedly in the best of everyone.

"Tell me what you think afterward. You forgot the last time. You give the best feedback when you have a fresh memory."

I smile fully, not feeling the need to shield my gratitude from them. "Promise." I pick up the macadamia nut cookie to show how serious I am.

"Trying to make me jealous isn't going to work." I hear Taylor's voice just as I watch Danni enter the elevator.

"I didn't know you could get jealous of cookies." I take a small bite, edging a macadamia nut with my teeth. Taylor laughs.

"I can't be jealous of someone who doesn't even know what your favorite cookie is." She turns to snatch the macadamia nut cookie out of my hand. "You hate macadamia nut." With every word, she breaks the cookie into pieces before crumbling them onto the ground. She plucks a chocolate chip from the tray before taking a bite. "And although chocolate chips are your favorite, you only like them when they're soft with a bit of crunch, moist enough to be almost undercooked, but gooey enough to be delicious. If you haven't bothered to tell her to take the cookies out of the oven before she thinks they're ready and allow them to brown on their own—it's because you don't want her to know."

"Them." I correct without commenting on her assessment.

"What?"

"They're non-binary." She huffs and I smile in glee at causing her annoyance for once... or twice.

She tosses the chocolate chip cookie to the side before holding the red velvet cookie to my face. "And we might hate each other now, but you would never break Daddy's heart by eating someone else's red velvet cookies."

Her dad makes red velvet cookies once a year at Christmas. They created the tradition when Taylor was young and wanted to leave cookies for Santa that he would never forget.

She drops it back onto the tray before standing. "That would be like me telling your mom your Tia's mole is better than hers."

Her eyes narrow at me before being replaced once again by her sunglasses. "What's Chasity's plan here? I didn't realize the rooftop was so massive. I've never gone beyond the greenhouses."

"Outdoor living for exhibitionists." *For you.* "Think nudist spa. It's going to be pretty restrictive. Voyeurs will only be allowed at the greenhouses." People should be able to be naked at BED without the expectation of sex or a performance.

Taylor's eyes roam over the remaining construction. "That'd be cool."

I smile. "Are we going to talk about last night?"

"What is there to talk about? You did your job, right? Kept me in line."

If I wasn't paying attention to her face, I would've missed the way her cheeks raised and her lips puckered to smooth out her expression.

"We should probably talk about it if you're going to be going through my closet."

She turns away from me. Her shoulders jump up and down in my black hoodie, with CREW sprawled across the back. She couldn't have been more obvious. I don't mind her in my closet. Or in my bedroom. I miss her wearing my clothes. And I miss tearing them off of her.

She composes herself to face me again. "I don't remember reading any rules about not going into your bedroom."

I shake my head. "Come here." She walks slowly to me, delaying her punishment.

"Your girlfriend is watching you."

I don't try to hide my happiness at her words. I smile fully, brushing my lips lightly against hers. "I know."

This rehearsal is just a test, a mockup to see what works in the space and what doesn't. As badly as I want to undress her, I don't. Her SoCal blood would freeze in this weather. Stripping her would only be for my pleasure and not for the sake of the production.

The garden is supposed to have a softer touch to it than the hotel. The show we're testing today is sensual and subtle. Just two women enjoying their time together. The show will probably evolve into offering more sexual acts, but not today. Besides, I like Erica too much to kill her.

Taylor is here to take on the role of the baker. She discards my hoodie to replace it with a long-sleeved pink top with embroidered strawberries. It's cute and looks like something a wholesome baker would wear. The thought of tearing that sweater off of her and tasting her, picking her up, sitting her on the counter, and spreading her thighs fills my mind. I could have Erica do it, but then—well, you know.

We pair the strawberry sweater with an apron. Chasity and I disagreed on this one. The employee aprons are custom made by a sweet little old lady in Nevada. They're cute and give a false appearance of innocence. Everyone loves them, but I didn't want the same look for the show.

I won in the end. When the show launches, the baker will wear a solid black French maid apron with a red and black double skirt and lace underwear.

"Alright, everyone. Quiet on set!" The story of the baker and her wife is supposed to be butterflies and red roses. There are supposed to be small kisses and intimate touches with cute laughter and inside jokes. Their whispers are supposed to make everyone jealous of missing out on their world.

Taylor and Erica do it beautifully. And I am so proud. Erica is not a professional actress in the traditional sense of the word. Sure, the work they do on the show is technically acting, but Taylor has been working since she was in diapers. She graciously works Erica into the scene, walking her through her lines seamlessly.

I wrap the rehearsal late in the morning, knowing members will be antsy if they can't access the rooftop for too long. Besides, I have other things I need to do. I send Erica off to her classes before turning my attention back to Taylor.

"I'm sorry."

Her apology is a shock to me, though it shouldn't be. She's always been good with that. Throughout our entire relationship, she's taken accountability even when she shouldn't have.

"I know my actions hurt you last night—and while that doesn't excuse how you reacted, I take full responsibility for my actions."

I can tell by the way she has her hands folded in front of her and tilts back onto the heels of her sneakers that she's pleased with herself.

"How did I react?" I did what was necessary at the moment. From the time she woke up, she was hell bent on embarrassing me.

"You don't think dragging me up a flight of stairs naked isn't an overreaction?"

"I think you took your clothes off because you like it when I drag you around naked."

She steps forward, her arms crossed over her chest. "And making me act like a cat?"

"Did I, though? Or are you just fantastic at following my instructions?"

"It would make sense. My obedience is the perfect testament to your relationship with Sara. Did you ever figure it out?"

"Figure what out?"

"If you used her to get to me."

We've managed to go this long without talking about Sara. It's been years. Her memory has tainted enough. Taylor is determined to make it not real. She wants me so badly to convince her that what we had was a fabrication. But we're not a fantasy for her to unlock when she's ready.

We are real.

"Taylor." I cradle her face in the palm of my hands, the tips of my fingers caressing the nape of her neck. "I love you." The three words quake out of me and overflow like an exploding volcano. Her head whips back in shock, almost sliding from my grip. I hold on. "I love you. I love you. I love you. I loved you for eleven years before I ever knew I wanted to be in your life."

She places her hand over my own. Her brown eyes stare straight into mine.

I keep going. "The two years we spent together were the best years of my life. Choosing you was the first choice I've ever made for myself. By choosing you, I finally chose me."

Whatever thoughts she forms from my words, she blinks away.

"I'll remember you for that, always. I'll love you for that, forever.

There is nothing you can say to me to make any of that go away." I allow my hands to slip away from her smooth skin as she steps out of my reach. My heart feels heavier than it did this morning.

This must be what goodbye feels like. When it happened the first time, I never allowed myself to feel it. There was always a plan to get back to her, eventually. Sometimes I got antsy and had to quell the urge to run and find her before anyone else claimed her heart.

It happened a lot whenever she made a rare appearance with anyone people weren't used to seeing her next to. Dating rumors always followed, especially if it was a woman. People wanted so desperately to know that side of her. They complained about how private she was. Even when we broke up, no one knew how or why. Except Nicole and maybe Eryn. I'm sure she told her manager, Zara, something to explain my absence. Everyone who warned her against dating me in the first place.

I rekindled my relationship with Chasity not because I was ready to forgive her, but because I needed a place for Taylor to go and be herself without worrying about there being too many eyes on her. It may all be for nothing if she decides she can't forgive me. I'll be okay with that, I think, knowing that I did everything in my control to help her heal without destroying herself in the process. I'm partially to blame for that, I know, but one thing I have learned about Taylor is that, while she has learned how to smile in the spotlight, she does an even better job at preserving her happiness even when the applause goes away.

Chapter Twenty-Five
Taylor

Leanna wasn't lying about how nice her room is. Keeping to Chasity's theme, Leanna's Lover room is adorned in a variety of purples. A deep eggplant purple colors the walls. Her white bed is decorated in lavenders, lilacs and magentas. A bucket of plum-colored rose petals sits on the table next to her door.

It took me a while to remember where Leanna's room was located. In the end, I had to guess. I knocked on three different doors before she answered, dressed in a BED-sponsored silk robe, an eye mask sitting on top of her messy hair.

I started crying again before I could apologize for waking her. Leanna ushered me into a hot bubble bath. I stopped a few minutes ago, instead concentrating deeply on blowing bubbles out of the palms of my hands.

Lovers' bathtubs aren't separate from the bedrooms, though I can tell the toilet and the sink are somewhere more private. Leanna's jacuzzi tub is right next to her hotel window, which would usually be a good thing for me. Except today, when my mind swirls with confusing thoughts about Gabriella. Last night I decided I was angry at her, then felt guilty for hurting her by inviting Mama Mae's girls back to our suite. And today, I loved performing for her in a different way. I forgot about that. Forgot about that part of us.

I believed her when she told me she loved me, like I believed her the first time. It was right for me to apologize for what happened last night. I was wrong, and I hurt her. The problem is, her love was never enough for her to decide to not destroy me. She never stopped to ask herself how badly her lies would hurt.

Leanna hasn't asked me any questions since I arrived. After stripping me of my clothing and placing me in the tub, she sat on the floor next to me, which is where she still sits now. A knock on the door sounds. I stiffen. Leanna notices and reassures me before getting up.

"I ordered lunch."

The breath once caught in my lungs flows through me, relieved. In my distress, I hadn't noticed her making a call.

The lunch is a pastrami sandwich with mustard and pickles. No cheese. Cheese on pastrami should be a crime worthy of a punishing stay at Hotel BED. Leanna must've asked me my order, though the memory of her ever doing so is not one I can conjure up. She sits a plate of chocolate-covered strawberries on the end table next to me. I eye them suspiciously. Some are covered in peanut brittle, which would be amazing if they didn't remind me of the former love of my life. Or the present, whichever, hell, I don't know anymore.

I pay the same amount of scrutiny to the pastrami sandwich I hold in my hand. "Where did you get this from?"

Leanna shrugs. "At one of the restaurants, I guess. It was on the menu."

I nod. Her answer puts me at ease.

"Do you want to talk about what happened?"

I shake my head, placing the half-eaten sandwich back onto its plate before standing. I accept the towel she hands me and use it to dry my feet before stepping out of the tub. I put on a pair of cotton shorts and a T-shirt Leanna has laid out for me. She moves from the floor to the bed, tapping the space next to her with her fingers. I accept the offer, snuggling underneath the plush comforter, missing the heat from the bathtub.

"She made you cry again."

I don't speak. She won't understand it if I try to explain.

"I saw the show."

I look up at her.

"It was sweet. You really are a talented actress."

I refrain from saying "duh" aloud. I have been acting since I was an infant. Switching into acting mode is easy for me. I've done it my entire life.

"You didn't enjoy it?" she asks.

"I don't know." I think about it. Acting is work like any other job, but I do like doing it. Although it was a possibility at some point in our careers, Gabriella and I have never worked together on set before. Not like that. But the situation also caused some confusion. I got to work with Erica, whom I hated less than twenty-four hours before. She's green with the dramatics, but otherwise pleasant. And then there was Danni, who has a thing for Gabriella. I couldn't tell how Gabriella felt about them, though, which was frustrating.

I don't explain this to Leanna. Instead, I tell her the other truth. "I don't think I know who I am." She looks shocked at first and then confusion settles onto her face.

She opens her mouth to speak and then closes it again.

"I mean sexually. Gabriella is practically my entire sexual history. How do I know that what I like is because of me or because of her?"

Leanna nods slowly in understanding. My tense muscles loosen at her reaction.

She scrambles to the other side of the bed, retrieving a notebook and pen from the end table's top drawer. "We should make a list." She draws two straight lines, forming three columns. On the top of the right column, she writes *do's*. In the middle, she writes *maybes*. And on the left, she writes *don'ts*. "Ok. Let's start with the basics. Men. Do you like men?"

I nodded. I'm pretty sure I like men. Leanna writes *men* under the *do* column.

"Kissing?" She flutters her eyelashes at me.

"Yes."

"Now we're getting to the good stuff." She presses the tip of the pen to her chin. "Oral sex?"

"Absolutely." The thought of my tongue sliding between a set of beautifully moist lips sends renewed energy up my spine. I love oral sex.

"Anal sex." She hovers the pen over the *dont's* column. I nudge her playfully before confirming the placement. She laughs. "I don't blame you. I've given it, but I'm not too crazy about receiving it myself." I appreciate Leanna letting me out of the hot seat to disclose her personal information. I give her shoulder a tight squeeze in gratitude.

"Ok. Vaginal penetration?" She's writing the word down under the *do's* column before I even have a chance to speak.

"That obvious, huh?"

"Ok. Third base?" She arches a brow before shrugging the thought away. "How do you feel about threesomes?"

"Confused," I answer honestly. In my mind, threesomes are hot, but that's also what's confusing. Anything hot in my mind has been hot in reality—with Gabriella's presence. I've never had a fantasy that she didn't infiltrate.

I tell this to Leanna, who doesn't balk at my explanation.

"So you have to choose one on your own. You should pick different couples. How else would you know if you prefer to be joined by men or women? Just because you like men doesn't mean you want to be with one in that way."

She makes a good point. I remember Trice's earlier instructions and pull up my phone to the BED app. I scroll through the ads for private parties and spot one that looks promising.

Women Loving Women couple seeking a new third. Minimal experience required. Stop by for a chat at Decadent this afternoon.

I show the ad to Leanna. She's adamant I don't qualify as having minimal experience, but also doesn't think it's something that can't be faked ("You're an actress, duh!") I don't know if I want to be a piece of a throuple. And I have no clue if they will even accept me as a temporary member of the hotel. I'm going to try. It's the whole reason I agreed to come to this hotel in the first place.

We scroll through the remaining ads for more potential connections. We reach out to two others; a Rose Gold couple and a Platinum Lover couple. Leanna thinks all three options would serve as excellent opportunities for me and if given the offer, I should take them.

I'll only be at BED for another day and a half. If I'm going to make this happen, it has to be quick. I've never had so much sex with so many sexual partners in such a short amount of time.

"First time for everything, right?" Leanna appears happy with our accomplishments, which reminds me I need to loosen up. This is a good thing. This is what I wanted. What I originally planned for. I really need to get my shit together.

There is less of a crowd in Decadent than there had been for dinner before, which now seems so long ago. Worry sets in about being able to find the couple from the ad. They didn't add any names or other identifying information to make it easy to locate them. After looking around for a moment, I ask the hostess if anyone is holding any meetings inside of the restaurant. She smiles, nods, and then beckons me to follow behind her. And I do.

I spot the women immediately after rounding the corner. They sit in a section of Decadent I haven't noticed before. This section is darker, and more discreet, with booths spread out away from each other to give a sense of privacy.

They whisper as I approach. I can tell they are both older than me, but not by too much. Perhaps in their mid-to-late-thirties. When the hostess stops at the table to introduce me as their guest, they both smile and gesture for me to have a seat.

I thank them both and throw a smile I hope displays innocence and vixen all in one.

"Ok. I just have to say, we're both big fans."

My smile freezes.

Their smiles grow wide.

"Oh my God, thank you!" I say with some relief. On the one hand, I hate the idea of being recognized in a place like this. All week, I could randomly hear Zara's warnings looping through my brain, but not once have I noticed anyone taking any photos or videos of me and if one had surfaced, I'd know by now.

"Huge Fans." The woman with the short, light brown curly hair leans forward. She has a mole underneath her left eye that I find adorable. For a second, it reminds me of Gabriella's freckles. A pinch of my wrist, my own doing, reminds me to stop thinking about Gabriella.

"We watched both of your greenhouse performances and this morning's show was just wild. It was so much fun. When you came on the screen, I just screamed." She threw her hands up as her partner nodded in confirmation. "And now you're sitting right in front of us." She gives her partner a look I can't comprehend.

I express my gratitude, giving the best expression my media training offers. I'm honest because there's nothing I can lie about. I'm really twenty-five years old and yes, I live in Los Angeles. When they ask about my Gold membership status, since it is not usually held by a single member, I am honest about that as well.

I tell them I'm an old friend of Chasity's, here to celebrate her birthday, and as a welcome present she gifted us all temporary Gold memberships. A mixture of emotions crosses over their faces. First, they look impressed.

"Well, since you're friends, that means you'll probably be back to visit at some point. We're not here every weekend, but if we can connect before, I'm sure we can plan to be here all at the same time."

I nod in agreement, although a long commitment isn't currently in my plans.

They don't ask about my sexual experience at all, too blinded by my time in the greenhouse, I suppose, though they never saw me have sex with anyone, but myself. They invite me to their room for breakfast tomorrow morning, and I try not to appear too excited. Besides, I'm an experienced member with a reputation to uphold.

The other two meetings go just as smoothly. The Platinum couple saw neither of my greenhouse shows, but they'd heard whispers of the "new curly haired member" and caught Gabriella's production on TV this morning. They loved it. They spent a considerable amount of time recapping it on my behalf, as if I hadn't lived it a few hours earlier. "It was so cute I looked right at her and said 'Babe, we've got to find her' and then we got your message and couldn't believe it." The conversation about me ping pongs between them, with no room for me to speak. In the end, we agree to meet at one of the outdoor pool areas for our "date" tomorrow afternoon.

I'm joining the Rose Gold couple tomorrow evening. I'll have to check out of Chasity's birthday dinner early to make my date with them. Before I'd left our initial meeting, the Rose Gold couple offered me a suggestion. "You should talk to the Drama Queen about putting you on stage. She's always looking for outstanding talent."

The BED equivalent of a stakeout is sitting outside a cafe in Lipstick Alley, a section of the hotel Leanna told me about. At first glance, Lipstick Alley seems to be plucked out of some sapphic rom-com. Women of all varieties roam the cobblestone-covered hallways here. We sit in front of a pink cafe, clinking heart-shaped tea cups together. The Alley is freaking adorable. Definitely not Chasity's idea at all.

Watching other women love each other becomes depressing. I've spent the last few years in mixed company, trying to escape the reminder of the good times. I'm supposed to be listening to Leanna explain which couples she thinks I should approach for more opportunities. How she knows which ones are open to adding to their bedroom, I do not know. I nod as if I'm listening intently while sipping my hot spiced green tea.

Britney walks by with a group of fluffy-tailed kittens—the ones with two legs instead of four. She waves goodbye to them when she notices us at the cafe.

"Where's your tail?"

She waves off my teasing to grab a seat from a nearby table. "What are you ladies up to?"

"Scouting for women Taylor can have a threesome with," Leanna says without taking her eyes off the walkway, still scrutinizing every couple that passes by.

Britney is taken aback by her answer, which surprises me. "And what about us?" She motions a finger between her and Leanna.

Leanna answers before I can think of a response. "We're too close to Gabriella. It has to be someone she doesn't know." Leanna speaking so matter-of-factly on my behalf is astonishing.

"We just met her. I don't think that should count." Leanna and Britney continue to disagree with each other over my personal goals. I sit back in silence. Shay emerges from the crowd, alone, snacking on a pretzel. She makes eye contact with us, but continues on her walk without speaking.

"She's so fucking rude." Britney's head shakes disapprovingly at Shay's behavior. I wonder if she's still angry about the spa incident or if something else has happened between them since then.

"You know what's weird?" They stop to stare at me, Leanna's eyes finally leaving the walkway. "I never worried about her cheating on me."

"Did she?" I shake my head at Britney's question. I didn't think so.

"I never cheated on my girlfriend." Leanna's eyes glow with confidence. She places her hand on top of the one holding my teacup. "And I would never cheat on you." I laugh when she reaches over to rub her nose against my cheek. It's a cute Leanna thing to do.

"Britney?" It's rare for Britney to be this quiet. At my question she looks up, her eyes are sadder, her lips turned down into a frown.

"It's complicated."

I don't press her.

Deciding to abandon the search for a new couple, we shop instead. Britney and Leanna's knowledge of the hotel is far greater than mine. While I focused on exploring the sexier side of BED, they know more about the fun side.

I eat cheese and they drink at Pour, Hotel BED's wine cellar that only serves fancy booze and expensive cheese. The cheese is delicious and I try every kind they offer. Our nails are done at Opulence in plush massage chairs with nail technicians who bring out glasses of champagne, chocolate-dipped macaroons, and hazelnut shortbread cookies.

For the first time, I experience the different pools and smaller lounges. More members recognize me from this morning's show or mention my other past work. I smile at the compliments, my uneasiness about it lessening more as time passes. I steer the group away from where I think I stumbled upon Paradise Row.

By the time we roll into Exquisite, it feels like I'm actually on vacation. Outside of BED, one would consider Exquisite to be a strip club, except the women aren't nude. There are three exotic dance clubs within BED, based on the sexual preferences of the members. Exquisite is for those who want to watch women perform. There's another club for mixed genders and then also one for men. I would do fine at any of the three, but surprisingly, Britney has a preference.

I'd assumed Britney to be bisexual like me, but I was starting to wonder if I had been wrong. Being at BED is a lot different from being at Chasity's Orange County mansion. Although we lived together back then, we didn't hang out with each other aside from planning discussions and late night visits from Leanna.

At the center of Exquisite is a stage with six poles attached to the ceiling. In the space between each pole is a cage. The set-up is exciting. It's unlike anything I've ever seen before. I jog unceremoniously to one of the empty seats. Dread fills my belly when I remember, "Shit! I don't have any money!"

Britney laughs. "Who needs money when you're at BED?"

That's not how it works. That's not how any of this could possibly work. The dancers have to be tipped. They've worked hard to craft their talent. I move to get up to find the closest ATM.

Britney pulls me back down. "Relax." She pulls out her phone. "You do it on the app. It's fine." I follow her instructions to find Exquisite under the venue tab and then select the time of the show.

A countdown begins. The lights dim. The show starts with all six women appearing onstage. They move in unison. Their neon outfits glow in the darkness. Once I take my mind off their bodies, all varying in shapes, sizes and beautiful hues, I focus on the show. The dance is not just a dance. It's a performance. I'm able to follow it easily. It's a story of love and support. A woman with a broken heart being rallied by her closest friends. I pick her out immediately. She dances the hardest. The others follow her lead, moving slow and then fast, climbing a pole and then dropping again with an unspeakable rhythm. I have never seen anything like it before.

The leader's bikini is splashed in splotches of hot pink, lime green and purple. Her hair is straight and long. I think she's a little older than I am, but not by much.

Leanna nudges my shoulder with hers. "This can be on your list."

She's right. I hesitate to call her a stripper. She has yet to shred one piece of clothing.

"I've never had a lap dance," I speak loudly into Leanna's ear so she can hear me. She wiggles her eyebrows at me before grabbing my cell phone. I watch her find the colors of the dancer's outfit, something I didn't even think to do.

When she presses it, another message pops up. *You are now in the queue.* I look at her questioningly.

"They only get naked in the private rooms." She places my phone back in my hand after increasing the tip amount. "The tip decides the order."

I nod, gathering all the information she's explaining to me.

"Let me know if you need any help. You still have that threesome to cross off your list."

I let out a slow exhale at Leanna's words. The images don't help me steady my heartbeat. Maybe I should do it. Leanna, me and the dancer—whose name I haven't even learned yet. Leanna turns her attention back to the show before I have the chance to respond. Waiting is probably a good idea. My rash decisions at BED haven't served me well so far. I'll meet with her first and then decide.

I continue to watch the show while dancing in my seat. Anything else would be a distraction and completely disrespectful to the performers. As a fellow artist, I know my place and the rules. A look around the crowd confirms everyone else has the same thought as I do. They move in their own spaces, maybe connecting eyes with someone else across the room. My eyes connect to a figure. She's not looking at me. Her eyes are trained on the lead dancer. I don't think she's one herself. The outfit is wrong. She wears a black leather jacket, a white T-shirt and ripped jeans. There's something about her that feels familiar, though I can't place it.

The show ends with thunderous applause. Unsure of where I remain on the list, I increase the tip amount again. It takes a few minutes before a new message displays on my screen, directing me to room five.

Britney goes into her room first. She tipped the dancer with dark brown skin, shoulder-length locs, and a hot pink bikini. "I'll see you guys at dinner." She has a hungry look in her eyes and a grin for a smile.

I leave Leanna at the bar and make my way down the illuminated hallway. The room is small, but cozy. A cushioned chair sits in the middle, facing an even smaller stage. *Cute.*

The dancer walks in. She's smaller than she looked on stage. Her outfit is now a sparkling silver, matching her silver chain and ID combo. She's unmatched. That information should be irrelevant to me. I'm not a real member of the hotel.

She starts small talk. She must see that I'm nervous. I answer all of her questions about where I'm from and what I do for a living. She's from Arizona and is studying to be a nurse. Nerves kick up again as the conversation moves on. I realize, as pretty as I think she is, I don't want to have sex with her. There's a part of me that believes I should and I'm somehow supposed to, but another much bigger part of me doesn't feel the same way.

My muscles relax, but I notice she continues to talk about random topics. "Is something wrong?" I ask as several more minutes pass by. Her eyes shift to the door and then down to the carpet.

"I'm not allowed to touch you without permission."

Asking whose permission she needed would be futile when I already know the answer.

"That's okay. You don't have to, but if you need to talk about anything, no one will know what happens outside of this room."

She cocks her head to the side before her eyes narrow at me. Slowly, a smile spreads across her lips. "That would be true, except she's already here."

Chapter Twenty-Six
Gabriella

THE EXQUISITE DANCERS ARE easy to manage. They are complete professionals and rarely need me for much. Still, like any excellent manager, I check in to assess the needs of the show regularly.

I didn't expect to see Taylor and her friends seated in the front row. Leanna can't seem to decide what she wants. I'm sure she's fucking crazy. I can see it slowly simmering behind her eyes, but for whatever reason, Taylor doesn't see it. You'd think she'd be more adept at recognizing us by now.

I easily identify Taylor's unique ID on the tipping system. She's not tipping nearly enough to make it to the top spot. No worries. I'll make sure Shawna rests for the next person. Shawna doesn't argue when I explain her role. I walk through the open door only a few seconds after she does. Taylor, enthralled, is completely oblivious. The problem is not her finding other women attractive. I'm in absolute love with a warm-blooded woman, not a corpse. I don't need Taylor to only have eyes for me.

I was ready to call it quits last night and let it all go with Taylor, but this morning had been good. We both need to sit down and talk about what happened and where to go from here. All she had to do was sit and wait. There are plenty of other nonsexual activities to engage in at BED.

But she had to walk into Exquisite.

Shawna exits the room as I always meant her to. Taylor displays a false look of innocence. Her bright eyes don't seem at all surprised that I found her. She leans back enough in her chair for me to sit in her lap to face her. I take a deep breath, pausing with my eyes closed for a few seconds before opening them again.

Her hand is mid-air, inches from the space in between my eyebrows. She smooths out the skin there with the flat of her fingers. I force the tight muscles to relax.

"Don't tell me you're jealous," she teases. It's almost enough to lift my spirits. I'm not jealous. I'm confused.

"Please tell me what you want." I hope my usage of the word please sends a message to her I'm tired of asking. Taylor is looking for something I haven't been able to give her. I need to know what that is.

Taylor's eyes travel from mine down to my lips and then lower between us. "I think this is the first time I've held you in over three years. You feel so good." Her hands travel up my back, tickling my skin. She continues moving her hands up and down my spine, drumming her fingertips against me.

"I miss you." I'm scared, but I say it anyway. There's so much between us we haven't talked about.

"Me too."

Her hands weave their way from my back, across my breast and up my neck. My shirt lifts, but she doesn't move to undress me. Her lips pucker against my collarbone, my jaw and my cheeks. Feeling unsteady, I pull at her elbows, begging for release. Her eyebrows crease. Her eyes darken. I'm losing this moment.

"Please tell me." Before it's too late.

Her hands return to me, this time wrapping around my waist. "I thought I needed to come here because I didn't know who I was without you. I was supposed to figure that out."

I don't understand what she means. Taylor is one of the most confident people I know. It's one reason I fell for her, the reason I love her, still.

"How?" I mean, how is it she thought she didn't know herself, but Taylor answers another question.

"Sex. I was going to come here and have a lot of sex with different people to figure it out." Her words connect the dots to her behavior this week. Asking Trice about the orgy floor. The Kitchen. Mama Mae's girls. Everything makes sense except the why.

"How do you not know who you are?"

She looks at me. Her eyes shift from side to side. She shrugs. "Before we broke up, you ruled me. I've tried hard to untangle us. How do I know how much of it was you and how much of it was me just desperately wanting you?"

My heart drops at the heaviness of her words. That I owned Taylor is hurtful. Yes, she belongs to me, but not in that way. Never like that. Taylor always did what she wanted and was always free to do as she pleased. I controlled nothing about her life. I just tried to go along with it.

"Hey." She cups my face with both hands. Her voice is low and smooth. "It's okay now. I figured it out."

I pull away from her. I twist to stand, walking to the other side of the room before Taylor has the chance to pull me back. The sadness in my chest drapes over my heart. Years ago, I would've never been able to call it that. To slow myself down enough to recognize my emotions before I react has taken a lot of practice, most of which I threw out the window the moment Taylor walked into the hotel, but I'm doing it now and facing a heavy truth. I've been sad from the moment Taylor came to BED. I'm not the person Taylor thinks I am and I refuse to be the villain here. Not then. Not for two whole years.

There's still so much for us to get through. I promised myself that when the day came, I wouldn't stay silent. She sits and waits with her hands folded in her lap. I'm surprised she hasn't left.

"There's a lot I want to say. I think I need time."

She gives a slight nod, her lips pressed together to keep herself from speaking. My hand brushes against the knob before turning it fully.

"I'll see you tonight."

Chapter Twenty-Seven
Taylor

TONIGHT DOESN'T COME FAST enough. The murder mystery dinner is the first event for Chasity's birthday I've attended in a while. I almost feel like a terrible guest, but then I forgive myself and move on.

Gabriella wasn't at the suite when I went to change, and one twist of her doorknob sent a new message—stay out. I don't think I did anything wrong by revealing to Gabriella my reason for coming to BED. I don't know what upset her, but I can wait. It's not like our lives are over once I walk out of the lobby doors.

Dinner takes place in a room I've never been in before. It has the same old glam feel of The Kitchen. My sexy detective costume is a period piece. Chasity stands at the table in her brown detective bodysuit, complete with a cape and hat. My outfit also includes a cape and hat, but I'm wearing a tight dress. Britney's cape does nothing to cover her crop top, also brown and checkered, but her skirt is long enough to conceal the area where her underwear would be if she were wearing any. Leanna's outfit is like mine, but a looser fit. More flirty than a pencil skirt. Shay opts out of the sexy detective trend, showing up instead in a trench coat and heels.

Britney leans over to whisper, "I guess we know who the killer is."

I don't spot Gabriella until I notice the cameras. She's not at all dressed like a sexy detective. In typical crew fashion, she's dressed in all black, watching the screen of a handheld monitor. I wonder if she's had enough time to think about our conversation from earlier.

Dinner is served without so much as a glance from her. I presume the comedians who perform at the party are members of the hotel. They're funny and I have no problem laughing at their jokes.

Gabriella is still watching her monitor when a woman screams. I jump and grip the edge of the table. The woman stumbles to the center of the room, her long gown dragging behind her. Her fingers clutch at her throat. Her eyes are wide.

"She's been poisoned!" Britney stands and shouts. An audible gasp sounds amongst the guests. I feign shock, cupping my hands around my mouth to conceal my giggle. The woman falls gracefully to the ground. Her arm outstretched, eyes closed and hair falling over her face.

Shay runs over and leans close before looking back up again, her eyes serious, her breath measured. "She's dead." Gasps again.

Someone shouts out, "We have to call the police!"

"No police!" Chasity stands, commanding the room. "There's too much at stake. We have no choice but to solve this on our own. Close the doors. No one may leave until we find the killer." The doors shut with a bang. I suck in my cheeks, desperately trying to maintain my composure.

We are each handed notebooks and a pen and told by Chasity to interview the party guests and capture the killer. "My friends. Please do me this one last favor. Please save my hotel." She places her hand over her eyes and pretends to weep. Shay swoops in, pats her on her back and helps her to her seat.

I survey the room, tapping the tip of the pen on my chin.

Poisoning is an old trick. I doubt the mafia guys would use it to complete a killing. They have other methods, like kidnapping, stabbing and shooting. Maybe cutting off a finger or two. I ignore them.

My eyes travel to a group of women sitting to the side, looking bored and mum. They may try to throw suspicion off themselves. Most women don't like gory things. Poison makes less of a mess. I make my way toward the group. A cameraman follows behind me. The thought of Gabriella keeping track of me is exciting. I wink at the lens.

"Hello, ladies." They return the greeting, looking both surprised and impressed that I came to talk with them. I sit on the small coffee table in the center of their group, pull out my notebook and begin my questioning.

"Were any of you ladies familiar with the victim?" I keep notes. The stories these women weave are truly remarkable. It must've taken Gabriella months to plan all of this on top of everything else she's responsible for at the hotel.

Betty points out a man she saw arguing with the woman outside of the restroom. She couldn't hear what they were saying exactly, but it sounded heated.

Christina says she had seen the victim around the hotel, but she'd seemed like a loner, never around anyone or hanging out with any group. Not even at a private party, and Christina would know, she goes to all the parties. She winks at me when she says this. I avert my eyes to the scribbled words in my notebook.

The man Betty pointed out denies he had any confrontation with the victim tonight. He sits with a group of men in business attire. He boasts about being an entrepreneur and a very busy one at that. "We don't have arguments. We have discussions." He can't tell me much about his business other than he works in 'sales'.

I notice one man look away while I speak with the victim's lover. I approach him, ask if he wouldn't mind helping me out of my dress to use the bathroom, and walk away. He looks surprised, but follows. The cameraman follows, too. Once out of earshot of the group, I ask, "How long have you been sleeping with her?" He doesn't deny it. That would be hard to do with tears spilling out of his eyes. *He's good.* He rants about how poorly the victim was treated by her lover. She was always alone and he, the lover, always had an excuse why he could not be there for her. She caught him in many lies. Once, when he was supposed to be out of town on a business trip, he was gambling away his money in the casino. The same casino he lived in. What an idiot. "I love my cousin, but he didn't deserve her heart." Gasp! Sometimes, it be your own people.

Britney, Leanna and I reconvene at the table to compare notes. Our shy victim's name is Maliyah. She's young, only about 22 years old. Her lover, Brandon, is a little older, around 28 years old.

"He's sketchy," I say. "But I don't think he's a killer. A cheater, maybe."

"She's a cheater, too." Before I can agree with Britney, she continues to make her case, including some of the information Leanna has gathered.

Our helpless victim, Maliyah, wasn't just sleeping with Brandon's cousin. She had weekly romps with his boss, his younger twin brothers, one of the pool bartenders, and was a regular breakfast-in-bed recipient. She thought she was queer for five minutes, but after having a rendezvous with one of the Exquisite dancers, changed her mind about being sexually attracted to women. The nerve!

"I have to say, though, the twin brothers thing is kind of hot," Britney grins.

I have to agree with her. If Maliyah was with the twins in the same bed, at the same time, then kudos to her.

Leanna chimes in. "Any of these men could've killed her."

I search for Gabriella and find her in the corner of the room, speaking with a member of the crew. I excuse myself from the table. She's done with her discussion by the time I reach her.

"Can we have a clue?"

She pulls a folded piece of paper out of her back pocket. Surprised, I reach for it.

She pulls it away, laughing. "Just kidding."

She unfolds the blank piece of paper.

"No clues. You ladies are just going to have to talk it out and work together." She makes to move around me. I stop her, grabbing her waist.

"And when are we going to talk it out?" I hope I don't sound as desperate as I feel. I miss her in ways I haven't allowed myself to imagine in a long time.

She wiggles out of my grasp and steps out of my reach. "You should go back to the game."

My feet move where she goes, though I try not to touch her again. "I don't want to go back to the game. I want to talk to you." My wasted words slam into her back. She stops only to allow the cart of desserts to push through the door Chasity demanded stay closed. It's Danni. I catch their words as they pass, smiling at Gabriella and completely ignoring me.

"See you tonight." They snatch a treat off the cart and hand it to Gabriella.

Gabriella accepts it. "See you."

So this is what it feels like. Gabriella has never cheated on me. I legit never had to worry about her being with another person. My mind is a tornado of memories. I don't even remember standing there until she finally speaks to me.

"You should do what you think is best for you."

What I think is best? *Fuck her*.

I don't know how I manage to walk with the weight of my heart bearing down on my feet. I make it back to the table. Leanna tries to hold the hand I tuck underneath the cloth. I make a fist. The party isn't as fun as it was five minutes ago.

"Who else was Maliyah sleeping with?" I need this game to be over. The heart in my chest is too constricting. It's getting harder to breathe. I can feel my eyes watering, begging to release the pain I've built up these last few days over an already overflowing well. I need something else to focus on. This stupid game.

I have a hard time believing Maliyah's lover killed her. He was too sloppy to be a shrewd businessman; all ideas and no business. They were broke, but somehow managed to stay in the hotel.

Britney shrugs her shoulders. "I think that's all of them."

I disagree. It takes more effort than usual to stand. I slide my notebook off the table, leaving it hanging to my side. I'm going with my heart on this one.

She looks up at me as I approach. Shay, flanking her on the side, has an eyebrow raised. The notebook drops on the table with a loud bang. "You killed her."

Chasity laughs, placing her hand over her heart in shock. "Excuse me?"

"You. Killed. Her." I repeat it louder to the silent audience. "Loverboy is full of shit. He's a businessman with no money, and yet he spends hours gambling in your casino. No one here has mentioned anything about her having a job or income. She should be completely reliant on him, except she's not. They're here because you let them be here. She belongs to you, not him. You treat him like a kid at an arcade, feeding him money to distract him, when really you're fucking his girlfriend. You don't care about the other men. Men are no competition to you. None of them have partners, so at best they're at the lowest tier, if that. You didn't get mad about her sleeping with other people until she slept with the dancer."

Chasity's eyes narrow at me. The corners of her lips twitch.

"You killed her because she disrespected you by being with another woman. Where's the dancer now, Chasity? Where'd you bury the body?"

Chasity places her hand over her lips, the tips of her finger brushing underneath her nose, her eyes slant to the corner.

"Yeah, jealousy's a bitch and so are your friends, " I say to her before turning my back and walking away. The round of applause that follows helps to lift a bit of the heaviness from around my heart. I pause. My eyes float to Gabriella, handheld in hand. The cameras are still rolling.

I'm wrong.

I rethink my theory. I'm confident most of it is right, but there's something I'm missing.

"A Boss Bitch never gets her hands dirty," I murmur.

Chasity can't help but smile at my words. I turn to Shay, untie the knot of her trench coat, and reach for the handcuffs she has tucked underneath. I drop them in her lap. They clatter against each other with a clang. "May I?" She brings her wrists together. Her eyes are dark and threatening, but I can tell by the way her lips twist, she's trying not to smile.

"All hail Piper Paige!" The audience acknowledging my old TV moniker brings me back to reality. The sound of the cuffs tightening around Shay's skin ends the game.

My feet carry me to the restroom. I fight the urge to splash handfuls of water on my face and ruin my makeup. The door to the restroom opens and I brace myself, convinced it's Gabriella coming to find me. It's not.

She reminds me of Chasity. She has the same deep brown skin and straightened hair. But while Chasity's is straightened regularly at a salon, and probably the one she has built here at BED, I'm certain this woman's hair is not.

"Good work out there." She joins me at the sink. Her back presses up against the basin closest to me. I thank her. The unbuttoned long-sleeved white collared shirt is tucked into a stretch black skirt with suspenders.

"I'm Reese."

"Taylor."

"Oh, I know. Everyone's been talking about you. What are you doing tonight?"

I had made no plans for after we had solved the murder. Truthfully, I thought I was going to spend the night with Gabriella, talking about the present and mending the past, but that seems unlikely now.

"No plans."

"Good. I'm going to be conducting a showing on Peek Street tonight. If you're in the market for a new house, stop by." She hands me a business card. A photo of her with her name, Reese Williams, Realtor, is scripted on the front. "The address is on the back." I turn the card over at the same time I hear the door to the restroom shut.

Midnight. House 8727.

Chapter Twenty-Eight
Gabriella

I DON'T SEE TAYLOR again before I wrap up the crew. Her performance tonight was phenomenal. She's a natural at getting the crowd's attention and earning their respect enough to root for her. Somehow she's always the underdog against the big bad threat. And this time, she faced off against the Queen and won.

Shay was pretty salty about it. She loves being a villain and when Taylor first got it wrong, albeit half-right, I could see Shay itching to stand and reveal herself. *That's a good girl.*

My decision to no longer pursue Taylor isn't an easy one. She needs more time. And I don't want to go through our relationship always wondering if she's really happy she chose me. I have to move on. Hopefully, by the time she decides, it won't be too late.

I make a quick stop to the suite to retrieve my jacket before joining Danni in the kitchen at Delicacy. It can get cold there sometimes and despite my ability to brave the Las Vegas winters, I'm still a warm-blooded girl from San Diego.

I enjoy watching Danni work. They technically aren't off the clock just yet, so I sit and wait while they prepare the stock for tomorrow's morning rush.

"You put on a great show upstairs."

They're always complimentary. There might not be anything I can ever do to piss them off. I thank them before dipping a clean spoon into a batter of chocolate chip cookie dough.

"You're going to get sick from doing that."

Danni slides the bowl out of my reach. I pull it back. "Lies." It's true. I've been eating raw cookie dough for years under the threat of illness. It has yet to happen. I stop only when I realize I won't be able to get a second spoonful without contaminating the rest of the bowl. Danni chuckles at my predicament, but doesn't offer to help.

"So, the girl, the one who cracked the case. She's your ex, right? The one the email went out about."

I nod in the affirmative. Chasity sent a warning email out to the managers about over-indulging her friends with too many private party invites. She specifically warned them against Taylor, who she said was an old friend of ours. The email doesn't say that Taylor and I used to date, but the implication was clear.

"How'd it end?"

"If I tell you I'm the one who ruined it, will you kick me out?"

"No way. I still see you guys hanging around each other. Couldn't have been too bad."

Oh, it was bad. Even with the amount of time that has passed, I still believe that to be true.

Danni looks down at the tray they're busy scooping groups of cookie dough onto.

"I lied to her. It maybe would've been okay if I had come clean sooner, but I didn't. I waited years and when she found out what I had done, she left." I hold my breath for Danni's reaction. I don't tell Danni anymore than that because it's not just my story to tell.

Danni's eyes shoot up at me. "OK, well. You seem sorry for it. And that's what matters at the end of the day."

I watch them work in comfortable silence, the swoosh of the dishwasher the only noise present. Danni's huff brings my attention back to them. "She's pretty."

"She is."

"I don't think I'm bad looking."

I try to maintain a blank expression. "Not at all."

"She seems pretty smart."

I nod. "Has a graduate degree and everything."

Danni tips their head to the side. "I have a degree in culinary arts and a diploma in pastry and baking."

The smile on my face grows easily. "I believe you."

Danni tears me off a piece of the new cookie dough she's kneading. I accept it graciously, plopping a small ball of it into my mouth.

"Do you still love her?"

"Always," I say it without hesitation.

"Wow, that much, huh?"

I don't want to disappoint Danni, but I have to tell the truth. It's what they deserve.

"There is no version of this world that exists where I don't love her. I don't think we have to be together just because we love each other. Sometimes it just doesn't work out that way, but whoever comes after her has to understand that."

Danni is quiet for a few seconds, their knuckles rolling into the dough they turn over again and again. "I understand."

Chapter Twenty-Nine
Taylor

THE SUITE IS PITCH black by the time I get in. I have about two hours before I'm scheduled to meet with the realtor. I couldn't find Gabriella before leaving the party. I asked Shay, but she feigned ignorance. I need to talk to her. The decision we make tonight will decide whether I take a walk on Peek Street.

The knob to Gabriella's door twists open this time. Her bed is neatly made. I flick off the light she left on in her closet. She must've been in a hurry. My shoes are off before I climb onto her bed. The minutes tick by slowly. I jump at every sound that so much resembles a door being pushed open or slammed closed.

I wait. And I wait. She never comes. My anger grows as quickly as the pain in my chest does. She doesn't get to do this to me again. My hand wraps around the handle of the lamp on the end table, fully prepared to toss it across the room. I pull at the cord. It snaps out of the socket, but then wraps around the knob on the end table. I pull again. The drawer shoots out, revealing Gabriella's toys.

The lamp crashes to the floor. I tug at my skirt, lifting it higher above my thighs and then over my hips. My fingers dip into the drawer and pull out the first toy I come into contact with. My tongue runs across the head of the hot pink wand. It's clean.

There's so much I've gone through because of her. So much

that I have deprived myself of. I press the button, sending the toy whirling into action. One hand grips the top of the comforter while the other maneuvers the toy around my most sensitive area. The pleasure is instant. It's not long before I'm wet, my arousal soaking through the fabric she'll likely sleep under tonight. If she ever comes home.

I add and remove pressure, keeping the toy planted exactly where I need it to be. The memories of us flood through my open thighs. Her dark eyes, dark hair and dangerous smile, stealthy and crooked like the assassin she is.

The killer of my heart.

My wild breaths easily overpower the quiet technology, no doubt advertised on whatever box Gabriella pulled this thing out of.

I ride it like she would want me to. Training the wand over my clit until the wave is too intense to take. "Shit!" I pull it away, take a few deep breaths and try it again. Gabriella would love to watch my breath catch and my hips shake uncontrollably while not being able to breathe. I move the wand downward, using it to caress the inside of my lower lips. I should've taken my clothes off. The cape is smothering. My detective ensemble now keeps me from accessing my body.

I hike my thighs up higher. It's what Gabriella would do. My head presses as far back as I can manage. My fingers wrap around my throat. "Please," I beg softly at first. I pulse the wand upwards, tapping it against the base of my clit, pausing my breath with each tap. The wand lingers for longer each time, building into the right amount of intensity. "Please!"

I'm desperate for release. Desperate for her to feel and remember me this time. She must've forgotten who we were, who she turned me into. I spent years resenting her and then believing my moments with her were something that I needed to reclaim.

I was wrong.

I fantasize for her.

I scream for her.

I come for her.

And not because she ever forced me to, but because doing so made me feel more alive than I ever felt on any set. It didn't matter who was watching, as long as she was there.

Memories of us pressed together behind open windows, doors, and in public spaces coax what I need out of me. Her commanding voice whispers in my ear as if she's lying next to me, compelling me to keep my legs pulled back and the toy trained in its place. Like she taught me. My hand grips my neck tighter with each promise she makes of love and forever. I remember every word.

My hips rise and fall with each addition to the mess we make together, producing a different sound than the last. This is us. A messy blend that works together to create magic. She never asked me to beg. And I never had.

Her punishments were lessons for me to savor for another time like this one. When I needed to look back and be reminded of what I loved about our time together. Her best weapon is her touch. From the moment her fingers grazed against my skin, she changed me. Without words. Without ever seeing her eyes or feeling any part of her body press down on me. I loved her touch.

Words can't escape the restriction I created. I gasp for breath. Gabriella stands in the doorway watching me. Her glare is encouraging. I spread my thighs wider in defiance, daring her to stop me. The evidence of what we've built together seeps down my inner thighs into the soft comforter. She can never forget us.

The intensity of the vibration reverberates down onto my clit. It's too much. The pressure turns into pain. I move it around, per her silent instruction. I lift and then I press. Lift and then press, again. My hips and my whimpering maintain the rhythm. She doesn't care if I can barely breathe as long as I reach our goal. I can do that for us. She's taught me how. While our love story is permanently written on her skin, our heartbreak is embedded into my chest and I hold it over my heart like a shield.

The pieces break away with each quiver. My scream catches in my throat as I explode, quaking, holding the toy as steady as I can until all air exhausts out of my lungs and no strength in my legs is left. Through the flutter of my closing eyes, I lose all sight of her. Gabriella's gone and she's not coming back.

Peek Street is dead at midnight on a weeknight. The lights shine on the cobblestones my heels tap against. There's no audience, and no shows are being performed. The door opened easily enough. There was no sign telling anyone to stay away. Everyone can't be still at the murder mystery party. They did not invite the entire hotel to Chasity's birthday festivities. Something's wrong.

My steps slow every time I near an alleyway. I look through more nooks and crannies than I noticed during my two previous trips here. I wipe my hands against my dress to rid them of sweat and contemplate going back in the direction in which I came. But where? Gabriella isn't home, and she showed no interest in talking to me tonight. After days of trying to explore all that Hotel BED offers me, this might be my last chance.

House 8727 has a small porch out front. The steps squeak under my weight, announcing my arrival before I can knock. The door swings open to reveal Reese. She's dressed in the same outfit as before.

"Please come in."

I cross the threshold, instantly surprised by how nicely House 8727 is decorated. It reminds me of a model home in a new housing development.

"This is a three bedroom, two bath home. The old owners were using one bedroom as an office, but you can easily convert it into a nursery." She says it all with a smile, wide and white.

I stumble with my response, "Uh, yeah, sure. That sounds great." Reese walks me through the rest of the house, pointing out building details I don't care enough to memorize. "The home has a new roof and a new HVAC unit, a must in Las Vegas."

I follow her down to the basement, a space she swears I could convert into a mother-in-law suite. I could've sworn Vegas homes didn't have basements, but I digress. As I descend the steps, lights flicker onto the white walls. My suspicion is confirmed the closer I get to the last step. The room is aglow with white, thick, long-stemmed candles. A single row of candles creates a circle in the middle of the room, surrounding a table. The only piece of furniture around.

Reese steps over the candles and I follow suit. "The house was built in the early 1900s." The cape slides off my shoulders. She drops it underneath the table, safe from the flames. The dress goes next. She tugs a little harder to get it over my hips. I step out of it. "Leave the shoes on. He'll like that."

He is a surprise to me. Before I can ask questions, my ass is sliding across the table. Reese takes no time undressing, spreading her legs across my hips.

"They say the original owners come back at the sound of a moaning woman." The glint in her eyes is sinister.

"Come back?"

"Yes. The wife murdered her husband here when she found him having an affair in the basement, in this very spot. Legend has it, one or both of them return during moments of intense passion. With there being two of us, we're bound to have the desired effect."

The words Reese explains to me scatter through my brain. What. The. Fuck. Having sex with a ghost is not on my fucking checklist.

I skipped the lesson on how to tell someone to get the fuck off of you. Respectfully. I buck my hips upward. Reese misunderstands, "Oh yeah, you're so ready for this." I am so not ready. Reese unlatches her bra and flings it across the room. "Come get us, Daddy!" She bounces up and down on top of me. Her performance is confusing. My bra and panties remain in place. Reese isn't paying attention to me at all.

Her hands cup her breasts. Her hair swings from side to side. She's moaning as if I'm giving her the best orgasm of her life, except my hands are pinned to my sides and my thighs are shut tight.

Bangs sound above us. For a second, I think Reese may be right. She seems unfazed by our new visitors, however. If I fling her off me, she'll sustain burns on her skin, or worse.

Bright lights spill down the basement staircase. Reese continues her bouncing. Her shouts drown out their commands. I strain my ears to listen, but can't make out the words. Multiple sets of black boots come thundering down the stairs.

They pull Reese off me; her wails still echoing in the room. I am given no time to stand. I'm thrown over a set of muscled shoulders with cuffed wrists and ankles. I scream, knowing no one will hear me. I kick, knowing there is nowhere for me to run. They wrap a blindfold around my head as they carry me away.

I can hear chains rattle as they walk. They speak to no one.

Not even to each other. I try to keep track of where we might go, but my attempts are futile. I don't know the hotel well enough to remember the layout. Even if I had, the group seems to change directions often. Getting on and getting off the elevator, going up and down different flights of stairs. It's baffling.

My journey ends once I'm thrown down on a hard surface and my blindfold is removed. The cuffs around my ankles are detached, but my wrists remain chained to a row of gold bars. I don't argue with my captors. I know they won't have sympathy for me. They are the property of Chasity.

They pull a thin sleeveless shirt over my head and yank it down to cover the rest of me. As it has no sides, I'm not sure if it can be called a shirt. It's a dress made for a prisoner, kept together by the belt he tightens around my waist.

Gold handcuffs. Gold chains. Fancy fucking jail. Chasity is a damned pretentious kept wench with too much money to spare. Her wives have built her an expensive torture chamber to carry out her fantasies as she pleases, and every day I spend in this hellhole becomes a new nightmare.

When the last click of the cuffs can be heard, my captor, whose identity I may never know, kneels to my ear and whispers, "Welcome to the Dungeon."

Chapter Thirty
Gabriella

MY FOREHEAD BOUNCES OFF the corner of the mattress, barely missing the wooden bedpost. "Shit!" The throbbing of my heartbeat is understandable given my near death experience. I unwrap the cord I tripped over from around my ankles before scrambling to turn on the light.

The lamp that is usually on the end table is now on the floor. Apparently being used to disguise my murder as an accident. It's too late for housekeeping, which means at some point, Taylor went ham on my bedroom, though the lamp seems to be the only thing she attempted to destroy. It plugs up fine once it's back in place.

The pink toy in the center of the bed gives me pause. *What the fuck. Did she have someone else in here?* No. She'd never do that. Taylor would never have sex in my bed with someone else. It only takes seconds before I'm pounding on her door. When there's no answer, I turn the knob and push. It's empty. She didn't stay home last night. It's almost one o'clock in the morning and I can't think of where else she would be instead of in bed with someone else.

Leanna is a safe bet. Someone she already knows and has already been intimate with. Leanna would be easy. I could go there now, except I can't because I don't know which room Leanna is checked into. I could find out, but that would involve waking people up in the dead of night to drag my ex-girlfriend back to my suite.

And what if she's not there? I take a deep breath, trying to calm my spinning thoughts. I don't feel this crazy when I'm with anyone else. Danni is so loving and understanding. Maybe that's where I'm supposed to be. I remember my words to Danni from earlier. *Just because we love each other doesn't mean we have to be together.* Taylor can make her own choices and her own mistakes.

I close the door to her bedroom and walk back to my own. I clean the toy with soap and warm water in the bathroom sink. On a hunch, I check my top drawer. It's mine. The bed smells like me and her and no one else.

My shower is longer than it should be. I moisturize the parts of my skin that need it and then dress in a white beater and gray sweatpants. I leave the vibrator where it is, on the side of the bed she should be on. The sheets are cool against my body. The top of the blanket is still damp. I'm certain now no one else was here with her, but I'm less certain about the message. Did she leave her scent behind as a gift or as a warning?

Chapter Thirty-One
Taylor

I'M NOT THE ONLY prisoner here. Multiple members sit chained against the velvety smooth black wall. Dimmed gold scones provide spare lighting in the small space. Only darkness is ahead. Reese is locked in further down the row. She's not screaming, bouncing, or shaking uncontrollably anymore. She doesn't look at me to offer any apologies. I look around the jail and realize no one looks nearly as annoyed and angry as I do. The rattling of my chains is the only sound that echoes in the darkness.

We sit silent and unmoving for a long time. Chasity forgot to install a large, gaudy gold clock in the room for our convenience. Just kidding. She did that shit on purpose.

Bodies shift to alertness when small noises echo around the room. First, a door opens. Then come the footsteps. A single set. A clatter of unfamiliar noises follows close behind until more footsteps come. Something scrapes against the floor. Chains rattle. Something squeaks. Murmurs increase. More footsteps. A door closes with a bang. And then silence. People around me continue to adjust themselves. The atmosphere is suddenly more lively. They're expecting what's coming and I'm dreading it. A ray of light peeks underneath a curtain separating us from the rest of the room. A single pair of footsteps click against the shiny, cold floor. They're coming toward us.

The sound of a motor lifts the black barrier to reveal the rest of Chasity's stupid fancy courtroom. I'm the only one who groans. Smiles lift on the others' faces. It's showtime for them. For me, it's a persecution.

The bailiff, if you want to call her that, wears a black leather brigade harness and barely anything else. She's extremely tall with thick thighs and a muscular build. She walks past me and stands in the middle of the group. Her black leather jockstrap leaves her backside completely exposed. The two straps, placed beneath her cheeks, propel them upwards until they reveal a nice round peach. I can't be mad at that, at least.

"Heather C., Platinum, first offense." The leather clad bailiff yells out the name as one would in any real life courtroom. She stands stiffly with her back straight and her hands clasped in front. Heather giggles and flutters her eyelashes in response. Her cuffs and chains are the same color as the necklace around her neck. Platinum with key and pendant. *Lover.*

The bailiff snatches away the thin cloth that covers Heather's body within seconds. Heather's smile doesn't falter as she's uncuffed from the bars and led into the bigger room. We all watch as her body is bent forward and her head and hands entrapped into an old pillory. Or at least the idea of a pillory was old, but this one is new. It's jet black—of course, but also includes a long bench to place each leg bent at the knee. She is wide open for all of us to see. There are two more restraint chairs identical to hers, all spread out to not obstruct the view of the audience—us.

Off to the side, there are three more court officers. They dress in variations of leather. One man's leather harness ends with a built-in cock ring. A female officer is similarly dressed as the bailiff, but with no bottom covering. The other female officer wears a black harness that extends around her spike-decorated breasts. In her hands, she massages the only thing that's not black; a lime green dildo attached to a black and white frilly strap-on harness.

The entrapped woman faces a very sleek and modern bench where the judge sits. The judge's robes are the only thing that hasn't changed. He looks like a modern judge you would find in any hall of justice today. He bangs his gravel against the desk at the start.

"Lover, how do you plead?"

"Guilty," she says without pause. Her voice is breathless and rushed. She's ready.

"Very well. I sentence you to the Seethe for four hours." He bangs his gavel again, but they do not release the woman. Instead, the bottom-naked officer moves from her post and positions herself behind her. Heather is up high enough so that the woman only has to bend slightly to eye what's in front of her. She wets her lips with her tongue. Heather's hips wiggle in anticipation. The tip of the bailiff's tongue lightly touches Heather's lower lips. She traces the outline of the skin there as if wetting a delicate piece of paper. Heather's body shakes in chains. Her breaths echo against the dark walls. The court officer's tongue slides and dips in excruciating precision.

I hold back my shock, my mouth agape. I'm never one to shy away from public sex or intimacy, but this is on a level I am unprepared for. I discreetly engage in my secret fantasies. For me, public means in the comfort and safety of my bedroom, even if someone is listening in. This is not that. These people are doing it out in the open. Everyone else wants to be here. I've been forced into this torture chamber and I want out. At no point did I think this was what being at BED was going to be like. I regret agreeing to come here and giving Chasity another chance. Again.

I fruitlessly try again to rattle the chains of my cuffs as the bailiff returns to the group to gather another prisoner. She doesn't spare a glance at my feeble escape attempt. This time, when she calls the next name, her voice raises in volume in competition with the moans and shouts from Heather.

Heather's punisher adds two fingers to her arsenal. Her pace has changed. The visual evidence of Heather's arousal is hard to deny. We can all hear the impact of the court officer's actions and witness the twisting of Heather's face. Before they entrapped her, she was confident. Now, she gasps for breath. Heather's clenched teeth and vibrating moans are all the defense she has against the court officer's brutality as she clasps Heather's clit between her two fingers and slides against it.

"Margaret L., Rose Gold, second offense." I'm shocked to see Margaret raise her hands, as high as her restraints will allow her to. She's a tiny older woman, perhaps in her sixties. Her gray hair is immaculately done in large, cascading curls. Margaret is more than ready. The thin cloth is torn from her body as quickly and as rough as it was for the inmate before her. She growls at the bailiff in response. Margaret's chain and key shine the same color as the cuffs that adorn her wrists and ankles.

As Margaret's body is lowered onto the equipment, Heather lets out her final moan, her voice quivering in an elongated "yeeesss." Her officer dislodges herself and walks over to someone off to the side, who waits patiently until she approaches and cleanses herself of all remaining fluids. I give Chasity mental kudos for hygiene, while still harboring my hatred for her.

"Partner, how do you plead?"

"Guilty, Your Honor," Margaret speaks loud and proud.

"Very well. As this is your second offense, I sentence you to six hours in the Forest."

Margaret's laugh is filled with gratitude. She wiggles her hips, points to the officer with the cock ring and beckons him forward. His grin is devilish. His strut is confident. He enjoys playing with his new toys. He pulls at her hair and smacks and jiggles her ass before rubbing the head of his against her center and slamming inside. I wince, but I'm sure I'm the only one. Margaret is overwhelmed with joy. She doesn't scream out "Yes!" Margaret shouts out, "More!" And the louder she screams, the harder he smacks her. Her screams soon become muffled as the naked officer places herself in front of her, lifts one foot onto the pillory and guides Margaret's mouth to where she demands it to be.

I am so transfixed by Margaret's punishment that I almost miss Heather being carried away by a group in expensive suits and high-collared capes. They have sentenced her to the Seethe. *Vampires.*

My eyes shift back to Margaret, who they've sentenced to the Forest. That could mean anything. Fae. Werewolves. Witches. For six hours.

The bailiff approaches the group again. I squirm. I'm understanding the point of the judicial performance. The pre-sentencing is carried out before us all to prepare us for the hours-long sentence dealt by the judge. There are multiple prisons, each offering differing experiences. If they enjoy themselves, they commit more offenses to reap the rewards of the punishment. The more offenses, the more holes that are filled. The process either serves as encouragement or a deterrent. I can't tell which. I'm not sure if they tie the prison options to benefit status or not, which still leaves me in the dark.

"Reese P., Platinum, third offense."

My accomplice waves her hands, palms out, and is eager to capture the bailiff's attention. Rage erupts inside of me. She did this on purpose. She set me up. With or without Chasity, I'm no longer sure. But with three offenses, she knew exactly how to land herself in the Dungeon. And she dragged me along with her. They lead Reese to the only torture trap that isn't being used. Her face gives nothing away. She doesn't display the same level of excitement as Heather or the same sass as Margaret. Her platinum chains slowly slide against the floor as she walks leisurely to her fate.

"Partner, how do you plead?"

"Your Honor. I truly apologize for what I have done. A villainous gold-chained slut led me astray." My jaw almost hits the floor at her words. The others quickly accept guilt and their rewards, but Reese, Reese is putting on a show.

"Be that as it may, Partner. This is your third offense. You know the rules and yet you chose not to follow them. How do you plead?"

"If it pleases you, your Honor. I am guilty." Reese drops her head in shame.

"Very well. I sentence you to eight hours in the Chambers." Reese raises her head to meet the eyes of the judge, tears now glistening down her cheeks. "Thank you, your Honor. I promise to make you proud."

Just as Margaret is being carried away by a team of bare chested men in torn shirts and jeans, the female bailiff stands behind Reese, carrying a black double-headed dildo with her. My muscles tighten as I imagine the impact that Reese is about the feel. The bailiff works one end of the dildo inside of Reese, stuffing her to completion before sliding it back out in one swift motion. Reese's sounds are barely audible. She stutters out gasps, her jaw never given enough time to close. After one swift exit, the bailiff takes her weapon and swings it upwards, beating it against where I know Reese's clit to be. She repeats the motion; beating Reese's skin and then inserting the dildo before pulling it out again. She repeats the process for both ends until it shines with Reese's slick juices.

The officer who slammed himself inside of Margaret minutes before turns away from the hygiene crew and slides between Reese's waiting lips. The bailiff carrying out Reese's punishment from behind squirts a bottle of lube down the crack of her ass. With one side already embedded inside of Reese, the toy is bent and positioned against her anus before it is pushed inside. A sound erupts from Reese's busy throat.

Another bailiff enters from the side dressed exactly as the first one. As he passes his predecessor, his hand offers a gentle pat on her shoulder. The new bailiff's body blocks my view of Reese.

"Taylor T., Gold, first offense." This one does not shout. His voice is even, but weighted like stone. While the former bailiff spoke out into the group, when her replacement says my name, he looks at me directly.

I don't acknowledge him before he moves toward me. If I try to run, I'll most likely trip. If I try to fight, I'll lose. Dread fills my gut as my heart beats faster against my chest. Nothing about this experience has been enticing to me. Sure, I'm plenty moist between my legs after watching many sex acts take place before my eyes. But I have no desire to engage in this nightmare. I can check this off my list of shit I have no interest in.

I resist having my body lowered into the pillory. I know if they lock me in, I'm as good as done. And that's when the trouble starts. The bailiff is strong. He twists my arm to get me to submit. He's strong and I'm stubborn. As we struggle with one another, I glimpse a blue bob from the corner of my eye.

"Trice!"

The bailiff stops. Trice looks at me in shock, with big eyes and her hand clasped over her mouth. "Help me!" She shakes her head from side to side wildly, pressing one finger to her lips. "Help me!" I yell again. When she makes no move, my agitation grows bitter. "You're supposed to be my fucking babysitter!" Abandoning me, she flees the room through the side door the new bailiff previously emerged from.

"Significant, are you aware there's additional punishment for yelling in the court?" My eyes stay on the door Trice has just flung herself through for a few seconds after the Judge's question.

"No!" The defiance in my voice is apparent. *Fuck this guy.* "How the fuck am I supposed to know that? How the fuck was I supposed to know that any of this was going to happen? I had no idea that I would be kidnapped for trusting another member. This hotel is supposed to be a safe place and yet I've been abducted, handcuffed and held against my will. I do not consent to this bullshit circus. You will release me immediately!" To my surprise, the judge looks both amused and skeptical. He shifts his eyes from me to the bailiff.

"What are the charges?"

The bailiff releases his tight hold on my chain to respond. "Your Honor. She breached a home on Peek Street without the prior approval of the appropriate authorities." The judge smirks. "Significant, how do you plead?"

"Not guilty! This bitch–" I point to Reese, who's still in the process of having two dicks jammed inside of her, and sigh in defeat. "I didn't know what she was planning. How has there not been an investigation? I am a victim of all of this. If you want to punish her, fine. She deserves it. I have done nothing wrong."

I hold out my chained wrists in front of the court. Any second now, they're going to be cut right down the middle and fall to the ground. I'll leave out of the same door that Trice escaped through and run right out those black iron doors.

"Who does this Significant belong to?" His amused expression tells me the judge is enjoying the difference in pace and performance. It has probably been a long time since he has seen someone come into the court and not be a willing participant.

"I'm not sure, Your Honor. I will check." Reese lets out a final groan. The pillory she's locked into shakes as her body shudders against the metal.

A group of leather-strapped court officers come and carry her out of the room. The judge and bailiff talk amongst themselves over a screen. I'm sure they see now that they've made a big mistake by imprisoning me, an honored guest of the hotel's boss. A phone rings from somewhere I can't see. The judge answers it swiftly. He speaks no words. Only grunts in acknowledgment to whatever he's being told on the other end.

When he ends the call, the bailiff returns to my side, once again gripping my chains. "I accept your plea of not guilty."

I've won.

"And for your first offense, I sentence you to five hours at the Palace, with extra time for defiance." My stomach drops. My protest lodges into my throat. The gavel bangs. "Take her to the Queen."

The scream erupts from me as soon as a group of knights files in to take me away. My bare feet stomp on top of the bailiff's black boots. He doesn't utter a whimper. My fingernails claw at stale air when I attempt to pierce his skin. I stand rigid and refuse to move. The knights don't hesitate. They grab my chains from the bailiff and pull me away, scraping the heels of my feet against the floor. Each step down the long dark hallway reveals more to me about the mystery of the Dungeon.

I keep telling myself to remember the path I'm going, but my mind is too distracted to strategize. Behind clear glass panes exist exotic worlds where prisoners are locked in tiny cages, awaiting their time to serve for their crimes.

We pass rooms bathed in bright blue lights. The creatures are hard to miss. Their blue bodies. Their elongated skulls. There are more people trapped in cages, but there are also others spread out onto flat surfaces that are not quite right. They're too rigid to be beds. The structures look too modern. Too futuristic. And then suddenly, I know exactly what I am seeing. Aliens. I've heard about people having desires with fantasy characters before. I am not one of them.

It's obvious which window belongs to the Forest. The Forest is covered in greenery, complete with tall trees, tree stumps and twinkling lights like fireflies. Somehow, they have managed to turn the ceiling into a picturesque night sky. I watch as a group of witches surround the cages of inmates before they carry my body up a flight of stairs.

The scenery changes quickly. While the lower level comprises multiple realms, this floor is strictly for the Palace. From wall to wall, a long red carpet passes underneath me. Everyone looks normal here. Those milling about the hallway are dressed regally in tight bodices and big gowns, but this is dark royalty. There are no bright whites, reds and golds here.

The walls are dark. Not black as it had been in the courtroom. Like a shadow gray. No windows here for me to look inside of. No way for me to grasp what I have gotten myself into or what dangers are coming my way.

They push open a set of ornate double doors to reveal a medium sized bedroom. Instead of separate cages to hold prisoners, they built the cages underneath the bed. Luckily, for the time being, they are unoccupied. I don't notice the black restraints until the moment I'm thrown onto the mattress, face first, and tied down. I try to fight, but they're smart. And quick. They rip the thin fabric from my body and snatch away my bra and panties, exposing every visible and vulnerable piece of me.

None of them stop to look before they exit.

Frustrated with losing this tortuous game, I scream. I keep screaming when I hear licks smack against flesh. I scream through the pleas that seep in from my neighbor's walls. I scream until my voice grows tired and hoarse. I scream until she comes.

She is not Chasity. She is too dark and wicked for bright whites, reds and golds. I knew it as soon as my eyes landed on the Palace floor. The Queen here is not the ruler of the hotel, but the ruler of the Dungeon. The Queen of the Dungeon is the most ruthless of them all.

Fuck Shay Salvador.

Shay strolls into the room in her blood red dress with every intent to taunt me. It's the hem that gives her away. It drags across the black floor with a heaviness that takes both grace and a certain amount of misery. She wears it well.

There is nowhere for me to look except at her. Turning away will take more strength than I have available to give. We were always more acquaintances than we were friends, but I always still saw Shay as a part of the group. I guess I was the only one.

"Well...well...well. Look who can't seem to stay out of trouble." Her long, jet black hair swishes back and forth as she paces at the side of the bed.

"You set me up," I croak out of an aching throat.

She laughs. "Please. Like I don't have better things to do all day. You broke into Peek Street, so you have to face the consequences like every other member here." She leans up against something I can only describe as a torture device with belts and shackles attached to it. My body shivers involuntarily at the thought of being trapped in that thing.

"You can try to tell me that the Girl Scout failed to mention it to you while you were on the tour that led to your record breaking performance, but I won't believe you, and lying to me will only add more time to your sentence."

Trice's earlier words about Peek Street being the only place inside of the hotel with a curfew come floating past thoughts I have about my hatred for Shay. Shit.

"No. She told me, but no one said anything about consequences. Why wouldn't you be able to walk down Peek Street after dark? And besides, they invited me. The doors were unlocked, and no signs were telling me I wasn't supposed to be there."

Shay gives a twist of her lips and a slight shrug before answering. "Not my problem. I don't make the rules, I just enforce them." She almost looks bored talking to me, as if my body displayed in front of her is not enough to keep her attention.

She continues, "Besides a personal guide, the hotel provided a manual, which you decided not to read."

I don't bother telling her that no one reads the *fucking* manual. I exhale a deep breath and gather the strength required to lift my head and face away from her. It's useless. She'll blame me for everything, no matter the justification.

I shouldn't have come here.

Shay's voice continues to drone on in the background. I do my best to shut her out by humming a song that fills my eardrums. It's a popular song sent to me by Gabriella's little sister, Maricela. When I try to sing the words in Spanish, Shay's voice breaks through. I stop speaking and resume humming at a louder volume.

I don't realize Shay's lecture has ended until she rounds the other side of my bed and bleeds into my eyesight. Instead of staring at me and gloating, she sinks to her knees and rests her arms on the edge of the bed. Her chin cradles on her crossed wrists.

The look in her eyes is softer. There's still a bit of anger in them, but tortured and wounded.

She moves her lips and I stop humming. When she receives no response from me, she repeats her words.

"Do you love her?"

I only nod.

I tangle the words I choose not to say in my throat. When I try to speak, they feel sharp and dangerous. So much happened tonight. My emotions shifted all over the place from the time I woke up. Last night I felt guilt and shame for what I had done. This morning I was jealous, playful and filled with hope. If I'm honest with myself when that hope shattered, I did what I knew would get her attention — I misbehaved.

Fantasizing about rebellion has always been easy because Gabriella has always been there as a soft place to land. No judgment. No lectures. She's given me the space to fly free since the moment we met in a hotel room in Hollywood.

"I never let her go."

Shay's chin rolls to the side in question.

I think for a moment whether I want to continue to say everything I've been keeping to myself aloud. "After everything that happened, holding her in my arms was too painful and locking her inside of my heart was too dangerous. People could see it. They watched and waited for me to become agitated and unpredictable. When I tried to run, they caught me. When I begged for her, they told me not to cry."

They were my sister Eryn and Nicole. The only two people who knew what happened. I don't register the tear that rolls down my cheek until Shay reaches out a long, strong finger and wipes it away. The other becomes absorbed into the silk sheets, leaving behind a cool, wet spot.

The smile I give Shay is probably only the second one I've ever offered. The first was in a mansion in Orange County, hundreds of miles away.

"I could only keep her in my head. Sounds strange, huh?"

She shakes her head in reassurance and allows the rest of the tears to fall.

I continue, "I can dream about her all day. I used to tell her I loved her after she fell asleep and now she tells me. Every night. Without even having to be there."

Shay doesn't know what it was like for us back when we were happy and running towards each other instead of—in my case — running away.

She rises to her feet and turns toward the door, her long train trails behind her.

"You know, I'm a big believer in actions speaking louder than words. Gabriella and I share that belief."

The restraint around my ankle tugs until my ankle is freed. Shay concentrates on the others without matching my gaze when my neck swivels around to face her. Since she refuses to look at me, I listen to her words carefully.

"Even though she wasn't there that summer, she loves this hotel. She had hoped that when you saw it, you'd love it too."

My feelings about BED are difficult to decipher. I forced myself to go that summer. It was an excuse to get out of my parents' house and escape everyone's concerned glances. I never mentioned Chasity to them. For Nicole, it would've been a dead giveaway. I only explained I needed to spend time away from the city for a while. Somehow, they believed me.

No one outside of us will ever know what happened that summer. I did not know then that Gabriella would one day make BED her home.

The muscles in my feet and wrists bend and stretch for relief. I'm so tired. My body aches in places I think it shouldn't. The icy breeze from the AC hovers down, producing a scatter of goosebumps on my skin. If she notices me shivering, Shay doesn't comment.

"You have a decision to make. You can leave this room or you can serve your sentence. If you decide to leave, know that it's your heart you're leaving behind. If you decide to stay, your escorts will be here soon to transport you to your assigned quarters. Know that staying doesn't grant you a fairytale, Taylor, but it'll bring you one step closer to forever."

Chapter Thirty-Two
Gabriella

THE ROOM LIGHTENS FROM the brightness of my cell phone screen. Annoyed, I click the buttons on the side to silence it before turning it over on its face. The end table vibrates. I wait for it to pass, gritting my teeth. I scoop it up angrily the third time, pausing when I see Shay's name outlined in white. I'm halfway out my bedroom door before I hear her first words.

"You're not gonna believe who's here."

No. The knob twists. I push the door open to an empty room. Taylor never came home.

"She's not approved to participate in the Dungeon, Shay." In disbelief, I search her bathroom anyway and find it in the pristine condition only she could leave it in.

"I know that. The patrol got a little lazy with verification. I'll deal with them later. Blame Chasity for waiving the new member protocols and believing that her friends were just going to have a normal girls' weekend, especially Taylor, who we all know has an appetite for trouble. Hell, I'm surprised Britney hasn't come sauntering down here."

The only rules I thought about pertaining to Taylor were the ones designed to keep her safe while she was visiting. The Dungeon is so far out of her element that it didn't even cross my mind. She's a rule breaker for pleasure, but a rule follower by societal standards.

The type of chase the Dungeon offers isn't the type that interests her.

"I need you to do me a favor." The steps it takes for me to get from Taylor's bedroom door to my closet feel minimal. I gather everything I need and toss it all in a bag never intended for this type of use.

"I knew you would say that."

"Shay–"

"Yeah, I know. You love her." She inhales a deep sigh and blows out a long breath. "You're lucky I didn't send her to the wolves." Shay sucks her teeth and makes more exasperated noises through the phone. "I've already transported her. Even sent the Link to help keep her calm."

"Thank you."

"Just remember, no matter what happens, you deserve to have someone love you as much as you love her."

"She does."

I allow the phone to slip from my ear and land on the stuffed duffel bag. My attire for tonight is simple. There's no need for formality when I'm about to rip my heart out for the woman I love and ask her permission to put the pieces back together myself. Fixing me is not Taylor's problem. Healing is and will always be my responsibility.

The day she left was the day I started planning her return. There was so much I needed to say that I didn't think she'd understand. If Chasity hadn't sprung this week on me, I'd be more prepared, but fate has a funny way of leading you to destiny. That's *my* beginning, anyway.

I fell in love with a girl who danced in a Christmas musical and was shocked when later I saw her on my television screen. Since my sisters were fans, listening to her shows from the kitchen became easy. It was better if I couldn't see her, knowing I'd never have her. But then that changed. It was only supposed to be temporary. Until it wasn't.

One day, her fantasies transformed into dreams of us and I didn't know what else to do except hold on. Even then, I knew losing her would be devastating, so instead of telling her the truth, I squeezed the life out of us. It was selfish, arrogant, and came at a steep price. I'd never felt so lonely before in my life. Fighting is what I'm used to, but you can't fight with ghosts.

At this time of morning, the hallways are empty. Only the Dungeon is awake now. The Dungeon is Shay's playground. Designed to meet the fictional sexual needs of BED members, Shay runs the show there. The route to the Dungeon is a secret from those who are not Dungeon staff. The Dungeon casts remain in character at all times. Competition to get into the Dungeon is fierce. You have to break the rules just enough to get caught, but not bad enough to have your membership terminated. Leave it to Taylor to make it to the Dungeon during her first week here.

We divided the Dungeon into different realms of pleasure. The more offenses, the more probability someone has of experiencing them all. Of course, it's not all up to chance. Behind the scenes, there are training and class completions taking place to ensure qualification to the next level. Can't undergo an anal probing without certification that you've completed the course and have provided written consent for the procedure. Shay isn't a complete monster. Whether she takes part in disciplining the members changes each day. Lately, though, her preference has been more focused on employee performance.

I take the back way to the Palace and bypass the busy courtroom. Though I've helped design sections of it, I have very little to do with the Dungeon. My performers are all I have to worry about to manage my department. Shay has to keep eyes on the cast and the members and whatever chaos they create to gain access to her world. I don't envy her at all.

Each realm appears quiet until you step out into its atmosphere. The forest is filled with nocturnal sounds of insects, some cackling from the nearby covens, and throaty gurgles that could mean pain, pleasure or both. Twigs snap underneath my shoes the further into the forest I walk. Some come out to investigate. They all go back inside their respective spaces.

Trice sits on the railing of the building I've spent the last year constructing, swinging her legs back and forth and rocking to a tune in her head. She hops off and lands on the forest floor as soon as she notices me.

"What did she do this time?" I stifle a yawn and attempt to look more alert. This is the Dungeon's busiest time, and it's usually when I'm lulled into a deep sleep.

"Got caught on Peek with a Platinum. Serial Dweller." A Dungeon Dweller is someone who loves to be jailed in the Dungeon. For some members, an experience in the Dungeon is their kink. Dwellers go to any length they can to gain the attention of the Dungeon Patrol. Breaking into a home on Peek Street is a popular choice, but you can only break the same rule so many times before it results in the revocation of your membership. They'll have to think of something else next time.

"How long did she get?"

"Five hours." I glance at the time on my phone. It's a little over 2:30 a.m. She'll be out by early morning. Not too bad for a first offense.

"Is she pissed?" Trice chuckles a bit, crossing her arms over her chest. "Put up a bit of a fight. Marcus is pissed that I told Shay she was here. He hoped she'd be sentenced to the Chambers." I can't recall who Marcus is, but I make a mental note to have him reassigned. Or fired.

"Thanks for everything, Girl Scout." Trice's pout as I reach to pat her on the head surprises me. "What's wrong?"

"That's it?" She cocks her head to the side and holds her palms face up. "You don't need me anymore."

I smile, although I try not to. With her, I always do. She's the type that locks happiness in like a memory. She remembers every expression of glee and uses it like a weapon. I don't need her to remember the moment that may shatter me—again.

"This is the end. I don't know what will happen after today, but thank you."

She nods slowly at my words and finally begins to put one foot in front of the other. I place one foot on the first step and pause when I hear her voice behind me.

"If it works, can I be in the wedding?" I look back at the hopeful gleam in her eyes. It reminds me of Taylor before everything broke. I miss that about her. Maybe after today, I'll see that look in her eyes again.

"If it works, I can guarantee you an invite."

Trice's shoes glide across the grass in the artificial moonlight. Again, I try my damndest not to smile.

"Then I'll let you get to it."

The two-story motel is white on purpose. With a blank slate, it's easy to disguise for every occasion. We installed the glowing motel sign a few weeks ago. Valentine's Day is the official preview. There'll be blood and chaos during Halloween. Guests may check-in for love, but they'll never check out. It's bound to be overbooked. Incorporating pieces of her into the hotel was one way I grieved our relationship. My therapist was the first person to encourage it. She said it was important to honor the ones we lose to move through our grief. So, when my ex-best friend called me to help build her hotel, I built a stage for Taylor to signify our first beginning and repaired my relationship with Chasity to signify a new start.

It all kept going from there. There are pieces of Taylor scattered throughout the property, resources to remind me of what I lost and what I cherished. I've missed her terribly, but I have survived. I know I can go through life missing her. Waking up next to her every day is my dream. Loving her is a strong preference. There will be no one else.

I pass the empty receptionist desk and make my way down the dimly lit hallway. Some paintings that were once hung have fallen onto the floor. Her doing, probably. Even with Trice present, she had to put up a fight. The classic motel keychain dangles from the lock. This key looks nothing like the ones that hang from our necks to announce our status.

Taylor sits on the couch with her knees folded underneath her. The only light in the room comes from the open window. She wears the silk purple robe that's placed in every motel room closet.

"I wore a T-shirt the first time." She fiddles with the edges of the robe she didn't bother to tie around her. "It was weird when I first walked in. Like déjà vu."

The room is almost identical to the first one we spent time in together. The layout is the same. The colors and fabrics are more to her tastes.

"Did Shay send you here to punish me? You picked the perfect place if you plan to torture me with my memories."

She would never make this easy.

I put the duffle bag on the floor next to the bed and remove my jacket. "Shay doesn't send me anywhere."

Taylor shrugs with her head down, studying the stitches on the robe. "She sure doesn't send you home." Her eyes flick up at me and away again. She shakes her head with her eyes squeezed shut. "Sorry. That's not any of my business."

I remove my shoes in silence. My shirt and pants follow. The sports bra lifts over my head and falls to the floor, along with my underwear. I cross my legs in front of me and wait with my eyes closed. The only sound I hear is the thump of my heartbeat. It increases in anticipation and slows when I attempt to soothe it.

"What are you doing?" she whispers close to my ear.

"Remembering," I whisper back with a surprising crack in my voice.

"You weren't the one sitting there last time."

"I know."

"Then why are you in my spot?" The seriousness in her voice threatens to tug a smile onto my lips. I remain in place committed to the plan formed in my brain years ago. My ears strain at a new rustling sound. I anticipate the creaking of the door opening and the slam it makes when it closes.

It never comes.

Instead, I feel the mattress dip in and my body rocks to the side. Taylor slides her thighs in place with her ass planted firmly in my lap. "I told you, you're in my spot." Her breath is barely above her previous whisper. My lips part while hers rains down on my jaw and neck. Chunks of comforter gather in my fists at the urge to wrap my arms around her. Her kisses trail down to my chest. I suck in a breath at the feel of her tongue swiping over my nipple. The cut of her teeth bearing down on my flesh sends my hips rising.

"There. All better now."

My eyes fly open to meet hers. A smile spreads across her wet lips.

"What?"

She takes a deep breath and slowly exhales. Her hand that was placed on my hips trails up my side. I fight against the laughter her touch produces. "Ask me again why I'm here." Her gaze travels away from my face to the spot underneath my breast where her name lives. Her fingers trace the cursive lettering now.

"Why did you come here?" I ask.

"To find you."

She looks at me with her hand still pressed to my side. "I thought I was coming here to find freedom and replace the memory of you. Except, turns out you're my favorite memory. I've been running around this hotel to run right into you."

"I hurt you."

"I know. And I forgive you." At my skeptical look, Taylor continues. "Look at where we are right now." Her eyes sweep across the room. "No one shares this memory except us."

"Taylor. I lied to you."

"Did you lie about loving me?"

I shake my head. I tried. For weeks, I came up with a million excuses about how none of it could be real and how it could never work.

"If loving me was real, I'm confident I can forgive the rest. I've had time and I miss you."

"I've missed you, too." My fingers tuck into her hair and gently scratch her scalp. Her eyes flutter close for a few seconds. Watching her soothes the anxiety in my belly and pokes at distant memories of a better time. "I'm sorry I didn't protect you." From me. From her. Sometimes I forget which one of us came first.

Taylor doesn't speak right away. She rests her cheek in the palm of my hand and then shakes her head. "You didn't need to protect me." A small smile tugs at the corner of her lips. "We locked eyes over the head of a barista, remember?"

I allow my smile to match hers. "We locked eyes over the ass of a reindeer while you wore antlers on your head." She cringes at the memory that fills my heart with happiness.

One eye peaks at me. "That was an original piece."

I laugh and both our bodies vibrate.

"You're all I remember about that moment. You were the only thing that mattered."

"You're changing our beginning."

"No. I'm correcting it. I fell in love with you for the first time at seven. Again at fifteen and for the last time at nineteen. My love has never stopped. It has only grown to match the size of my heart every time we find each other. We locked eyes during a winter play, then in a crowded room and finally in a cafe."

"I love you, too." Our lips melt together and my arms lift to hold on to her naked skin. She feels like a dream—delicate to the touch. My lips follow hers in protest at the impending separation. Her eyes brighten with every sweep they make over my face.

My spine straightens to attention at the sound of her words. "Now get out of my spot."

Chapter Thirty-Three
Taylor

I DON'T KNOW IF my heart has ever felt this big. My girlfriend's back. God, I've missed her. She's the same while also being different. Her hair is longer and in the Vegas winter, her skin is paler. Working indoors all day probably doesn't help either. I've checked her body as best as I can for anything that wasn't supposed to be there. After all this time, only my name remains.

"You should probably leave before my ex gets back." My reclaimed spot on the bed is warm from Gabriella's body heat. A smirk plays on her lips even as she glances at the door.

"Oh?" she asks mockingly. "You're rooming with your ex?"

"Yeah, she's obsessed with me. Not that I can blame her. If she finds you here, it won't be good."

Gabriella leans against the couch. She's still naked, a fact that my mind is having a hard time ignoring while my acting skills take control of our present situation.

"How did she become your ex?"

I shrug and allow my body to lean back on my elbows. It's a dangerous question. I need the answer to push our game forward and not tear us further apart. "She wasn't used to handling girls like me. I'm delicate and she was-" I look up into Gabriella's gaze. "-rough."

"And that's a bad thing?"

"Obviously," I say dismissively while crossing one leg over the other and turning so my ass points to the forest window.

Gabriella's eyes follow my movements. My muscles tense as I watch her drop to the floor and crawl to the bed on her hands and knees. I feel more than one ache run through me. She crawls over to me and stops with her face a mere inch from mine. "Something tells me you like it rough."

The unmistakable click of her blade and the cold kiss it presses against my skin springs joy into my heart and temptation to my middle. The tip of the blade pokes my skin, but not enough to puncture. She drags it across one cheek and then crosses over to the other.

"So, tell me, does your ex not know how to take care of you, or does she know you don't like to be treated like a princess?"

"I could be a princess." My voice shakes at the feel of the blade's descent. On instinct, I pull my knee up higher to allow the blade space to move. It's an automatic response. One I've been trained for. The steel smooths out the wetness between my inner thighs. My breath hitches while Gabriella swishes the blade back and forth to spread out my excitement.

"A princess that comes on knives?"

"I...don't. I wouldn't."

She dismisses my words with one command:

"Open."

My lips unlock and my tongue rolls out. The knife leaves behind warmth when she extracts it from my skin and lays it flat onto my tongue. The taste of me increases the wetness that forms in my mouth after such a delicious treat. My lips close over the blade and I pull back slowly until it's free from my mouth, clean.

Gabriella sucks the back of her front teeth repeatedly in admonishment. "Someone's not telling the truth." She rolls from the bed and back down to the floor. The sound of a zipper racing across fabric encourages the movement of my hips that I have been attempting to conceal. "What did your ex do whenever she caught you in a lie?"

Instead of peeking over to see Gabriella, I look behind me at the window. "She'd punish me," I answer honestly with the confidence in my voice to imply the detail is relatively small.

"Did you like it?" Gabriella's voice is louder now that she stands. My eyes travel down to her hips, to the strap-on she's secured. This one is thick, jet black and veiny. The first one she used on me was caramel colored. It looked angry, and felt like it too, but I had deserved it. I had been a very, very bad girl that night.

I try not to spring my thighs open at the first sight of it. That would get me into even worse trouble.

I swallow down the anticipating flow of saliva. "I - I guess. It only hurt a little." One of Gabriella's eyebrows rises. The toy springs up and down as she moves closer to fill the space between us.

Her soft hands clench my throat in her hold. "If it only hurt a little, she didn't do it right." With every word, she pulls me forward until my parted lips rest on the tip of her toy. Her free hand tangles itself in my hair. "Show me how much you like being punished, Emmy."

I fight the urge to control my movements, allowing her to pull me all the way forward until the head of the dildo tickles the back of my throat. No gagging is necessary. I became an expert a long time ago.

Hair pulling? Check.

Choking? Double check.

Dominating, ridiculously sexy, strap-wearing girlfriend? Triple fucking check.

I look up at her in time to see her looking down at me with her mouth open and eyes half-closed. She's always loved watching me. I add the right amount of pressure. Even though she can't feel it herself, she can see my cheeks deepen, my lips pout out and hear the loud pop they make when she pulls me off of her. The toy shines after my performance. I lick the tip, running my tongue along the thin line of the head, knowing she can envision me doing other things the same way.

No class at BED could rival my personal lessons. I've been trained for Gabriella's pleasure. When she watches me, I do as expected, performing exactly the way she taught me. If her hands are at my throat, I obey. When she smacks my ass, I hike it up and wait. Knowing whatever punishment she's delivering to me, I've earned every lick. Fingers sliding inside of me? Yes, please. Tongue fucking me? Thank you, ma'am. When she tells me to come, I do it. Like a good girl should.

Applying a small squeeze to my throat, she pushes me backward. I do as I'm told. In anticipation of her next command, my thighs fall open and she nestles herself in between them. The palm of her free hand smacks against my vulva and I struggle out a breath at the impact and dig my ass deeper into the mattress at the pleasure.

"Did that hurt?"

I shake my head while staring her directly in the eyes. My feet shuffle against the comforter to open my hips wider. I always push and challenge her, savoring my punishment and expecting a reward for finally listening to her commands and following her rules. Both are enjoyable. I get excited at the prospect of disobeying her and also at the idea of receiving her praise.

She probably should've done something about that sooner.

She strikes me again and again. Her palm glistens in the lamplight each time she pulls away. The response from my body only validates my behavior and her eyes narrowing at my refusal to admit to pain motivates me to continue to endure it.

I focus on her grip on my neck as a distraction. Her hold tightens every time her hand swings back and then loosens upon contact. I know it's to allow the words she desperately wants to hear to escape. The wet, splashy melody we make together gets louder.

"Looks like you're the one I should be more worried about and not your ex."

She gives me no time to respond. My neck is released and I'm pushed onto my stomach with my breasts pressed onto the comforter in seconds. Her wet hand lands on one cheek and the sound is louder than what we've just created. The sting settles on my skin longer, too. My back curves into the position she wants me in with my ass hovering above the rest of me.

"You've always been a bad girl, haven't you?" She repeats it while she spanks me. Her hand inching low and lower each time the words 'bad fucking girl' expel through her breath. The tingle spreads from my meat to my center. Without the distraction of her constricted touch, I use the sheets crumbled into my fists. She strikes me again. This time, lower, grazing the edge of my most sensitive area with her pinky finger.

I wasn't a bad girl until I met her. Until she pushed all of my fantasies out of me. She made me trust her and forced me to expose them.

So, really, this is all her fault.

Two fingers slide between my folds. I push against them, the top of me staying flat and obedient. Her tongue flicks out as a replacement. I let out a shuddered, breathy moan. She keeps spreading and licking with the occasional smack. I keep my ass right where she wants it, the view perfectly angled for her to feast.

The last smack is hard and loud. The hair tug forces me onto my back. She wastes no time spreading my thighs apart again, pushing my knees far back until they settle underneath my breasts.

"Sore, yet, baby?"

I shake my head again and fight the urge to move my hips in search of friction. My arousal's journey down my labia to kiss the crack of my ass before absorbing into the comforter is an excruciating one that reminds me just how hungry for her I am and have always been.

I steady my eyes from rolling to the back of my head at the feel of her hands on the backs of my thighs. She rocks her hips forward and the black head nudges its way through my opening, past my drenched vaginal muscles and settles itself inside in one swoop.

"Fuck!" I can't help but call out. It's been a long time. There's nothing like this hiding in my drawers at home. Gabriella has never permitted me to have one, and I've never gotten this far with anyone else who might possess one.

She rocks into me at an agonizing rhythm that forces the lids of my eyes closed. She brushes into my clit with each stroke and my nails dig deeper into the silk sheets. Gabriella's pace slows momentarily and I feel the sharpness of her teeth bite down on one nipple before she wraps her tongue around the brown bud.

I know what being punished by Gabriella feels like. I know it makes my heart thunder in my chest, my breath catch in my throat and my body scream. Only for her. Always. She's what I've been running from and towards at the same time for the past four years. No one's ever been able to match her because I never belonged to them.

I belong to her.

My clit pulsates, my pussy clenches and Gabriella grinds out my orgasm. Without her weight, I would've spiraled out of control. My body jostles and humps against her. The flood is so overwhelming, for a second I wonder if I'm going to be able to handle it. She doesn't let up, keeping me spread with her hands on the back of my thighs. I let out a deep breath when the intensity recedes, but groan again when she places a hand between us and uses the other to remove the harness.

We're far from being done. This is only the beginning.

Chapter Thirty-Four
Gabriella

MY SLOW WHINE IS just enough to keep her awake. She's notorious for falling asleep after sex. But not tonight baby, we have so much more we need to talk about. Light sweat covers my body. I missed the feeling of my body on top of hers, the sounds she makes when she's too overpowered to use words. Usually, the sensations that I feel from her—her quaking thighs, her clenched fists, her lips folded between her teeth — are enough. But this time, I'm going to need her to speak.

Right after this.

My hand settles at the base of her throat. I'm careful to place my palm against her collarbone and not on her trachea. I flatten her thighs to open them and nestle in between, hovering my pussy over hers. When I move, my clit hits against hers, creating the friction I need to release the orgasm I've been building since I walked in here.

Taylor's favorite position is whichever one I place her in. She likes them all and works to exploit the time I keep her locked into one. The first time I slid my wet pussy against hers wasn't a spur of the moment decision.

It was a punishment. That she has since enjoyed dozens and dozens of times.

Her hands grip the sheets instead of my waist. She knows she's at my mercy. Our position gives me a perfect view of her titties jiggling as the mattress bounces beneath us. I'll consider this an intermission to the pain she is supposed to be feeling right now. The pain she so bravely told me she has never felt before.

"God, you feel so good." Her fingers release the sheets to settle into her hair while she mumbles other praises I'm not supposed to hear. She grips clumps of hair into her fists and pulls. I know what she wants, but she's not going to get it yet. The thought of the games she likes to play and the words that always remain unsaid sends a shockwave in between us.

My speed increases with our slippery wet lips melting against one another, our clits bumping along to our impassioned tempo. My thighs clench. I spasm above her. Her screams encourage my finish, my voice joining hers. It takes a while for the shockwaves to cool. I breathe through the rush, completely aware of Taylor dipping her fingers between us before raising them to her lips.

I fight the urge to join her in tasting us and bend to kiss her instead, sucking the remaining flavor of us from her tongue. She pulls me against her.

I pull away.

I use her fingers to trace across her skin. She takes over when we reach between her thighs. Four fingers glide over the flood I helped her create. I bend to suck one glazed finger into my mouth. The taste of her melts onto my tongue and warms my cheeks. I bite down on the tip of her finger. A nip. She inhales a breath, but does as she's told. Three other fingers curl away and leave one behind.

"One at a time, Emmy." The permitted finger slides in easily and becomes coated in her when she slides it back out again for inspection.

"I can take more than one." I can hear her disappointment through her pout.

"Are you challenging me?" I ask her. She shakes her head, but there's something in her eyes I'm weary of. "What's lesson number one?" My eyes route from the view of her pussy to her face and I see her bite down on her lip.

"I will do as my girlfriend says." She pouts as she recalls the line. The point remains as she works one finger into the slippery slot. My thumb grazes over her clit, causing her hips to rise.

"Behave. Your poor ex." I tisk. A strangled cry of frustration reaches my ears. I could punish her for this.

I settle myself over her face. A quick look back tells me she's still following instructions with only using one finger to please herself.

Her tongue swipes up slowly. I suck in a breath. You can never forget how good it feels to have your pussy quivering in the mouth of the one you love. And Taylor was always so damn good at it. I was her first, but she's a natural. I barely had to teach her anything. My body being at Taylor's mercy is rare and not because I don't like it. Prioritizing her pleasure over mine was an old habit built before her time.

I loved her before she drank from me the first time.

I worshiped her after.

I grip the only part of her I can, tugging on her hair to steady her rhythm. Patience. I had to teach her patience. She listens, returning to the gentle strokes that compelled me to lose my initial breaths. My hips grind against the flat of her tongue. Her eyes never swerve from mine. Her lips close around me, sucking and humming, sending shockwaves through my clit.

"Fucking shit!" No longer able to hold up my body weight, I fall forward with my palms slamming down onto the blanket. She releases me long enough to wiggle her tongue at the entrance, sliding it inside.

"Fuck, Emmy." I can barely get out the words. My legs shake

uncontrollably. My core tightens with every thrust. She sucks and laps up every ounce of my arousal she's responsible for. I buck harder against her, losing control. Her teeth tug at the skin of my folds. The tip of her tongue tickles the most sensitive piece of me. She's exactly where she needs to be. My eyelids drift shut. My body stiffens. The release rattles through me as I ride out the assault.

"Fuck!" she growls when I pull back from her kisses, only to moan when I wrap my lips around her tongue. Our full lips meet hungrily, sucking, pecking and licking all over.

It's been four years too damn long.

"Last one." I don't bother with a toy for this one. I trace my fingers down between her breasts, over her pierced belly button and down, sliding my fingers through the thick stickiness of her. She takes a quick breath and shifts. My knees sink into spots already wet from our time together.

I spread her open, revealing the hidden pockets of nectar trapped between her folds. I lick them free. She shudders underneath me. I deliver long, pressured strokes against her clit before I trail the tip of my tongue across her lips. She rocks, whispering the same words I praised her with before.

"Fuck."

I do it again and again. I insert two fingers into her at the same time I squeeze two into mine. My thumb does the same work for me that my tongue does for her. The noises coming from her are loud. My kisses barely steady her. While her head stays in position, her thighs threaten to close with every pump.

I increase the speed, pulling my two fingers in and out. She claws at the sheet in the small spaces next to her. My fingers rub against her in fierce repetition.

"Fuck! Fuck! Fuck! Fuck! Fuck!" she screams until she comes.

I stay with her bouncing orgasm, never letting up on the

pressure. Her toes straighten. Her body twitches. I let go. Her muscles collapse in exhaustion. I let out a breath, completely unaware I had filled my lungs. I lose count of the amount of kisses I plant on her cheeks. When I look up again, she's asleep with her eyes closed and her face resting to the side.

It's a good thing the sheets are silk. I didn't think to pack the room with extra headscarves and I doubt they have any in the Dungeon where comfort is an inconvenience. She hates sleeping without one, but tonight she's too tired to care. I grab the thickest blanket I can find from the closet and drape it over her before sliding underneath it myself.

A few coiled strands obey me enough to move out of her face. A kiss on her cheek doesn't wake her. I place another on her jaw and then a third on her lips.

The love I feel for her is overpowering. A burst of sunshine and happiness scattered with rainbows, with a hint of fear. The morning will be a new day for us. "I love you," I whisper in her ear.

Please, don't let me let you go.

Chapter Thirty-Five
Taylor

IF FANTASIES ARE MADE to break you, then dreams are meant to heal. The dampness of my skin is the first thing I notice. The warm and toasty feeling wrapped around my body is a contrast from the drab coldness I felt last night. My eyes flutter open before closing again. I want to stay in this large heated bed with pressure on my back and with Gabriella's arm wrapped tightly around my middle, keeping me close.

My body hasn't lain beside anyone else since her, and being with her right now is magically fulfilling in a way that I never expected. This time, I don't want to run. I want to stay. There is so much we still need to talk about. I hope when she wakes up, she's willing to listen.

Shay doesn't knock when she comes in. She's trailed by a crew of cleaning staff. Mountains of sheets and comforters line the hallway behind her.

"Time to check out." She drops a set of folded clothing next to me. I assume my tattered detective uniform is somewhere at the bottom of a trash can.

"Does my girlfriend know how rude you are?" I say it because I know she'll hate it, but also because saying the word 'girlfriend' sends a glowing spark through my chest. Gabriella's lips press against my upper back. I conceal the breath I release out in relief.

Even if Gabriella felt it, at least Shay didn't see it.

"Of course. She has to keep someone around to remind her you're a bad idea." Her taunting smirk bears down on me.

"Shay." Gabriella's arm tightens around me at the same time she sends out her warning.

"It's fine." I turn to look at her, removing the bulk of my hair from the side of her face. "Forever is a long time to be a bitch."

Shay and Gabriella talk more before we leave. I keep most of my business to myself by ignoring their conversation and traveling the short distance to some of the other bedrooms. It doesn't look like the rooms are being cleaned as much as they're being decorated. The coloring in our room is unique. An array of pinks and reds sprawl out in the others.

Gabriella finds me bent at the waist in a chest of toys, trying to make sense of one I've never seen before. Each toy is individually wrapped in the treasure chest replica.

Ignoring my look of confusion, Gabriella grabs the toy and tosses it back into the box without explaining. "Forget you ever saw this." She knows I won't.

Our hands embrace without words. We leave the hotel and set out in the dark green forest. More light shines in than it did when I was dragged here earlier.

Our suite is understandably quiet, but annoyingly bright because of the opened curtains. I veer to the left and discard my newer clothing before sliding into Gabriella's bed. Silk lands on my face. "My scarf!" It's not spoken enough about how much comfort and warmth a black girl's headscarf brings her. Even when the pillowcases are silk or satin or any of the other fabrics good for maintaining the moisture of curls, the scarf remains essential. I tie it in the back before pulling the ends to the front and tying it a second time for security and comfort.

"We need to talk before I leave to check on the party set-up."

The crease in the middle of my forehead forms before I stop it. "You don't have to be everything for her, you know." It's unrealistic for her to be Gabriella Flores, writer, director, producer and party planner of Chasity's dreams.

Gabriella doesn't respond to my last statement. "We need to talk about us," she says as she lies down on her side, shuffling in close to me until our noses touch. "We need to talk about the past."

"Will it change anything?"

She thinks for a moment about my question. "Yes. I'm hoping it'll save us in the future."

I let the crease in the middle of my forehead stay this time.

She chuckles and rubs one finger across my wrinkled skin. "Please."

I take a deep breath, forcing the fear down into the base of my belly. She's been so brave this whole time. I've done nothing this week but terrorize and taunt her, throwing other women in her face, trying to scramble into different beds. This is the least I can do.

"I'm sorry." My throat clams up and prevents me from saying the rest.

She runs her fingers through my hair, scratching my scalp with the tips of her nails. "Me too. I'm sorry I made the wrong decisions for us. There was a part of me that didn't think I deserved you. When I had you, I told myself I needed to do whatever was possible to keep you."

I lean into her touch, not wanting it to ever go away. "I don't wanna lie and tell you I know exactly how I would've reacted then. I don't. If you had told me sooner, maybe we could've figured it out."

"I don't know if there was a sooner. It all happened so fast that

I only knew I needed to keep it from falling apart. I failed."

"You didn't fail." I press my lips to the back of her hand, which still faintly smells like us. "You've been through a lot. I think we both needed space to figure it all out."

It's no secret that Gabriella, the oldest daughter of immigrants, works her ass off. When she's home, Gabriella zips around the house doing everything for everyone before they ask. Gabriella's parents have always been nice to me. Even after the breakup. I know she paid for most of her sister's Quinceañera a few years ago. I was too afraid I'd see her to accept the invite.

Maricela accepted my shopping spree gift as an alternative. She was excited to show me pictures of her champagne-colored ball gown. It was a beautiful A-line princess dress covered in crystals and complete with detachable puff sleeves. I think she kept the sleeves on the entire time. She should've. The damn dress cost over $1500. And that's not including the elaborate decor Maricela talked about, the massive cake they ordered, the food and the venue.

Maricela's a stunner. Equally as gorgeous as Gabriella, except she straightens her curly hair and is more extroverted. Araceli's quince should be this year, too. And Maricela is graduating from high school and heading to college in the fall. I hadn't asked Maricela about it, but I had wondered how Gabriella was paying for it all.

Her mom owns her own business and her dad works at the airport and I think does other jobs around the community. I've picked this up mostly from gathering pieces of information here and there. Gabriella has never really talked about it and her family seems bad with communication. They say things without actually saying them—a lot. If you're around long enough, you pick up on the subtle communication cues.

Our fingers intertwine on top of the blanket. Her nails are

longer than she usually kept them. The muscles in my cheeks relax into a flat, neutral expression. "Should we talk about Sara?" It's hard to describe the mix of emotions that twist in my stomach at the reminder of her. Not that she'll ever allow me to forget.

Gabriella's ex-girlfriend is still around. She landed the villain role in a horror series and it's gotten her plenty of rave reviews. Her success has been painful to witness. I force myself to read every interview of hers, though I dread them. She hasn't mentioned me at all, which is a blessing I'm not sure I can trust.

Gabriella gives a slight shrug of her shoulders and a shake of her head. "No. She doesn't matter."

"Then we should talk about what happens after today. We live over two hundred miles away from each other."

Gabriella chuckles and settles on the pillow beside me. "That's basically around the corner."

"Glad to hear you're not worried."

She opens her mouth and then closes it again. Her lips part to allow a deep breath to push through. "I'm scared out of my mind."

"Why?"

"I don't think I can lose you twice." A single tear crosses the bridge of her nose and rolls over her freckles. I've never seen her cry. Even on the day I left, there were no tears. She'd had a lot of anger. Red had shown through her cheeks and her grip around my waist had been deadly, but that's how I knew she loved me.

"You won't. We've both grown up a lot since then. I mean, look at you, *the* Drama Queen." The shaking from her laughter causes more tears to fall and a smile to form.

"I love you," she says while using the tip of her finger to trace my jawline.

"I love you, too."

Chapter Thirty-Six
Gabriella

THE ROOFTOP IS EVERYTHING I imagined it to be. After spending the day becoming reacquainted with Taylor's body and neglecting my party planning duties, the team proved they could construct the set-up without me looming over them.

I left her in bed, confident she'll show up on time. The last 24 hours have been an absolute whirlwind for us, and we made it out intact. There's a part of me worried about what happens tomorrow when she leaves. Now all there is left is to wait.

"Do you need me to help you bury the body?" Shay's in high femme mode today, dressed to the nines and for the gods. I could say the same for myself with my makeup done fully, my hair washed and curled expertly and my body strapped into a skintight dress. I'm even sure I'll be able to survive in the stilettos for the next few hours.

The twinkling lights overhead mix in beautifully with the glowing orbs. It's everything Chasity wanted, including the three-tier chocolate ganache cake decorated by Danni.

"Sorry to disappoint you, but our love lives on." I laugh before the undeniable look of disgust crosses her face.

"Fine. But be careful. The good ones always hurt the most."

I look down at her shiny gold key, identical to my own. "We'll see what happens. For both of us." I lay my head on my overprotective best friend's shoulder. "But now that we're together, watch what you say to her, okay? I don't want to lose anyone else." It's not a threat. It's a boundary. I enjoy the banter between Shay and Taylor. If it can stay respectful, I'm okay with it, but Shay doesn't always color within the lines.

Never offended by anything, Shay hunches her shoulders to sway me off. "Yeah, yeah, I got it. You love her or whatever."

"Or whatever."

Leanna shows up alone without Britney right before Chasity stands to give her speech. Leanna doesn't look at me. She's a pretty girl, outwardly meek but with devilish energy. There is something about her I just can't trust.

Chasity places her hand over her heart in deep gratitude. She's wearing all white, with speckles of gold splattered across her dress, her hair adorned by a gold headband only slightly resembling a crown.

"Words can't express how overwhelmed I am by all the love and support you have all shown me over the last two years. To my loves—" She turns to Camille and Caprice, holding their hands in hers. "I love you both so much. Thank you for always being there to love and hold me through all of my transformations. I would never be the woman I am today without the two of you."

The crowd awes and cheers. Chasity searches through the large group, her eyes landing on Shay and me.

"And to my best friends, the people I cherish the most in the world, Shay, the Executioner of My Worries and Gabriella, the Architect of My Dreams, I don't know how else to repay you for all that you've done for me and for this hotel." Her eyes drift into the crowd. I follow her gaze to a bright shimmer of white. A small laugh escapes her lips. "Except maybe I can repay you both with love." I catch the wink before she thanks the audience once again and encourages them to enjoy their dinner in the new garden and dining space.

Taylor glides past the sea of bodies in her white evening gown, identical to the gold one I'm wearing. Her hair is straight and flows deceivingly to the middle of her back. She wedges herself between a displeased Shay and me.

"Excuse me, Miss." I look around, but she's staring at me. "Yes?"

"Are you close with the boss?" A waiter brings her a full glass of champagne. She ignores it. Her eyes stay planted on mine.

"Chasity and I are old friends."

She looks impressed. Her bare shoulders shimmy in the fairy lights above us, but this time, not from the cold. She gathers one side of her hair and pulls it over to the other.

Shay, catching on, interrupts. "She's a manager here, you know." Her finger points at me directly.

Taylor gives a shocked expression, her manicured fingernails tapping against her lipstick. "Really?"

I nod, keeping my face blank and uninterested.

"Do you know who I could see about getting on stage?"

I wave my hand about in the air dismissively. "Auditions for the shows are closed," I say it definitively, bothered by the question and the attention.

Taylor pouts, her chin nearly resting on her collarbone. "But..." Her head pops up. Her eyes fill with hope. "I am considering holding private auditions for a very special role."

"What's the role?" She comes closer, her breasts pressing up against my arm. *My wife.* My heart skips a beat. I look from her eyes down to her lips. If I say what I want to say, the game will be over. It'll be too real to continue with that amount of pressure.

So instead I say, "My mistress." She gasps. Her mouth drops

open.

"Are you —" She looks around the room before leaning in to whisper, "–a submissive?"

"Hardly," I say over Shay's laughter. "My Significant is very busy." I look around the room as Taylor had done earlier. "Famous." Taylor's jaw drops open and she nods in understanding. "I need someone to fill her shoes when she's away. Now, are you ready to begin?"

Taylor's newly painted pink nails scrape against the tablecloth. She takes a deep breath before answering.

"Yes."

"Significant." I finish for her.

"Yes, Significant." The smile I thought I saw forming, dies.

I walk away from the cocktail table to take my assigned seat for dinner. Taylor follows. She stops the waiter from filling my glass by placing her hand on his elbow. Per my instruction, she can only shake her head with a forced smile while she wrestles the pitcher away from him.

A wave from Chasity authorizes his release. Taylor gently pours the water before sitting in her seat, leaving her glass empty. I told her she was to serve me. I said nothing about her being able to serve herself.

Good girl.

When my salad arrives, she scoots all the croutons off to the side. Every spoonful she places into my mouth has at least one slice of parmesan cheese on it. I give her permission to eat her own after I'm done.

With a keen eye, she inspects the temperature of my steak, not allowing the waiter to leave until she's done. After it passes the medium rare quality check, she cuts it into bite-sized strips, before feeding it to me. This time, I won't make her wait. She alternates between feeding herself and me through the rest of dinner.

She takes my napkin off my lap when I stand to use the restroom and folds it back onto my lap when I return to my seat. She smiles and bats her eyelashes as she does it. For those who don't know it's an act, they compliment me, raising their glasses in praise. I'm slightly amused and highly aroused.

Chastity stands once more. "I want to take this time to thank the wonderful kitchen for creating this beautiful dinner we've all had tonight." The audience claps. The waiters bow their heads in gratitude.

"Tonight is a celebration of not just the day when I was born, but also what we have been able to build together. Where you sit now will serve as the home to hundreds of our guests who want to have the experience of BED, but the privacy of their oasis. The members who convene here all have something in common, and that something is what Hotel BED strives to provide: the ability to be free." More applause, this one more energetic than the last.

My heart thuds in my chest. I pluck at the gel polish securely attached to my fingernail. "Welcome to the Garden..." Her eyes sway to mine before sweeping to Taylor "...of Emmy."

Chapter Thirty-Seven
Taylor

THE SMALL AMOUNT OF water I attempt to sip while listening to Chasity's speech gets caught in my throat. I grab for the white napkin in my lap, concealing my panic. I can't tell if Chasity's grin is devilish or angelic.

At the time that Chasity announces the name, a statue is revealed. It's not gold, but black marble. I saw it covered the day we shot the show, but thought nothing of it. I spent four years hating the woman who spent four years planning my return.

The Peek Street rooftop was the only place I learned to get to in BED by heart. It was the first place where I felt at home. And it was created by the one person I swore I hated with my entire being, but loved with my whole heart.

The Garden of Emmy is just as Chasity said, an oasis. There's a bistro and a lounge area. A private pool area and a gaming area. There's a spring water mud pool, hot and cold plunge pools, a shallow lounge pool and a saline pool (or Epsom Salt pool, as my family would say, and Chasity's too, for that matter). The same massage amenities offered at Embrace are also offered here as well.

The guests stand for the start of the tour. While my legs follow, my feet have a hard time moving.

"What if I hadn't come?" The face my eyes collide with isn't Gabriella's. I look around. She's nowhere close.

"You weren't supposed to." Shay's glossy jet black hair trails down her back. She doesn't look at me when she speaks. Her eyes study the statue. "She kept hoping you'd keep giving Chasity a hard time. Scared, I think."

"I love her." Saying the words sends my heart fluttering with hope and memories. I knew I meant the first time as much as I know I mean it now.

"I know. That's the scary part for all of us." Shay grabs a champagne glass from the nearest table, one I'm almost sure wasn't hers. She takes a sip and sets it down again. "She's already inside. If you take too long, she'll think you've changed your mind."

Shay looks down at the front of my dress. I follow the trail of her eyes and try to spot the smear of food or droplets of moisture on the gown. I find none. The garden is empty now of guests and there's no one else around to witness whatever plan she has forming in her mind to embarrass me.

"You should pay that necklace a little more attention."

"I don't remember you being this cryptic," I say while lifting the key of the necklace and studying it carefully.

"And I don't remember you being this clueless."

I try my best not to roll my eyes at Shay and her unreasonable expectations of people's behaviors. First large membership manuals and now tiny inscriptions.

The smoothness of the key remains unchanged each time I roll it across my palm and between my fingers. When I find nothing unusual, I turn my attention to the pendant. Those etchings are still on the back, but on the other side is a phrase I didn't see. My eyes strain in concentration and determination to decipher the wording. *Make every second count. From the beginning.*

"What is that supposed to mean?"

Shay smirks and gives a slight shrug. "I'm the messenger, not the interpreter. You're supposed to figure it out." She walks away and heads toward the path the tour took earlier.

"Shay," I call after her. Though she pauses in step, she doesn't turn to look at me. "It was a tough summer for all of us." Shay resumes her walk without a glance in my direction. Chasity brought together a group of young girls with broken hearts and gave us a task we each used as a distraction from our problems. Though the distraction worked, our problems never went away. We were all changed by the end of the weeks we spent together. I've assessed and reassessed whether my changes have served or hindered me. I'm still not sure I know the answer.

I leave the garden the only way I know how; past the greenhouses and down the elevator to the tower. Earlier I had to show my invite to gain elevator access, but the party has mostly dispersed, Chastity has made her great reveal, and now the masses at BED regain their full amenities.

My heels click against the cobblestoned street and I am grateful that someone had the foresight to build Peek Street as an indoor activity. I scan the crowd enjoying dessert at Delicacy. She's not here.

I pass more people on the way to the theater and notice for the first time the way they all look at me and whisper. They all smile though no one approaches. I keep walking. It was bound to happen, eventually.

I pull at each theater door handle until one finally opens. The music is the first thing I hear. Gabriella is the only face I see. She stands in the middle of the snow-covered stage surrounded by twinkling Christmas trees and the backdrop of a waterfall of warm white lights. An orchestra stands behind her playing a timeless Christmas classic.

I take it all in on the way down to the stage. Little specks of snow shine in her hair as it falls from the ceiling—or somewhere. I slip off my heels and feel the tiny sheets crunch underneath my toes. I'm shivering though I haven't felt a bit of wind blow.

"I don't know why I'm crying." My vision is blurry when I look at her. The tears started when I took my first step down the aisle. I don't dare to wipe them away. She should know how much this means to me. My tears are in acknowledgment of her efforts to repair what we both broke.

Gabriella's hands grab mine and she pulls me in. I go willingly, completely lost in her brown eyes. Her smile makes everything feel good. She presses her lips to my moist cheeks and my skin tingles in her care.

"I love you," I repeat the words with every new kiss she plants on my face, knowing they mean the same.

When my face is free of tears, she stands back to look at me. Still smiling. Still happy. Still the girl I never knew I was dreaming of.

"My biggest regret in life is losing you," I say.

The corners of her lips tug her smile into a small frown. I squeeze her hands in reassurance and she speaks.

"I missed you every day, but knew I had to earn your love the right way this time. In truth. I have loved you since I was 7 years old when you stood on a stage just like this one. And I have loved you ever since. There was a moment when I didn't think loving me was something you would be willing to do. You were the most beautiful girl on earth. People flocked to you like butterflies. You have fan clubs and merchandise and—I'm just a girl from San Diego. I'm nothing to you."

I shake my head at her words because they aren't true. She is everything. The tears return as I release the words from my throat. "You're not just a girl from San Diego." She blinks away the droplets of water that escape past her eyes. "You're mine." I feel it in every fiber of the muscles that stretch across my bones. Gabriella belongs to me as much as I belong to her.

That's what being here at BED has taught me. Without Gabriella, I would be fine on my own. I'm strong, resilient and kind. I have a wonderful family and supportive friends. There's nothing I can't do.

But with Gabriella, I am whole.

She takes a deep breath and continues with her eyes on mine again. "I did it wrong, Emmy. There were so many opportunities for me to be honest with you. I was scared I would lose you and I lost you, anyway."

I playfully shrug my shoulders. "We were on a break."

Gabriella's lips stretch wider than I have ever seen. "For four years?"

"Uh-huh." I look around the snow-covered stage and the members of the orchestra, who have continued to play Silent Night on repeat.

"It takes a long time to build something like this," I say. "I had to be patient." Gabriella releases one of my hands to tug me toward the closest Christmas tree. I step lightly to not disturb the landscape. Small wrapped Christmas presents sit underneath. She opens the first one.

The small gold ring looks nothing like the others. It's a simple, thin band. The nine heart-shaped rings she gifted me before are at home in my jewelry box. I could never part with them.

She slides it on my finger and reaches for the next box. She doesn't stop to look at me again until there's one ring left and two empty fingers. "Taylor Marie Townes, will you be my girlfriend?"

Her question melts my heart into a puddle. There's only one right answer to this—the one my heart wants. "Yes."

All nine rings are identical. They're more subtle against my skin.

Not that the others ever bothered me before. I wore those proudly and will wear these the same.

The last box she pulls from the tree is larger and square-shaped. This one, she unwraps slowly, pulling at the strings of the ribbon at a pace that allows me to hear it separate from the paper, even with the music playing.

Once finally free, she hands me the notebook. I look down at the cover and recognize her writing.

From the beginning and to the end.

The first page is a note from her saying most of what she said tonight. The rest of the words ache and soothe me.

The truth.

"I won't ever lie to you again," she whispers beside me. I believe her.

The next page and every page after is us. The conversations between Daisy and Emmy.

The beginning.

"How did you get this?" I shudder to think of the deal she may have made with Sara to get this back. I'd forced it out of my mind completely. The damage had been done. My trust had been broken and my heart had been shredded. There was nothing for me to do. If it had ever gotten out, I'd have worried about it then.

Gabriella glides a hand across the printed words. "I've had it since the last time I saw Sara. I had it that night, too. When you left."

Sara lied as she has always lied. It's hard to say if knowing Gabriella had the notebook in her possession would've changed anything.

"I promise it's the only copy."

I press my lips to her knuckles and hope she hears the love that seeps through me.

"I know. I trust you."

We're the first guests at the new rooftop bistro on the restricted side of the garden. We're fully clothed, for now, but in the future, that's supposed to change.

"You think I can get the pastrami sandwich to go this early? I think I'm going to want it for lunch." And then after lunch, it's time to go home. Neither one of us have mentioned I only have a few hours left here.

"Yeah, I'll have them deliver it to the room, so it's still warm." She kisses my knuckles. We haven't let go of each other's hands since we got out of the shower this morning. I knew I had a problem when I followed her to the bathroom and sat on the floor until she was done. I knew she had a problem when she didn't tell me to go away.

Nicole is going to fucking kill me.

I groan more outwardly than I intend to.

"What's wrong?"

"Nothing." It's almost the truth. "I'm going to miss you." That is the truth. If we're going to be honest with each other, this is a good place to start. She lifts from her seat long enough for our lips to meet. Our hands still clasped together.

"So what's the plan? You always seem to have one." I tear off a piece of the bran muffin I'm eating.

"Believe it or not, I didn't think this far in. Vegas is further than San Diego, for sure, but I think it'll be fine. We'll figure it out."

Her smile is something I can get used to. She does it more often now.

"When are you going to see your family again?" We could meet there. I take the drive myself every other month, which is probably something else we should talk about. I spent so long blocking out any news about her I didn't realize how estranged she had become from them.

"Not anytime soon." She glances up at someone who walks by and waves and then turns her attention back to me again.

"Mari's going to UC Santa Barbara, right?" Gabriella nods. I wait for her to notice I didn't ask her a question. UC Santa Barbara is a good school, but more known for their partying than for their academics. "Are you nervous?"

She shrugs. "Mari has to make her own decisions."

I guess I'm the only one who tried to talk her out of it. I know their mom wanted her to stay closer to home, but she didn't push it too much after Maricela said she'd be closer to me, which also isn't accurate. Santa Barbara is at least two hours away from L.A. on a good traffic day.

We leave the bistro and spend the rest of the day in the garden. I gain great amusement when members ogle at Gabriella mingling with the little people. They don't bother us too much other than to introduce themselves to her and compliment her on the shows. They speak to me, too, to tell me how much they enjoyed watching me on the hotel's new streaming network. I smile and nod appropriately. My actual show will premiere this upcoming Tuesday when I'm long gone from BED.

I have my pastrami sandwich at lunch with no need for delivery, since we still haven't left. We have a private show in one of the other greenhouses. By the end, tomatoes become my new favorite and we somehow manage to not get any dirt in any of the important places.

When it's time, I gather my bags in silence, including the extra one to fit all the new items from BED that Gabriella insists I take with me. It's odd stepping back into my bedroom after abandoning it and moving into Gabriella's.

Trice meets us at the top of the lobby. I'm more happy to see her than I thought I would be. She gives me a smile and a hug. I don't let go when she does. "Take care of her for me, please."

I feel her body wiggle in my arms.

"I will. Scout's honor."

I don't know what that means, but I trust her.

The pit in my stomach and the tears in my eyes surprise me a bit. I thought I was prepared for this goodbye. A few days ago, I was trying to escape. Now, leaving feels like the hardest part.

Gabriella wraps her arms around me and I revel in the dozens of kisses she rains down on my face. "I love you." She pauses when I say it, so I repeat it.

"Come back." She says the words, but somehow I know what her heart means.

Don't leave.

I'm joined by Britney and Leanna on the way through member services. "I guess that worked out, huh?" Britney smiles widely at me and then at Gabriella, standing a few feet behind.

"Yup. Sure did." Leanna bumps a playful shoulder against me. The staff scans the pendants of Britney's and Leanna's necklaces before I hand over mine.

Near the exit, the employee calls back to me, "Oh, wait! You're forgetting your key." I turn back, confused. The chain swings from her closed fists. She looks down at the screen and back at me again. "You're Mrs. Flores' wife?" The words startle me. It's my heart that instructs my feet to move and allows me to catch the last glimpse of what I hope is my future, no longer shrouded with pain. I came to BED with a mission to find myself, and I recovered my heart in the process.

Gabriella still stands in the lobby, her arms crossed, talking to the newly arrived Shay.

"Yes." I reach for the necklace again, clutching the chain between my fingers. "Yes, I am."

THE END

Dear Reader,

Thanks for reading. If you have enjoyed reading Taylor and Gabriella's story, please consider leaving a review. It would be a enormous help. Hotel BED needs new members in order to grow, which means we have to find new readers.

Have you already read about the night Taylor explored her stalker fantasy? That bonus scene from the Intimate Beginnings of Taylor is available here.

Goodies

If you would like to see what happens when Taylor encounters her biggest fan, the bonus scene is available here.

If you would like to continue to discuss the Intimate Beginnings of Taylor, join Lavender's Intimate Suite, a group for all readers of the series to come together.

If you would like to read ahead to the future books before they are polished and published, join me on REAM here.

Acknowledgements

I WANNA THANK MY MAMA...again, because who knows who I would be if I didn't have you. Thank you to my husband for your patience and your grace.

Every time I start a new book I think, "Am I really doing this?" The fact that you have taken your time to read this means more to me than you will ever know. Thank you to my editor, Astrida, who for a long time was the only other person who had any knowledge of Gabriella and Taylor's existence in my brain.

Thank you to every character artist/illustrator I have ever worked with. Having you create them gave me so much motivation.

And lastly, thank you to every piece of me that had the power, strength and skill to push away the anxious thoughts and complete my dreams.

I love you, Lavender. Keep growing.

About the author

 **Lavender Quinn** is a lover of all things purple and sparkly. She's an avid believer of glitter when crafting, hot chocolate even when it's not cold out and eating ice cream when it's raining. She was born and raised in Los Angeles, CA in the same diverse community she strives to recreate and bring to life in her sapphic romance novels. When not writing about her daydreams and book wives, you may find her underneath the covers watching reality television in the dark, reading a love story, listening to music or silently dancing to the glow of candlelight.

www.Lavenderquinn.com